Ethan gazed at h̶e̶r̶ ̶s̶t̶e̶a̶d̶i̶l̶y̶. "What else? Don't look so miserable. Come on, Matilda. It can't be that bad."

"You're right. It's not bad. It really isn't. Because I'm happy about it. But it is...a lot. You know? It's not how I expected it to happen." Far from it. "So much for all our happy little plans..." she whispered, her throat tight again, her eyes blurring with a fresh surge of tears.

Ethan took Matty's hand and pressed another tissue into it. She wiped her eyes and then sagged against him.

They sat there holding each other for an indeterminate period of time. It was good in the most basic way. Just Matty and Ethan, sitting on the sofa together. She was a mess and he was there for her and everything felt better than it had in a long, long time.

"Whatever it is, just tell me," he said into the comfortable quiet that had settled between them. "Just get it all out and let it go."

Matty pulled away from Ethan and sat up straighter. As she met Ethan's beautiful green eyes, she felt such gratitude that she had a friend like him. And when she thought of it that way, she couldn't hold the truth back for one minute longer.

"I'm pregnant," she said. "Thirteen weeks. It wasn't planned but it happened. And this baby is *mine*."

Dear Reader,

Many of you may be followers of my long-running series of stories about the Bravo family. More than two decades after the first Bravo family story came out, I'm still having a great time writing the next one. And the next one after that...

Recently, I've been creating the love stories of Bravo family members who were children in the first books of the series. This story is one of those. Ethan Bravo is a small-town lawyer with a secret years-long crush he honestly believes he's put behind him.

But then Matilda Hunt, the widow of Ethan's best friend, Gabe, returns to town to take over her family's bookstore and raise her coming baby on her own. Her husband has been gone for three years now. And Matty is thirteen weeks pregnant by a man who doesn't want the child.

Right away, Matty reaches out to Ethan, her lost husband's lifelong friend. She's so grateful to connect with him again. Ethan's a man she can trust and count on. After all, he's Matty's friend, too.

Hope you enjoy this one. There's just something about longtime friends discovering that they could have so much more...

Happy reading, everyone,

Christine

HIS BEST FRIEND'S GIRL

CHRISTINE RIMMER

Harlequin

SPECIAL EDITION

Harlequin®
SPECIAL
EDITION™

ISBN-13: 978-1-335-40220-2

His Best Friend's Girl

Harlequin Enterprises ULC
22 Adelaide St. West, 41st Floor
Toronto, Ontario M5H 4E3, Canada
www.Harlequin.com

Printed in Lithuania

Recycling programs
for this product may
not exist in your area.

MIX
Paper | Supporting
responsible forestry
FSC® C021394

Christine Rimmer came to her profession the long way around. She tried everything from acting to teaching to telephone sales. Now she's finally found work that suits her perfectly. She insists she never had a problem keeping a job—she was merely gaining "life experience" for her future as a novelist. Christine lives with her family in Oregon. Visit her at christinerimmer.com.

Books by Christine Rimmer

Harlequin Special Edition

Bravo Family Ties

Hometown Reunion
Her Best Friend's Wedding
Taking the Long Way Home
When Christmas Comes
His Best Friend's Girl

Montana Mavericks: The Trail to Tenacity

Redeeming the Maverick

Montana Mavericks: Brothers & Broncos

Summer Nights with the Maverick

Montana Mavericks: The Real Cowboys of Bronco Heights

The Rancher's Summer Secret

Montana Mavericks: What Happened to Beatrix?

In Search of the Long-Lost Maverick

Montana Mavericks: Six Brides for Six Brothers

Her Favorite Maverick

Montana Mavericks: Lassoing Love

The Maverick's Surprise Son

Visit the Author Profile page at Harlequin.com for more titles.

His Best Friend's Girl is dedicated with much admiration and appreciation to Edmund and Xo Cat (pronounced Zo), two special felines who have roles in this story. They are the bookstore cats who live at Cloud Peak Books in the town of Medicine Creek, Wyoming.

While it's true that Medicine Creek and Cloud Peak Books came straight out of my imagination, Edmund and Xo Cat are the real-life beloved fur babies of readers Karen White and Michelle Church.

Of Edmund, Karen White writes: This is my emotional support cat, Edmund. He thinks he has to always be on the counter or the table and supervise whatever I am doing in the kitchen. He loves to be petted but will bite if he's not ready for you to stop when you are. He also loves to get the zoomies and run through the apartment growling like a dog. People who have heard him do this look at me in disbelief and ask, "Did he just growl like a dog?" And I say, "Yes he did! He does it all the time!"

Michelle Church has this to say about Xo Cat:
Xo Cat plays favorites with my husband!
She loved having him work from home during COVID.
She loves to make appearances on video calls.
And she makes us laugh all the time. I think tuxedos must be the biggest comedians of the cat world.

Many thanks to Karen and Michelle for allowing me to put their sweet cats in this story.

Chapter One

On the first day of March, after two long days on the road, Matty Hunt pulled into her parents' driveway towing a U-Haul trailer.

Her mom and dad came rushing out to greet her. Waving and beaming, they descended the front steps. Matty pushed the driver's door wide and slid out from behind the wheel, her boots crunching on clumps of old snow from a recent storm. The cold Wyoming wind blew her hair into her eyes. She guided it back behind her ear as her mom and dad came at her.

Her mom got there first. "At last!" Simone Gage cried, enfolding Matty in her soft arms. The well-remembered rose scent of her mom's favorite perfume mingled with the smells of pine and woodsmoke and the sharpness of the wintry air. It had been sixty degrees out when Matty left North Hollywood. Here in Medicine Creek it was in the high thirties.

"Here's our girl..." Neal Gage, his wire-rim glasses glinting in the gray afternoon light, piled onto the family hug. "It's so good to have you home..."

For a moment, they just held each other, the three of them, their little family reunited for the first time in almost a year.

And then her mom cupped the side of her face and chided, "You really should have let us come and help you. Packing up everything you own and then driving all the way from Los Angeles with a trailer hooked on the back is no job for a pregnant woman."

Matty laughed through a sigh. "I'm fine, Mom—great, in fact. No morning sickness at all in the past couple of weeks. And before I left, my doctor in LA gave me the okay to make the drive."

"But travel can be so stressful."

"It's done and it went great. I had a rideshare straight through to Salt Lake City. She was nice. She did half the driving, and we split expenses down the middle. It was fine—I promise you."

A pickup slid in at the curb.

"Here's Colin," said her dad.

All long arms and rangy legs, Colin Trask got out of the pickup and came up the driveway toward them. Colin was...what? Seventeen or eighteen now? He worked part-time at the family bookstore. "Hey, Matty." He gave her a shy smile.

"Colin! Good to see you."

Her dad tightened his hold on her in another quick hug. "I cleared plenty of space in the garage. Colin and I will unload that trailer for you."

"Thanks, Dad." She kissed his bristly cheek, and he and Colin got to work.

Matty and her mom carried her suitcases inside and up the stairs to her old bedroom, which had been redone as a guest room years ago. Long gone were the Paul Theroux, Bruno Mars and Rihanna posters Matty had once tacked up with push pins. Instead it was all very adult and tasteful.

There were framed posters from events at the bookstore and large botanical prints hanging above the tufted headboard.

In the thirteen years since Matty had moved to Los Angeles for her freshman year of college, she'd stayed in this room often. When she and her husband, Gabe, would come home to visit, they'd slept in here. And since Gabe's sudden death three years ago, she'd stayed here alone several times. She'd always thought the space was pretty in a generic sort of way. Now, though, it made her feel oddly disoriented—like she was suddenly a stranger in this place she knew so well.

She had a sudden overwhelming urge to jump up and get out—run downstairs and keep going out the front door, to zip right past her dad and Colin unloading the U-Haul. Her breath came too fast and her heart beat a wild tattoo under her rib cage as she pictured herself racing off down the street, never once pausing to look back.

Her mom brushed a lock of hair away from Matty's forehead. "You want some time to yourself to start unpacking, get settled in a little?"

Matty moderated her breathing and took care to answer in an easy tone. "That would be great."

"All right, then." Pressing a kiss to her temple, Simone said, "I'll leave you to it."

Matty rose and trailed after her. Shutting the door quietly, she let her head droop against it and closed her eyes. *What next?* she thought. The two words echoed in her head.

She did have a plan. She was home for a reason. Still, her life felt as though it had somehow gotten away from her. She had no idea what might happen next. Sometimes her lack of confidence in herself and her future terrified her.

How had she become so completely...unmoored? The

Matty Hunt she used to be had desire, determination and focus. Yet nowadays she couldn't help wondering where the old Matty had gone.

Head down, feeling crappy, she wandered back to the bed. As she sank to the cream-colored duvet, that sense of complete unreality rushed over her again.

Back home. In Medicine Creek. And this time to stay—with a baby on the way. Who would ever have imagined that could happen to Matty Hunt? Matty Hunt, who was a successful travel writer, one who'd made Los Angeles her home base and had no problem living out of a suitcase much of the year.

Matty Hunt, whose babies were supposed to be Gabe's babies, too.

Gabe. Even after three years, it hurt to think of him. She missed him still. The loss of him was a hollow place just beneath her beating heart. She knew she would never stop missing him.

Matty put her hand to her still-flat belly, closed her eyes and imagined sending pure love flowing straight from her heart, down her arm and out her fingertips, pure love transmitting through the cage of her flesh to where her baby slept. Her baby was very much wanted. And her choice to move back home was just that—*her own.*

She *wanted* to be here, she reminded herself.

And this disoriented, freaked-out, not-really-here feeling? It would pass, hopefully soon.

But it didn't pass, at least not right then. The rest of the afternoon went by as if in a dream.

Once her dad and Colin had unloaded all her things, her dad wanted to go with her to return the trailer. She insisted that she could manage it just fine. And then she got back behind the wheel of her Jeep Cherokee and headed for the U-Haul dealer in nearby Buffalo.

When she returned to Medicine Creek, she finished unpacking her suitcases and helped her mom with dinner. They sat down to roast chicken, baked sweet potatoes and a tossed salad. She wouldn't have minded eating in silence.

But she probably should have known that wouldn't happen.

Right away, her dad had a question about her ex-boyfriend, Ted. "So, sweetheart, any…change of attitude from the baby's father?"

A change of attitude? From Ted Lansing?

As though that could ever happen—as though she would even want it to happen. Because she didn't. No way.

"No, Dad," Matty replied firmly. "Ted is never changing his mind—believe me."

"Then you've had more talks with him?"

"No. I haven't spoken to Ted since I told him about the baby. You've already heard how that went."

Telling Ted about the baby had not gone well. He'd put up both hands and backed away shaking his head. *No*, he'd said, his eyes round with horror. *Uh-uh. You and I are already through, Matty, and I never signed on for any baby. Just leave me out of it.*

Her mom suggested, "Maybe he only needs time to—"

"Mom. Honestly. Ted has made it painfully clear that he doesn't want the baby."

For a moment, nobody spoke. Her mom and dad shared a speaking look. "Ah," said her mother in a soothing tone. "Well, all right, then."

Just in case they still didn't get the point, Matty clarified it for them. "I'm going to be a single mom. And I'm good with that. It is what it is, and I'm just fine with how it's worked out. I don't want to be coparenting with Ted. We broke up, as I've told you both before, and Ted does not want anything to do with this baby."

"Got it," her mother said.

Her dad patted her shoulder and predicted, "It will all work out."

"I know it will," Matty replied in a mild tone—and it *would* work out. She would make it so. "I love you both and I am so grateful for how good you are to me, but..."

"We love you, too," said her dad, reaching over and giving her shoulder a squeeze.

"Yes, we do," her mom agreed. "And what else were you going to say?"

Matty laid it on them. "I would greatly appreciate it if you would never mention Ted Lansing to me again."

Her mom glanced away as her dad looked at her with real pain in his brown eyes. The silence went on forever.

Finally her mom said, "It's that bad, huh?"

"Yeah," Matty replied. "He is completely out of the picture, and that is never going to change. Plus, it's all so...fresh, you know? One of these days, I'll be over it. Then maybe I'll share all the gory details with you. But not right now."

"We understand," her mom replied.

Matty felt terrible. Her mom and dad just wanted to help. And she really was grateful for their love, their care and their understanding.

But still, as the too-quiet meal continued, she kept picturing herself jumping up out of her chair and whirling for the front door at a run. She ached to fling that door wide and get out of there, to keep on running forever, never pausing, never once looking back.

She kept taking slow breaths, reminding herself that she was doing exactly what she wanted to do, that she was grateful for her baby, that everything really would work out just fine in the end.

Still, as each moment went by, her feelings of unreality only got more so. All she wanted was to get out of that house, away from the tenderness and honest concern in her dad's eyes. She just needed to be somewhere else, someplace where people she loved didn't have to wonder if she knew what she was doing, if she had any kind of real plan for her new life as a single mom.

Maybe she should go over to Heather's later...

Her cousin, who was her mom's sister's daughter, lived right there in town. Heather already knew all the gory details about the breakup with Ted. Matty had also shared the news of the baby with her.

But Heather had four kids and a loving husband, and after dinner would no doubt be family time. Matty didn't want to break in on that. Plus, Heather could get so emotional about things. The last thing Matty needed right now was someone to cry over her. She could manage the crying part all by herself.

So if not Heather, then who?

The answer came instantly. Ethan.

Ethan Bravo had been Gabe's lifelong best friend. Over the years, he'd become Matty's friend, too.

Yeah. Ethan...

Ethan would offer her drama-free support. Also, it really was past time to bring Ethan up to speed on all the stuff she'd never quite managed to get into with him since Ted Lansing had entered her life.

It would be tough, having a long talk with Ethan.

But she needed to do it.

"Sweetheart, did you hear me?" Her mom smiled at her across the dinner table.

"Hmm?"

"Pass the sweet potatoes?"

Matty blinked. "Oh. Yeah. Here you go..." She passed the bowl and went back to thinking about Ethan.

Thirteen years ago, when Matty and Gabe left after high school for college in Los Angeles, Ethan went with them.

She and Gabe chose UCLA, while Ethan went to USC. Four years later, they all three had their bachelor's degrees. That summer, Matty had found a slightly rundown but charming apartment in Los Feliz. She and Gabe moved in. A month later, when another unit became available, Ethan took it.

Matty and Gabe had quickly discovered their well-matched career paths—Gabe as a travel photographer, Matty as a writer. As for Ethan, he'd always wanted to be a lawyer. He'd started law school there in Los Angeles at Loyola Marymount.

But at the end of his first year as a graduate student, he'd said he was burnt out on LA. He'd moved home and ended up finishing his JD at the University of Wyoming.

Now he lived a few blocks from her parents' house. He'd partnered up with another lawyer right there in town. They shared a law office on Main Street.

Ethan didn't know about the baby yet. He didn't even know about Ted. So far, Matty hadn't been able to bring herself to tell her deceased husband's best friend that she'd met someone six months ago and three weeks later, that guy was living in her house with her—let alone that now she was having that guy's baby.

Before Ted, she'd only ever been with Gabe. That was how Ethan had gotten to know her—because she was Gabe's girl. Would Ethan be shocked that she'd lived with some guy she barely knew and also managed to get accidentally pregnant by him?

So far, she'd been afraid to find out. Their conversations had become infrequent. In the past six months, since she started in with Ted, talking to Ethan was downright awkward. She'd been evasive. He hadn't called her on that. She'd known that he was waiting for her to tell him what might be going on with her.

He hadn't pushed her, though. He never did.

But they were drifting further and further apart.

And she missed him.

She figured she could handle telling him the truth in stages. Maybe talk about the thing with Ted tonight and save the news of the baby for later. As of now, she'd only told her parents and her cousin Heather about the baby. She'd sworn them to secrecy until she gave them the go-ahead to start spreading the word. She needed to tell Ethan.

Tonight, she thought. *I need to go see Ethan tonight. I need to tell him about Ted, at least, so he has some idea of what is going on.*

As soon as she'd helped her mom load the dishwasher after dinner, she went up to her room. Her fingers were shaking as she texted him.

Hey. I'm here in town at my parents' house and I want to see you. Okay if I come over—I mean if you're free tonight?

She hit Send and stared at the screen. The check mark appeared: *Delivered*. And then it showed *Read*. Several seconds went by. At last, the phone dinged with Ethan's reply.

Matilda! I'm here. Come on over.

Her heart just melted. He really did want to see her. Suddenly she could take a deep breath again. She realized she felt better about everything.

She ran downstairs, told her parents she was going to Ethan's, pulled on her boots and her puffer coat, and set out.

The first sight of him put a big, fat smile on her face. He was waiting for her at his front door in his stocking feet. "About time you showed up. It's been too damn long." He held out his arms.

"Ethan!" She ran up the steps and jumped on him. He caught her, wrapping her up in a hug, spinning her around in the glow of the porchlight. They were both laughing as he let her boots touch the ground again.

"Safe flight?" he asked.

"I drove. And it was great. No problems."

"So how long are you staying?"

She just went ahead and told him. "Well, actually, I'm thinking the rest of my life."

"Whoa." He took her by the shoulders and looked at her for the longest time. "You're moving home?"

She nodded. "I'm essentially already moved. I'll be staying at my folks' house until I find my own place."

He shook his head. "I had no clue."

Guilt tugged at her. "I'm sorry. I... Ethan, I didn't know where to start—I really didn't." Unwilling tears welled in her eyes. "I, um...well, a lot has happened in the past several months. And that's why recently, I decided I needed a change, that I needed…" She didn't know how to go on.

"Hey." He pulled her close again. "It's okay. You don't have to explain anything. You're here and I'm glad…"

She buried her face in the warmth of his soft flannel shirt, breathed in his scent of soap and a faint hint of some woodsy aftershave, and let herself sag against his solid strength. He stroked a hand down her hair. It felt good, his touch—like all the comfort she'd been longing for lavished on her, at last. Then he caught her face between his palms and tipped her chin up so that she looked in his eyes.

"Let's go inside…" Grabbing her hand, he pulled her across the threshold.

She loved Ethan's house. It was roomy and comfortable. He'd bought it soon after he graduated from law school using trust-fund money from his wealthy grandparents. The main floor had an open-plan living area with a big, beautiful kitchen. There was a roomy laundry room and an office in the back. The bedrooms were upstairs. He even had a home gym in the basement.

Once she'd shucked her boots and hung her coat and scarf at the door, Ethan led her through the foyer to the great room. He gestured at the fat leather sofa. "Sit." She ignored his command and followed him to the island that marked off the kitchen. He turned to face her again. "How about a drink?"

"Got decaf by any chance?"

"I do. It's from the Perfect Bean. It's really good, too." The coffee house and roastery on Pine Street off Main had opened almost a decade ago. Matty and Gabe used to joke that no small town in America could get by now without a cozy place that offered espresso and lattes and whatever other fancy coffee creation one might desire.

"Decaf from the Perfect Bean, please." She took a comfy high-backed padded stool at the island as Ethan turned to the counter by the sink and started fiddling with a coffee machine. "So?" she asked. "How's Sylvia?"

He and Sylvia O'Grady, a local accountant, had been dating for over a year now. Matty had yet to meet her.

"Sylvia's good," he said.

"Meaning?"

"She's fine, honestly. We're still together—but right now, I want to hear about *you*." He slanted her a look over his shoulder, a thick wave of his brown hair flopping on his forehead the way it always did. "You, Matty Gage Hunt, moving home? Really?"

"Really. It's… I guess it's just time, you know. Gabe's gone…"

There was a silence. Ethan turned his whole body to face her. They stared at each other, the memories seeming to crowd the space between them. Gabe had died on an assignment to photograph endangered black rhinos in Africa for a big piece in a major magazine. His plane went down in the jungle.

She'd been told that he died instantly. Getting that news had actually made her knees buckle. One moment she was on her feet, staring at the solemn-faced policewoman she'd let into the North Hollywood duplex she and Gabe had bought the year before. The woman broke the news gently—and Matty crumpled to the floor.

"Matty?" Ethan looked at her with concern.

She shook herself. "Sorry…"

"Don't be," Ethan said, his voice low, his eyes dark with understanding.

"I'm thirty-one, Ethan. And I'm ready to…" She laughed, but it just came out sounding sad. "Settle down, I guess. Mom's going to retire in the next year or two. Dad retired in January."

"I heard about your dad retiring."

Neal Gage had worked as a critical care nurse at the hospital in nearby Sheridan for as long as Matty could remember. "They want to travel. Mom's turning the bookstore over to me."

"Damn. Never saw that coming."

"Yeah, well." She made jazz hands. "Surprise!"

He was looking at her so steadily. The wordless moment stretched out, full of all the things that had yet to be said. Finally, he spoke. "Go on, get comfortable on the sofa. I'll bring you your decaf, and you can tell me everything."

Five minutes later, he set her coffee on the low table in front of her and then dropped down beside her on the sofa.

She sipped. "So good. Thank you." He'd even frothed the milk.

"Talk to me, Matilda." Laying his arm along the back of the sofa, he turned his body toward her and hiked one stocking foot across the other knee.

She had no idea where to begin. So she just started talking. "I met this guy on Tinder six months ago…" Already her face was burning up. As for Ethan, he actually looked stunned. That made her laugh—a real laugh this time. "What? You thought I would be a sad, lonely, celibate widow for the rest of my life?"

"No. No, of course not. It's just, I…" He looked away.

"Say it," she prompted softly.

He groaned. But then he straightened those broad shoulders. "Full disclosure?"

"Please." She gave him an encouraging smile.

"I'm, uh, yeah…"

"Gee. Thanks for clarifying, Ethan."

He shrugged. "Okay, you're right. I'm surprised. I never thought of you with someone who wasn't Gabe, and I…" He shut his eyes and shook his head. "Aw, hell, Matilda. I'm sorry. It's just that you and Gabe were together since…"

"Ninth grade," she finished for him. And then, in an attempt to reassure him, she reached out and awkwardly patted his shoulder. "I know that it's hard not to think of me as Gabe's girl. I do get it, and it's okay. Because it's been hard for me, too—but anyway… Tinder. When it's just for tonight, right?"

"Right." He looked doubtful. Guarded, too.

She forged on. "Because that was what I wanted. Just a night with a hot guy. To start getting out there, to find out how to be more than a lonely, celibate widow, you know?"

"Matty, I—"

"Wait." She showed him the hand. "Just let me get through this?"

"Of course. Go ahead."

"I matched with a guy named Ted. He was nice looking and friendly."

"Was? Is he dead?"

"No. Ted is not dead." *Though he's dead to me.* "Anyway, Ted is a charming guy. And the night we had together was…" She frowned, thinking that the less she said about her Tinder date with Ted, the better. "Ted was smooth and easy to talk to. That night was okay. I got home to my empty duplex, and I didn't know whether to cry from this weird feeling of total loneliness—or to jump up and down that I'd finally put myself out there. I mean, it felt all wrong, to be with someone I hardly knew. But at least I'd done it. I'd slept with a man who wasn't Gabe. It seemed like a big step in the right direction, you know?"

"I get that, Matty. I honestly do."

She almost laughed. He spoke so slowly, kept his voice low and steady, as though he might be worried she was on the verge of losing her ever-loving mind. "Ethan?"

"Yeah?"

"I'm okay." She said that in the same low, steady tone he'd just used on her.

He drew a slow breath. "Gotcha. Continue."

"Okay. So anyway, Ted asked me out again, and I figured, well, the first night was okay, so why not? And suddenly, we're dating and then we're exclusive. And it's three weeks since that first night and he's at my place all the time…"

"So what you're telling me is that you fell for this Ted guy?"

"Fell for Ted?" She winced. "Yeah, that is what I told myself at the time. But looking at the situation in retrospect, did I really fall for him? No. Not by a long shot. What I'm saying is that, hey, at least he was there in the house with me at night, you know? Because really, Ethan, I've been alone for what seems like the longest time now…" Her throat clutched and her eyes were getting all misty again.

Ethan leaned in. She did the same. They were nose to nose. She could see the flecks of gold and amber in his eyes and smell his clean, familiar scent. "I should have flown out there," he whispered, "made sure you were doing okay…"

"You're the best," she whispered back. "But it was still

just something I had to work through. Nobody could do it for me—not even you."

"Still, I—"

"Wait." She put two fingers to his soft lips—and then quickly took them away. Sitting back a little, she asked again, "Let me get through this? I just need to tell you this...please?"

"I'm sorry." He retreated to his own sofa cushion. "Continue."

"All right. So, about Ted. Did I even like him? I really thought I did at the time. Honestly, Ethan, I'm not sure how it happened, but suddenly he was living with me. And I mean, looking back, I think I convinced myself that it was something good, something real, what I had with Ted. That it wasn't just a case of me trying to move on and making a hash of it."

"But it *wasn't* real?"

"No, it wasn't."

"Matty." He leaned toward her again. "Just tell me. What did this Ted guy *do* to you?"

"Oh, Ethan..."

"Just tell me what happened." His expression was blank, his eyes guarded. She had a feeling he'd already figured it out.

"Fine. Back in January, I flew to Scotland to do a piece on the pub scene. I was finished two days early, so I flew back. I thought I would surprise Ted, you know?"

Ethan nodded. His eyes stayed locked on hers. He definitely knew what was coming now.

She said, "I surprised him, all right. I walked in on him in my bed with someone else. I mean, it took me a minute to register what I was seeing. I just stood there in the open bedroom doorway for what seemed like half a life-time watching him nail some woman with pink hair and a full-sleeve tattoo of twining vines and roses…"

"And then what?" His voice remained low, coaxing, yet carefully controlled.

"Eventually the woman saw me standing there. She let out a shriek and shoved Ted off her. He turned around and saw me, too. And instantly he started talking, telling me I wasn't seeing what was right there in front of me. As he was gaslighting me for all he was worth, the woman ran around grabbing her clothes and throwing them on. Finally she snatched up her purse from the chair by the bed and sprinted out the door."

"What about Ted?"

"It took me longer to get rid of him. He just kept right on trying to convince me that I hadn't seen what was right there in front of my face—and then when that didn't work, he moved on to how it wasn't his fault that he'd cheated on me. He accused me of coming home early just to try to catch him in bed with someone else. He whined that he had to do *something*, that I was gone all the time, that he was a man and a man had needs and what did I expect him to do? I just kept saying, *Get out, Ted. Get out.*"

"Did he go?"

"Yeah. Finally. He threw a few things in a suitcase and left. I called a locksmith and changed the locks."

"Good." Ethan clasped her shoulders. Then, carefully, like she was something so precious and fragile, he pulled her into his strong arms.

She sagged against him, burying her nose in his shirt that felt so warm and soft and comforting and smelled like everything good. "Oh, Ethan. I've been wanting to tell you about Ted moving in with me for months, but I just couldn't work up the courage. And then, when I found him in my bed with someone else... Uh-uh. No way did I want to tell you about that..."

"Well, now I know. And I'm glad you've told me." He spoke quietly, still holding her. "And I sincerely hope that is the last you saw of Ted."

A tiny, ragged sound escaped her as she tried to decide what to say next. Her eyes filled and a tear trickled down her cheek.

"Matty?" He held her away again and met her gaze. "What is it? Are you okay?"

"Not really." She was whining, just a little, and so tempted to blurt out the news about the baby. But wasn't the awful story of Ted the cheater enough for one night? "I mean, Gabe and me, we always knew what we wanted. With Gabe, I was full of confidence, sure of how my life would go. And, well..." She gestured down her body with a sweep of one hand. "Look at me now..."

"Hey. Don't be so hard on yourself." He handed her a tissue from the box on the side table at his end of the sofa. "You're as smart and beautiful as ever."

"Yeah, right."

"I *am* right. You gave that fool a shot, and he blew it. He showed you who he really was, and you kicked his ass out. Good work." He seemed to mean that.

And suddenly she felt a lot better about everything. "Thank you." She wiped her eyes and blew her nose, then grabbed her coffee and had another delicious sip. "I, um, wasn't sure how you were going to react to the news that I let a complete loser move in with me..."

He pulled back a little. "Matty." His voice was calm, even tender. "Come on. Look at me."

With a sniffle, she straightened her shoulders and lifted her chin. "What?"

He stared back at her with years of affection and understanding in his eyes. "Ted's the loser. I mean, come on. What a clown to let *you* get away."

She grinned then. Slowly. "You always did know just the right thing to say."

"That creep is out of your life, right?"

"Yep. Ted is as gone as they get."

"*That's* what I wanted to hear."

She scooted a little closer and dared to lean on him again. He wrapped his arm around her, and she rested her head on his shoulder. "I was finally ready to move on a little. To get out there, meet new people, start picking up the pieces after losing Gabe, to make a life that was more than the next assignment. And then I messed it up royally and ended up making myself nothing short of pathetic."

"No. Uh-uh. Don't be like that." He waited until she looked at him. "You are not pathetic, not in the least. You're Matty Gage Hunt and you are strong, smart, and beautiful."

"Oh, Ethan. Thank you." She dropped her head to his shoulder again. "Too bad that sometimes, lately, all I feel is weak and gullible."

"You're way too hard on yourself. What happened is not your fault. You got out there, you took a chance on that guy, and he burned you. So you kicked him to the curb. Now you're free and moving on. Everything is going to be all right."

Was it? He didn't have the whole story yet. "Ethan."

"Hmm?"

"There's more." She gulped.

Because what was she doing? She'd said enough for tonight. She could tell him about the baby later. It was too much to lay that on him now.

She stared at the cheery flames in the fireplace opposite the sofa. It was so good to be here with him, at last. To be able to let go, to talk freely about her own complete foolishness, to break down and bawl like a little kid and get support and affection in return.

Yes, she'd already told her parents and her cousin Heather everything, including about the baby. But she'd tried to be strong around them, both to salvage some semblance of pride and also so they wouldn't worry too much. Now, though, with Ethan, she could let her pride go and sob all over his broad, strong shoulder.

He and Gabe had been like brothers, after all. That made Ethan family to her in the truest sense of the word. She should have come to him earlier, she realized now. She should have admitted the emptiness she felt in her heart, confessed to the lack of joy in her work and in every aspect of her life after it became a life without Gabe. If she'd done that, she just might have avoided all the ridiculousness with Ted.

But then she remembered the baby, and she shook her head. Given the chance to erase the ridiculousness with Ted, she would say no.

Because if there'd been no Ted, she wouldn't have the baby coming. The baby was well worth making a fool of herself over a bad guy. The baby had given her back what she'd lost when Gabe died.

The baby had given her love. And love, she knew now,

was so much more than an emotion. Love was also a promise. And a sense of purpose.

She pulled a tissue from the box and blew her nose again. Her face felt blotchy from crying, her eyes tired and swollen.

Ethan gazed at her so steadily. "What else? Don't look so miserable. Come on, Matilda. It can't be that bad."

"You're right. It's not bad. It really isn't. Because I'm happy about it. But it is...a lot, you know? It's not how I expected it to happen." Far from it.

It was supposed to have been according to the plan she and Gabe had laid out for themselves when they were still in high school. According to the plan, they were going to start trying for a baby when they turned thirty.

But Gabe never got a chance to turn thirty.

"So much for all of our happy little plans..." she whispered, her throat tight again, her eyes blurring with a fresh surge of tears.

Ethan took her hand and pressed another tissue into it. She wiped her eyes and then sagged against him.

They sat there holding each other for an indeterminate period of time. It was good in the most basic way. Just Matty and Ethan, sitting on the sofa together. She was a mess and he was there for her and everything felt better than it had in a long, long time.

"Whatever it is, just tell me," he said into the comfortable quiet that had settled between them. "Just get it all out and let it go."

She pulled away from him and sat up straighter. As she met Ethan's beautiful green eyes, she felt such gratitude— that she'd had Gabe, however briefly, and that Gabe had given her a friend like Ethan.

And when she thought of it that way, she couldn't hold the truth back for one minute longer.

"I'm pregnant," she said. "Thirteen weeks. It wasn't planned, but it happened. It's Ted's—except it isn't. Because Ted wants nothing to do with this baby. And you know what that means? That means this baby is mine."

Chapter Two

Ethan had no idea what to say.

Matty pregnant? By some cheating asshat who said he didn't want his own baby?

It seemed completely impossible. Unacceptable. All wrong.

Except…

She was looking at him so hopefully.

And she really did seem thrilled that she was pregnant.

He took her hands. She grabbed on, like she needed him to hold her steady. "You're happy—about the baby?" he asked. "You really are?"

A big, beautiful smile bloomed on her unforgettable face. "Yes! I am, Ethan. I am so happy."

He nodded slowly. "Well, then. I'm happy *for* you."

Her smile wavered. She bit her lip, uncertain now. "I need the truth from you. I really do."

He met her eyes and nodded again, more firmly this time. "Matilda, I am happy for you."

"Oh, Ethan!" And she threw her arms around him, laughing.

He laughed with her, holding her soft, curvy body good and tight, breathing in the well-remembered scent of her perfume, a scent of oranges and tropical flowers. "You're home now," he said, stroking her hair. "Things will only get better from here on out."

She pulled back to look up at him, her eyes red rimmed but her smile big and bright. "I think I'm all cried out."

It felt so good to have her here, to know that he could be there for her in the months to come. "So, then. Any other big secrets I need to know?"

"Hmm. I do believe that you know everything now—and *everything* is probably way more than I ever should have told you."

"Hey."

"Hmm?"

"Matilda, there is nothing you can't say to me."

"I know that. I do." Her soft mouth quivered just a little. "And I'm grateful. And the same goes for you. Anything you need to talk about, I'm here for it. I mean that."

"It's a deal," he lied with a smile. There were some things she was never going to know, and the way he saw it, that was for the best. "Can you stay a while longer? Let's hang out, stream a movie."

She said yes.

He offered popcorn. She said yes again.

He had a nice, big flat screen mounted above the mantel. They watched *Warm Bodies*, a love story between a zombie and a human woman. Because who doesn't love it when the zombie apocalypse meets *Romeo and Juliet*?

She said, "This is great, you know? Being with you again, having a good cry and feeling thoroughly supported and completely understood—and to cap things off, I get to munch popcorn and drool over Nicholas Hoult."

"Any time—you know that."

She was hogging most of the sofa by then, with her head on a throw pillow and her feet in his lap. It wasn't long before her eyes started drooping. He watched them flutter shut—for a moment or two. And then she would shake herself and stare at the screen, determined to stay awake.

But within minutes, her eyelids would get heavy again. He wasn't surprised. It was a long drive from North Hollywood. And tonight had been emotional. Plus, she was having a baby. No wonder she was exhausted.

Eventually, her eyes drifted shut and stayed that way. He left the movie on for a few minutes as he wondered if this was it and she was truly asleep.

When a gentle snore escaped her, he knew for sure she was over and out.

Carefully, he eased out from under her stocking feet and lowered them to the sofa cushion. He turned off the movie.

She didn't stir.

"Matty?"

Down for the count, she slept on.

With slow care, he slid one arm behind her back and the other beneath her knees. When he lifted her off the sofa, she turned her head into his shoulder and whispered something—he couldn't make out what. The small sounds made him smile again.

He'd missed her so damn much in the years since he moved home. But at least while Gabe was alive, he'd seen her whenever he and Gabe got together, which was a few times a year on average. Once Gabe was gone, he and Matty had vowed to keep in touch but they only saw each other infrequently and somehow the time between visits kept getting longer.

He'd had this idea that maybe it was better, for him and for her, to let the months go by without checking in.

Wrong.

He should have reached out more often.

Slowly, so as not to wake her, he carried her up the stairs to the guest room and put her down on the bed. Still sound asleep, she rolled to her side, tucked her hands under her cheek and murmured "Umm, yeah!" with dreamy enthusiasm. That made him smile again.

Turning for the closet, he got the big blue patchwork quilt his mom had made for him several Christmases ago. Shaking it open, he covered her with it.

And then he just stood there above her, staring down at her, thinking how good it was to see her, to spend time with her again—too good, really, and he knew it.

He was still having some trouble processing the things she'd told him tonight, mainly the stuff about the douchebag who'd messed her over—and left her pregnant, too. It was a lot to take in.

He grinned to himself. He'd always loved that adventurous spirit of hers. More power to her, to get out there and take some chances.

As he stared down at her, she shifted beneath the quilt with a heavy sigh. Ethan realized he'd been standing there like a creeper, watching her sleep for way too long. He shook himself and headed for his own room.

Friday morning, he was up at six. He spent half an hour in the gym downstairs, hit the shower and dressed for work. Before he left the upper floor, he tapped lightly on the guest-room door. When she didn't respond, he stuck his head in. She was still conked out. Carefully, he shut her door and went on downstairs to get breakfast started.

Twenty minutes later, he looked up from his phone to find her standing by the island. Her eyes were still sleepy, but she must have found the spare comb in the guest bath because her blond hair didn't look the least slept in. It fell thick and soft and wavy to her shoulders.

He held up the phone. "I just texted your mom that you're safe here with me."

"Thank you." She gave him that beautiful smile. And then she groaned. "Tell me the truth. I don't remember walking up the stairs. Did you actually carry me?"

"You were dead asleep. I tried to wake you up, but it wasn't happening. I considered covering you with a blanket and letting you sleep right there on the sofa, but the bed in the guest room is a lot more comfortable."

"Thanks. But I have to ask—how's your back?"

"Matty. Please. It was no trouble and my back is just fine."

"Whew. I'm glad to hear that. Having to carry a grown woman up the stairs is bad enough. I would hate to think you might have been injured doing it."

"I wasn't. Can we move on?"

She chuckled. "Absolutely."

"Wonderful. Coffee's ready—it's the real thing. I can make decaf if you—"

"Are you kidding? I allow myself one big mugful a day, and I'm having that now."

"Well, all right, then. Ham-and-vegetable scramble?"

"I thought you'd never ask." He watched her fill a mug, add milk and sip. "So good," she said with a sigh.

Stirring the scramble without looking at it, he stared at

her—Matty, right here in his kitchen, sipping her morning coffee on the second day of March.

And then, with a twinge of guilt, he thought of Sylvia.

He reminded himself that he had nothing to feel bad about—and yet for some unknown reason, he dreaded telling his girlfriend that Gabe's widow had spent the night in his guest room.

Ethan plated the eggs. They sat down to eat. And then, too soon, Matty was hugging him goodbye and heading out the door to return to her parents' house.

Sylvia called as he was leaving for the office. He let it go to voicemail and made a mental note to reach out to her when he got a spare moment during the day.

At home, Matty found her dad sitting at the kitchen table sipping coffee and reading the *Medicine Creek Clarion*. He glanced up when she entered the room. "Hey, sunshine. How's Ethan?"

"Doing great. It was good to spend some time with him, to catch up a little, you know?"

"It's nice that you two have kept in touch. There's coffee..."

"I had some at Ethan's. He made me breakfast, too. Has Mom already gone over to the store?"

"Mm-hmm..." He was reading again, his glasses slipping down his nose.

"I'll just grab a shower and then head over there."

"Sounds good..."

Forty-five minutes later, dressed for work in a short, fitted crewneck cardigan, a nice pair of jeans and tan boots, with her hooded puffy jacket for protection against the late-winter wind, she entered Cloud Peak Books on Hart Street, just off Main.

Her mom stood at the counter ringing up a sale. Simone gave Matty a smile and went back to chatting up the customer. Matty took a minute to look around, see what was new since her last visit months ago.

The store was a great space. White shelves filled with books covered almost every wall. Pretty tables of differing shapes and sizes offered attractive displays. White-framed arched windows faced Hart Street on either side of the front entrance. The walls were sky blue. Like the bookshelves, all the doors and trim were white. Origami birds and butterflies hung from the blue ceiling, on which Emmaline Stokely, a local artist, had painted clouds of different shapes and sizes.

On the wall at the rear of the store, between two sets of wide bookcases and surrounding the door to the back room, Emmaline had also painted a rendering of Cloud Peak. It was the highest peak in Wyoming's Bighorn Mountains. And it was beautiful, that craggy gray mountain, rising up from teal-blue mountain lakes known as tarns, and dotted with remnant glaciers.

The customer took his bag of books and turned for the street. Matty nodded as the man went by.

Her mom gave her a giant grin. "Mornin'!" Matty went to her. They shared a hug.

Matty said, "You mentioned the Cloud Peak mural. You were right. It's gorgeous. And I love the clouds on the ceiling. Emmaline is something else."

"Oh, she's good, all right. And worth every penny."

Edmund, the sweetest black cat in the world, was stretched out on a stack of nature books. He yawned, displaying a complete lack of teeth in the front. How he'd lost them was a mystery, but her mom fed him very soft food and he thrived on it. The story was that Edmund had wandered in the back door during a delivery about a decade ago. He'd never shown any inclination to leave.

When he swiped at her hand a second time, Matty scooped him up and cuddled him close. "How've you been, my man?" He purred in her ear.

Her mom asked, "How's Ethan?"

"Terrific, as always. We talked half the night. Then we tried to watch a movie, but—"

"Let me guess. You fell asleep."

"I did." She dipped to the floor and set Edmund down. He strutted off toward the front door as Xo Cat appeared from behind the register counter. Xo Cat (pronounced *Zo Cat)* was black and white—and a real comedian. She rolled to her side, batted Matty's leg and then rolled onto her back, her way of begging for a belly scratch. Matty gave Xo Cat what she wanted.

As she scratched Xo Cat's white tummy, Matty explained, "When I woke up this morning, I discovered that Ethan had put me in the guest room and covered me with a quilt. I slept really well, and now I'm ready for you to put me to work."

Xo Cat grabbed her hand with both paws and pretended to bite her. "Knock that off..." She laughed as she said it.

Xo Cat gave her finger one more nip, rolled upright— and dashed away.

Grinning, Matty stood. "Things do look great around here. How about I take the register? Or maybe you need stuff done in back?"

Her mom came out from behind the counter, clasped

Matty by the shoulders and clucked her tongue. "Go home. Take it easy, settle in. You can start working next week— or the week after that. There's really no rush."

"But I want to—"

"I mean it." Simone gave her shoulders a squeeze. "You should take a break. Give yourself permission to relax a little before throwing yourself right into a new job."

"Working here is hardly new to me, Mom." Matty had helped out at the bookstore since she was five. Admittedly, she hadn't been much use at first. But from the age of four-teen until she left for college, she'd worked in the store most weekends. And as soon as she turned sixteen, she'd gone full-time during the summer.

Her mom was shaking her head. "Go see your cousin. You know she's hoping you'll come by."

"But I really want to—"

"No. Decompress a little. Catch up with Heather. She'll be so glad to see you. She's been missing Leonie as much as I have." Leonie Bishop, Heather's mom, was Simone's younger sister. Last year, she and her husband, Darryl, had retired to Florida.

And Matty knew that look in her mom's eye. Simone was not going to give in and let her start working today. She might as well just give it up now. "You're sure?"

"You bet I am. I've got Colin coming in at four. If I'm suddenly overrun with customers before then, I'll give you a call."

"You'd better." Matty tried to look stern.

"Give Heather and the kids a kiss for me."

"I can't believe you're here!" Heather cried when she opened the door and found Matty standing on the front

step. "Come in, come in!" As Matty crossed the threshold
onto the slate-tile entry space, her cousin grabbed her in
a hug. "Home to stay, at last…" Heather's voice wobbled.

Matty pulled back to meet her cousin's brown eyes. "You
okay?"

"Fine, fine."

"Heather, you don't sound fine…"

"Well, I am, so let it be."

"But if you—"

"And you've come at exactly the right time," Heather announced briskly. "The boys are at school and the twins are
downstairs in the playroom with their princess castle. It's
actually quiet around here—for the moment anyway. And
how about you? How're *you* feeling?" She barreled right
on without waiting for an answer. "Oh, Matty. A baby at
last, huh?" Heather gave her a big smile—while simultaneously looking like she might burst into tears.

Matty took her cousin's hand. "Come on. Come here."
She pulled Heather into the living area and tugged her
down onto the giant sectional sofa. "What's the matter?"

Heather sniffled and raked her thick brown hair back
off her forehead. "Nothing."

Matty didn't buy that for a second. "Look at you. You're
all choked up. That's not nothing."

"Oh, Mat. Really. It's fine."

"What's fine?"

"Everything. I'm just so…happy for you. I mean, I know
it's not the way you thought it would be, what with losing
Gabe and then that awful guy, Ted, and now facing motherhood on your own. But babies bring happiness—just take
it from me. Babies are what life's all about, and I can't wait
to…" Heather paused in mid-sentence. Matty waited for

her to gather her thoughts again. Instead, Heather burst into tears.

Matty gasped. "Whoa, hey…"

"Oh, Mat. I just… Well, I mean I can't…" She spoke in a hushed voice—probably so the two little girls downstairs wouldn't hear—as tears rolled down her pretty, heart-shaped face.

Matty held out her arms. Heather resisted for about five seconds. Then, with a torn little sob, she collapsed into Matty's embrace.

"Oh, honey…" Matty rubbed her back and reassured her. "It's okay. Just let it out. Whatever it is, it will be all right…"

"Oh, Mat… No. It's not all right, and I don't think it's ever going to be all right again."

"What? Tell me…"

But Heather only shook her head and sagged in Matty's arms, clinging to her. Matty stopped asking questions and concentrated on soothing her using soft touches and whispered words of comfort and encouragement.

Once Heather had wound down a little, she drew back from Matty's hold with a shaky breath and instructed in a near-whisper, "Keep your voice low. If we're lucky the girls will leave us alone for a while."

Reminded of last night at Ethan's house, when she'd been the one breaking down, Matty promised, "I'll be quiet." She smoothed Heather's silky hair. "Talk to me, tell me what's got you so upset."

Silence.

Matty prompted, "Are you missing your mom, is that it?"

"Yeah," Heather confessed in a tiny voice. "I wish Mom was here. I miss Junior and Vernon, too." Heather's older brothers and their families also lived out of state now. "But…"

Matty waited for her to say something more. The seconds ticked by, the single word hanging in the air all by itself. "But what?" Matty asked at last. "Come on, now. Maybe I won't be any help, but we'll never know if you don't tell me what's bothering you."

Heather gave a sad little moan. "I'm just going to put it right out there."

"Good." Matty pressed her hand to Heather's round cheek. "I'm here and I'm listening…"

"It's Billy."

Matty waited for more. When Heather only sighed, Matty prompted, "What are you saying? Is Billy okay?"

"He's fine," she replied with a scoff—*and* an eye roll.

"But…?"

"But *we're* not fine." Heather leaned closer, her voice intense. "It's… Oh, Mat, it's our marriage."

"Wait. *What?*" Matty whisper-shouted. Because she honestly could not believe that. Heather and Billy were as solid as Matty and Gabe had been—as Matty's mom and dad, and Heather's parents, too. "Your *marriage?*"

"Yes." Another quiet sob escaped Heather. "Billy and me, we're…on the rocks."

"No way."

Heather sniffed. "Yes. Really. I hate it. I wish it wasn't true, but it is true. Sometimes I just don't know if he and I will make it through."

"But why? What happened?"

"Like I said, it's Billy."

"It's Billy *what?*"

"He's changed."

"But how?"

"He's turned selfish—selfish and completely self-absorbed. He doesn't listen anymore. He never hears what I'm saying. There's what *he* wants and that's all that matters. I just can't get through to that man these days. When I try to tell him how I feel, it's like I'm not even there. He talks right over me."

"You're serious? Billy?"

"Yes, Billy. How many times do I have to say it?"

Matty realized her mouth was hanging open in disbelief. Because Billy was a sweetheart. *Selfish* and *self-absorbed* were words she never would have chosen to describe Heather's husband.

Heather was scowling now. "Don't give me that look."

"What look?"

"Like there's no way that Billy could be the problem."

"Heather." Matty took care to speak gently. "I understand that nobody's perfect. Of course it's possible that Billy's at fault in...this." Whatever *this* was. "It *is* hard for me to believe, though."

"Believe it. Because it's true."

"But honey, Billy adores you."

"And I adore him," Heather said through clenched teeth. "We love each other. It's just..." Heather threw up both hands. "Matty, he's being totally unreasonable. He used to be so sweet. He understood what I needed. He wanted the same things I want. But not anymore. Lately he just wants things *his* way. He refuses to see my side of it."

"But I just don't—"

"You don't *what?*" Heather cut her off in an angry whisper.

"I don't get it, that's what. You talk about *your* side and *his* side, but your side and his side of what? I'm in the dark here. I don't understand what the issue is here."

"Mat. Just be on *my* side, will you please?"

"Of course I'm on your side. But Heather, I still don't know what's actually going on here."

"Just take my word for it." There was more sniffling. "He's completely unbearable lately."

"Oh, honey..." Whatever had gone wrong between Heather and Billy, Heather was truly torn up about it. Matty ached for her. "Come here..."

Heather scooted close. Matty put an arm around her. Heather laid her head on Matty's shoulder. "It's so bad between us. I don't know what to do."

Matty still longed to know what the actual problem was. "If you could maybe be a little more specific..."

"No. No, I can't get into it."

"But if you would only—"

"Mat. I mean it. I've said way more than enough."

No, you haven't, Matty thought as she resisted the urge to give her cousin a good shake.

Heather looked up at her through big, damp eyes.

And that did it. Heather would talk when she was ready to talk. Right now, she wanted blind support and comfort. Matty could do that for her. "Oh, sweetie..." Matty kissed her temple. "I'm so sorry."

"Thank you," Heather replied in a little-girl voice.

"And whatever it is, I'm here now. Any time you need me, you know you only have to call."

"And I'm grateful, Mat. I am." She huddled even closer and added plaintively, "I really am glad for you, Mat, and I'm so glad you're home. You're going to love being a mom. Everything's going to turn out great for you—wait and see.

But as for me and Billy, well, right now, I'm not so sure that we're going to make it."

Matty tried not to be impatient, but really, what was the problem here? She asked one more time, "What exactly is going on with you two?"

Heather let out a sad little moan. "It's just, well, we're arguing constantly now."

"About...?"

"Money. Money and how Billy wants to spend more time with me."

Last Matty heard, Billy's online farm-and-ranch supply business was a great success. "You have money problems suddenly?"

"Not really. It's just... Look. How many ways can I tell you that I don't want to get down in the weeds about it right now? It's just too sad and depressing."

"Of course, but if Billy wants to spend more time with you, I can't see that as anything but good."

Heather let out another pitiful little sound—and failed to elaborate.

It went on like that for several minutes more, with Matty gently pushing for details and Heather either ordering her to back off or remaining aggravatingly vague.

Then they heard small footsteps on the stairs that led down to the lower level, where the kids had their bedrooms and play area. Heather's three-year-old twins, Claire and Elissa, were on their way up.

Two blond heads poked out of the stairwell.

"We want snacks, please!" announced Claire as she reached the upper floor.

Elissa blinked at the sight of Matty—and then beamed her a giant smile of welcome. "Hello!"

"Hi, you guys!" Matty grinned back.

Heather put on a bright face for the kids. "Your aunt Matty is here!" The twins were actually Matty's first cousins once removed. But Heather had made it clear years ago that Matty was Aunt Matty to her kids.

Frowning, Claire stopped in mid-step. She turned to stare at Elissa, who stared right back at her. There was an entire conversation in that look. Matty bit her lip to keep from chuckling. Her last visit was eleven months ago. The twins were two at that time. Apparently they didn't remember her now.

They came running anyway. Meredith, the family golden retriever, herded them from behind. "Aunt Matty is here!" cried Elissa ecstatically.

Matty opened her arms and gathered them in.

After that, it was all about the twins. Matty hung around, enjoying her little cousins, sharing a snack with them. When she left at a few minutes before noon, it was starting to snow.

And she still had no idea what had gone wrong between Heather and Billy.

"Let's make it a working lunch," Ethan's law partner, Gavin Stahl, offered at noon.

Outside, the snow was coming down steadily. They put on their hats, tipped up the collars of their fleece-lined coats and walked fast to the Stagecoach Grill right there on Main Street. At the grill, they ordered French Dip sandwiches and discussed the status of a couple of cases.

Just as the waiter was delivering their sandwiches, Gavin's wife, Nicole, walked in. They signaled her over. A successful Realtor, Nicole was six months pregnant. It was Gavin's second child and her fourth. She'd been married before—to Ethan's second cousin, Ty Bravo.

Ethan watched the couple. They always seemed so happy together. Ethan had been fifteen or so when Nicole married Ty—fifteen and pretty oblivious, really. But even he'd noticed that Ty and Nicole never seemed to get along. It was good to watch her now, with Gavin. Clearly Nicole had found her man.

As he had way too often that day, Ethan thought of Matty and wondered what she was up to right now. It still seemed unreal to him that she'd come home to stay—not to mention that she, like Nicole, was having a baby. As much as it had surprised him that Matty had chosen to walk away from her dream career, he was glad to have her back in town, where the people who cared about her could look out for her.

On the table beside him, his phone lit up with a call: Sylvia. Guilt made him shift uncomfortably in his chair. He should have gotten back to her hours ago.

Promising himself that he would do that as soon he returned to the office, he sent the call to voicemail.

Half an hour later, the snow was still coming down. Nicole kissed her husband and went off to show a house right there in town. Gavin headed down to the courthouse in Buffalo for a child-custody hearing.

Back at the office, a potential client was waiting, a walk-in. Ethan led the tired-looking fellow into the small conference room. Mandy, the secretary/receptionist, brought them coffee.

After Ethan walked his new client to the door, he had other clients to contact and pleadings to write. The rest of the day went by at the speed of light.

He called Sylvia as soon as he got home that evening.

She didn't pick up, so he left a message apologizing for not getting back to her. His phone rang a few minutes later.

"Finally," Sylvia grumbled. "I was starting to wonder if you'd died."

He felt guilty again, and rightfully so. He really should have gotten back to her—or answered the phone one of the times she'd called.

"Sorry. It was just one of those Fridays."

"Well, I *was* hoping we could get lunch or something before I left."

He remembered then. She was flying to Denver to visit her sister for the weekend. "Damn. You're back Sunday, right?"

"Monday morning, actually." She sighed. "At least it's stopped snowing. My flight should leave on time tomorrow."

He really did feel like a jerk. Probably because he was one. "How about if I come over for a little while?"

"Ethan…" She was using her patient voice.

"Let me make it up to you," he coaxed. "Anything you want. We can go out. Or why don't you come here? I'll open a nice bottle of wine and fix us a nice dinner."

Another tired sigh. "My flight leaves at five in the morning, and I still have to pack."

"So that's a no?" He said it teasingly and got a reluctant chuckle in response. "I'm a jackass for not calling you back."

"Yes, you are."

"Sylvia, I really am sorry."

"Okay." Her voice had softened. "You're forgiven."

They talked for a few minutes—about the weather. About how they would go out for dinner Monday night.

"Arlington's, please," she requested sweetly. The steak-house and bar was her favorite.

"Arlington's it is. I'll make the reservation."

"That sounds nice…"

By the time they said goodbye, he felt pretty confident that she really had forgiven him. He was grateful for her understanding. Still, he hung up feeling not only annoyed with himself for managing to blow off his girlfriend the entire day, but also…

On edge, somehow. He kept remembering lunch with Gavin and Nicole, the way they'd looked at each other. Like they were partners in some great adventure. At one point, Gavin had reached over and put his hand on Nicole's rounded belly. They'd seemed so happy, so proud of them-selves and the life they'd created.

He wanted…

Before he could complete the thought, his phone buzzed in his hand.

He looked down and grinned when he saw he had a text from Matty.

I'm guessing you and Sylvia have plans for tonight?

He couldn't text back fast enough. Nope. She's got an early flight to Denver tomorrow, and she needs to pack. I'm all alone… He actually added a crying emoji.

Ethan. Emojis now? You clearly need company.

Does that mean you're on your way over?

Ten minutes later, the doorbell rang. When he answered, she was leaning against the doorframe wearing her hooded coat and carrying a plastic container, which she handed to him.

"Wait." He took it with reverence. "You didn't…"

"I did." She held up both hands, palms out. "I baked my fingers to the bone."

He stepped back. She came in and shut the door behind her as he popped the lid of the container and the beautiful smells of sugar, vanilla and chocolate drifted out. She used to bake all the time back in LA when they lived in the same Los Feliz apartment building. And when she baked back then, she always shared the results with him.

"Chocolate chip." His favorite. "And with pecans, too. You really shouldn't have."

"Hey. After my behavior last night, I had to do something to repay you—for listening to my endless whining, letting me cry all over your nice, comfy flannel shirt and then, when I dropped off to sleep in the middle of our movie, carrying me bodily up to your guest room."

"Hmm. When you put it like that, I might be a hero."

"Oh, you are. Beyond the last shadow of a doubt."

She hung her coat by the door and took off her boots.

He led the way to the main room. "Have you eaten?"

She was silent behind him. He glanced back at her, and she shrugged. "It's official. I am one of those friends who invites herself over and then, when she gets there, wants to know what's for dinner."

Chapter Three

Matty planned to help with dinner. It was the least she could do after how wonderful he'd been last night—and this morning.

And right now as well, for that matter.

"Let's cook together," she said and followed Ethan as he circled around behind the kitchen island. "Like in the old days."

Back then, Gabe never had much interest in cooking. Which was fine. Gabe did his share. He was always handy around the house. He could do simple electrical repair, unclog a drain, fix broken furniture, that sort of thing.

Ethan and Matty were the ones who cooked. During their Los Feliz days, the two of them had pitched in with meals. Sometimes they would cook at the apartment Matty shared with Gabe, other times at Ethan's on the floor below.

They'd been like a family, really, the three of them. And Matty had felt super sad for a while when Ethan suddenly decided he'd had enough of LA and moved home.

"What's up, Matilda?" His voice was warm and low, the auditory equivalent of a gentle hug. He was studying her face.

She folded her arms and leaned back against the island.

"Just thinking of that year we all three lived in Los Feliz. How we used to cook all the time, you and me."

His crooked smile said he remembered, too. "Yeah. We were pretty damn creative."

"There were a few gastronomic disasters, as I recall. But hey, give us a pound of hamburger and a bag of rice, and more often than not miracles happened." She crossed the space between them, hip-checked him away from the sink and washed her hands. "So whatcha got to work with around here?"

He had penne pasta and most of the ingredients for carbonara sauce. They improvised the sauce, and he had enough greens in the fridge for a tossed salad. There were ciabatta rolls in the freezer. Matty whipped up some butter with garlic and spices, spread it on the halved rolls and broiled them in the toaster oven.

It was a delicious meal. They high-fived each other and agreed that they hadn't lost their touch.

Later, they settled in the living area. He ordered Alexa to play their favorite tunes from the old days, and they talked about Gabe, about how much they both missed him.

It was so good just to be with Ethan. So easy and comfortable. The sadness that had dogged her constantly since Gabe's death faded when she was around Ethan. He was so good to her. Even in the worst of it, when she came home to Wyoming to bury Gabe, Ethan had been her rock.

The whole town had turned out for the funeral. Gabe's parents, who had moved to Texas a couple of years before, had returned to be there for the burial of their son. It was one endless, grueling slog, that day. The only bit of relief for her came the day after.

At that time, Ethan had an apartment in a four-unit building on Fort Street. She'd gone to visit him there and, just like last night, he'd looked after her. They'd passed a fifth of Jack Daniels back and forth and talked about Gabe. Eventually, the tears came. Ethan had held her and let her cry all over him for hours. She had no memory of how she got back to her parents' house that night. Ethan must have taken her over there.

The morning after that, she woke in what used to be her childhood bedroom with the world's worst hangover. Her head pounded and her stomach churned.

She didn't let that hangover slow her down, though. Her return flight was that day. She put on her dark glasses, drank three cups of coffee and boarded the first leg of her flight back to LA.

She didn't talk to Ethan again for several months after they put Gabe in the ground. At that time, it had hurt too much to have to deal with Ethan. Ethan and Gabe had been so close. The sight of Ethan, even the mere sound of his voice, used to get her aching for the love she'd lost.

But not anymore. Now Ethan was *her* friend. And being with him was all good all the time.

She said, "Thank you, Ethan. For tonight. And last night. And that night after the funeral when you got drunk with me and listened to me cry and carry on for hours."

He leaned in so they were nose-to-nose. "That's what friends are for."

"Well, it was a lot to ask of you."

"Not true." His voice was rough and low.

She took his big, long-fingered hand and wrapped both of hers around it. His green eyes probed hers. She laughed at his wary expression. "Not sure what I'm up to, are you?"

"Well, whatever it is, you look very serious." He made

a low, thoughtful sound. "I might be a little bit terrified of you right this minute."

"I don't want to terrify you, Ethan."

"Whew. Glad to hear that."

"I just want to be a better friend to you. I really do."

He squeezed her fingers. "Stop beating yourself up. You're an excellent friend. You and me, we're fine. Solid."

"You mean that?"

"I do." He seemed sincere.

Still, she knew that he was letting her off easy. "It's just that we've been losing touch, since Gabe died. I should have—"

"Enough. Life gets in the way. You were living in California or off on an assignment. Meanwhile, I've been plenty busy building my practice with Gavin. You and me, we had stuff to do. So shoot us."

"I'm glad—that you don't feel I disappeared on you. Even if I did. It was awful for a while there, and I was ducking everybody's calls."

"Matilda. You need to stop. You did what you had to do to move on. It's called life. Cut yourself some slack."

"All right. But I'm here now. And I'm going to do better. And you have to promise me that if you ever need me—for *anything*—you'll call."

"You got it, Matilda. I need you, I call you." He was grinning now. "Now can we please move on?"

"All right." She asked him about Gavin, his law partner.

"I got lucky. Gavin's a damn good lawyer and a good man, too."

"He married your cousin Ty's ex-wife, right?"

"Yes, he did. Nicole is a crackerjack Realtor."

"I hope they're happy, Gavin and Nicole."

"They are. She's pregnant with their second kid—and she and Ty share custody of the two they had when they were together."

"Life. Who knows how things will go? Who would have guessed that Ty would end up married to Nicole's best friend?" Sadie McBride Bravo, Ty's second wife, owned and ran Henry's, everybody's favorite diner there in town.

"Yep. Ty and Sadie have one little girl together."

"It's sweet," she said, "that Ty and Nicole both found happiness the second time around." She thought of Heather and hoped that things would work out for her and Billy. "I mean, you just never know…"

He peered at her more closely. "I'm confused. Whose marriage are we talking about now?"

"Not your lawyer friend's. Not your cousin Ty's, either."

Ethan just looked at her, waiting.

Flopping back against the sofa cushion, she frowned at the ceiling. "I do want to talk about it—with you, Ethan. Because I know I can trust you to keep whatever I tell you to yourself."

"So, you're swearing me to secrecy…"

"Mm-hmm. Total cone of silence. Strictly hush-hush."

He waited for her stop talking and then said somewhat warily, "No problem. I'm a vault."

She patted his knee. "I knew I could trust you—and it's my cousin Heather."

"Wait. You're talking about Heather and Billy? You always said those two are rock solid."

"I know, right? And they were. But apparently not so much at the moment."

"What's the problem?"

"I don't really know. I haven't talked to Billy yet. Heather seems to put the blame all on him. She's really unhappy. And she's so evasive. She cried on my shoulder and said how miserable Billy was making her. I kept trying to get her to explain the situation, but she just wouldn't do it. So here I am, very worried about her, and I don't really know why. I'm hoping she'll open up more at some point so I can understand what's going on." She leaned close to him again. "Sorry. Here I am laying this on you—and yet not really giving you any information."

"She'll tell you eventually."

"Yeah. I'm sure she will." Matty drew her knees up and rested her chin on them. "I just… Heather and Billy on the outs? Who would've guessed that could ever happen?"

"Most likely it's only a rough patch. I'm no expert, but it's not as though love and marriage are always easy. They'll work through it."

Matty hoped he was right.

A little while later, he offered hot chocolate. She said yes. They talked some more. The time just flew by.

It was a little past eleven when she said, "I really should go."

"Nah. You should stay. I have more hot chocolate. And my guest room is yours any time you want it."

Was she was tempted? Very much so. She'd slept better last night than she had in what seemed like forever. There was just something about knowing Ethan was nearby. It soothed her, made her feel safe. Like she could let down her guard, close her eyes, allow oblivion to settle over her, and nothing terrible could possibly happen. So far, at least, Ethan was the best thing about coming home.

But she couldn't just move in on the guy. "Thank you. I had such a good time. But really, I do need to go…"

He walked her to the door. She put on her puffer coat and gave him a hug and then went on out into the cold late-winter night. Halfway down the street, she turned to look back. He was still standing in the doorway. She loved that he had lingered there, watching out for her.

She waved and he waved back.

On Saturday Ethan put in a few early hours at his deserted office. As a rule at Stahl and Bravo, they didn't take appointments on the weekend. Quiet Saturdays offered time to catch up on whatever had slipped through the cracks during the busy workweek.

His half sister, Starr Tisdale, came by while he was working. Starr was married, with two grown children and a six-year-old, Cara Grace. She also owned and ran the local weekly paper, the *Medicine Creek Clarion*. Today she came bearing tall coffees from the Perfect Bean.

"What's this?" he asked, eyeing the coffees as he ushered her in. The absence of chatty little Cara told him his sister was probably sniffing out news for the *Clarion*. "As an attorney, I should warn you that everything I know falls under the heading of attorney-client privilege. You'll get nothing out of me."

"Don't take yourself so seriously," Starr advised drily. "I changed your diapers, in case you've forgotten."

"You had to remind me," he grumbled.

"Plus, I come bearing gifts." She passed him the cardboard tray of coffees. As soon as his hands were full, she reached up and ruffled his hair.

"Hey." He stepped back. "Knock it off."

She snickered. "You're still kind of cute, not to mention as annoying as ever."

"Let's sit down. Here or the conference room?"

"The waiting area's fine."

They sat in armchairs around a low central table. He sipped the excellent coffee and asked, "What's up?"

She had a few legal questions she wanted to bounce off him concerning water rights on the open range. He sipped his coffee and shared what he knew.

Then she said, "So I heard Matty Hunt has moved back to town…"

"That's right." He didn't mean to sound wary, but he knew that he did. His sister had that look—like she was after a story. But what kind of story? He didn't want Matty upset. She'd had a rough time, and she deserved to have her privacy respected.

Starr eyed him sideways. "Relax. This is hardly an inquisition."

He wasn't sure he believed her. He felt protective of Matty and probably always would.

His sister asked, "Is Matty home to stay?"

"What's this for, Starr? Over the Back Fence?" The chatty column that covered town and neighborhood news had been running in the *Clarion* since long before either Ethan or Starr were born.

"Probably. I'm not sure."

"Come on, big sister. Just talk to me."

Starr crossed her legs and leaned toward him. "I would love to interview her—about her writing, her career, about what's brought her back to Medicine Creek. I would make sure she gets to plug the family bookstore. It would be a win all around."

"So why ask me? Talk to Matty."

Starr looked at him so patiently. "I will ask Matty. But

you're her longtime friend. If I go straight at her myself, I might come off as pushy."

He faked a gasp. "What? You? No!"

Starr narrowed her eyes at him. "Don't be a smartass. Just ask her if she'll meet me for an interview."

"And if she says no?"

Starr was silent. Finally, she shrugged. "I'll get in touch with her anyway, see if I have better luck."

"So why not cut out the middle man?"

Starr considered his question. "Let's call it a form of professional courtesy. If you approach her first, it's a heads-up. She has time to decide what she wants to say when I reach out to her."

He thought about the baby, about the rotten jerk who'd screwed Matty over and now wanted nothing to do with his own child. Matty was going through a lot right now. The last thing she needed was his sister trying to ferret out all her secrets. "I don't know, Starr…"

"Oh, come on. The *Clarion* is hardly ambush journalism. It's a town paper, and I want the kind of story that I doubt Matty will mind sharing. I would just like you to let her know upfront that I respect her and admire her and I hope she'll agree to an interview."

When she put it that way, what could he say? "Fine. I'll talk to her. And if she doesn't want to do it, I'll warn her that you'll be in touch to try to change her mind."

Starr beamed. "Of course you'll warn her. I expect nothing less."

He called Matty as soon as Starr left. "Are you busy?" he asked.

"Are you kidding? I'm at my folks' house doing laundry. Because my mom won't let me get started at the bookstore until I've had time to *decompress*—her word—after my supposed grueling trip from LA. She says I'll need a week, minimum, before I'm ready to stock shelves or stand behind the register and ring up a sale. Not that I'm bitter about that or anything."

He pictured her looking grouchy in old jeans and a UCLA sweatshirt, her thick blond hair piled on her head in a haphazard way, soft corkscrew curls escaping, brushing against the side of her neck. "Your mom loves you," he reminded her.

"Yeah, well." He heard a mechanical clicking sound and then what was probably water pouring into a washing machine drum. "Love doesn't have to mean protecting me from what I would actually prefer to be doing."

"What are you up to tonight?"

"Nothing important, that's for sure."

"There's nothing important to do at my house, either. You should come over. We can do unimportant stuff together."

"And you should definitely be sick of me by now."

"No way. Come over. Six?"

"I'll be there."

That night, Ethan waited to bring up Starr's visit until after dinner. "She wants to interview you for the *Clarion*," he said once they were comfortable on the sofa with a scotch for him and a decaf for her. "She says she'll ask about your writing career, about why you've moved back to your hometown. She expects to talk about the bookstore, too."

"Did you tell her I'll eventually be taking over at the store?"

"I told her nothing."

She slapped him lightly on the arm. "Ethan, she's your sister. Be nice."

"That's what she said, more or less."

Matty shrugged. "Sure. Give her my number. Tell her to call me." He must have had a funny look on his face because she asked, "What?"

"Well, I don't know. I thought you would be more hesitant, I guess. More concerned about your privacy."

"Why?"

"Well, you just haven't had an easy time the past few years, and now there's the baby and maybe you want to keep that quiet for a while…"

Matty snort-laughed when he said that. "Please. I've got nothing to hide." She rested her hand on her stomach. "And what would be the point anyway? I'll be showing soon. There's no keeping this baby a secret. If some people are shocked that I'm going to be a single mom, well, I'll just inform them that the 1950s would like their morals back. Sheesh. Ethan, don't you get it? The only person I was worried about telling was you."

He blinked. "Me? Why?"

She glanced away and then dragged her gaze back to meet his. "Because before Gabe died, you knew me as someone pulled-together and confident. I liked myself that way. I liked seeing myself that way in your eyes. I just didn't want you to think less of me because of how I fell apart after we lost Gabe—or because of the way I ended up living with someone like Ted Lansing and then managed to get accidentally pregnant by the guy. It all makes me look like a ditz ball."

"You are not nor have you ever been a ditz ball—whatever that is."

"Really? Was I unclear? Fine. A ditz ball is a giant ball of ditziness."

"Right," he said. "Thank you for clarifying. And you are in no way a ditz ball."

She seemed to be studying his face, those blue eyes of hers wide, the corners of her pretty mouth turned down. Finally, she nodded. "Well, thank you. I feel better about everything just hearing you say that. As for your sister's interview request, yes. Absolutely. Give Starr my number and tell her to give me a call."

Again, they hung out all evening and into the early morning hours. She didn't get up to go until almost two o'clock.

When he opened the front door, it was snowing.

"Hold on," he said. "I'll walk you."

She rolled her eyes. "It's Medicine Creek. I can guarantee there's not a single criminal lurking out there between here and my parents' house. I will be perfectly safe."

He grabbed his sheepskin coat and his black Stetson. "I'm walking you. Let's go."

Outside, the streetlights made the snowflakes sparkle as they drifted to the ground. It was sticking a little, but most of it would be gone by noon.

They didn't talk, just trudged along. At her parents' house, he stood in the driveway and watched her run up the steps and let herself in the front door. Only when she was safely inside did he turn and head home.

At four o'clock he got a call from his mom. The snow was coming down thick and fast by then. It was calving season, and they could use another hand out at the family ranch. Ethan might be an ordinary townie now, but when they needed him at the ranch, he did his best to step up. He put on old jeans, work boots and a warm shirt, grabbed a heavy canvas jacket and his winter hat and headed for the Rising Sun.

At the ranch, he tacked up his favorite mare, Ginger, and rode out to look for newborn calves in distress. Whenever he found one, he hoisted the critter up in front of his saddle and took it to shelter where the little guy could warm up and dry out. In addition to the night calver, who had a day job at the local feed store and only helped out during calving season, Ethan worked with his dad, his half sister, Jobeth, who was older than Ethan but younger than Starr, and also with his brother Brody, the youngest of his siblings.

The night calver went home at seven. The family kept working. By eleven, the snow had stopped, temperatures were above freezing and all the warmed-up calves were on their feet and latching onto their mamas to eat. He joined the rest of the family at the main house for a big midday meal.

Everybody wanted to know how Matty was doing. They'd heard she'd moved home—because it was Medicine Creek and everybody knew everything that went on in their town.

Ethan reported, "Matty's doing great. She's really happy to be home."

His mom said, "I always thought she loved living in LA, traveling around, writing about faraway places."

"She did love all that. But now she's ready for something different." He sought the right words. "She's going to be working with her mom at the bookstore."

Last night, Matty had said she had no problem with people knowing about the baby. But Ethan wasn't going there. Not yet. Not without further instructions from her.

"Matty Hunt moving home to stay," Brody said with a puzzled frown. "Who would have thought that could ever happen?" Brody was twenty-three, with a bachelor's degree in ranch management. He planned to marry his longtime sweetheart, Alaina, and work right there on the Rising Sun alongside their dad and Jobeth.

"Matty seems pretty happy about the move," Ethan said. "She's, uh, ready for a change."

Was his mother looking at him funny?

Apparently so. Now Tess Bravo gave him a knowing smile. "So you've been spending some time together, you and Matty, since she came home?"

"Yeah, Mom. Catching up, all that—oh, and I think Starr might be interviewing her for the *Clarion*. Matty says she's game to do it."

"I'll look forward to reading that," his mom said. "And how's Sylvia doing?" she asked. It was a routine question. Sylvia was his girlfriend, after all, and thus of interest to his mom.

"She's great. Busy with tax season. She went to see her sister in Denver this weekend."

"Ah," replied his mom.

"Gramma, will you please pass the gravy?" asked Jobeth's little girl, seven-year-old Paisley. His mom turned to deal with Paisley, and Sylvia was forgotten.

After the meal, Ethan went across the yard to the house where Jobeth lived with her family. He caught up with his sister and her husband, Hunter, and ended up with Paisley chattering at him nonstop and her little brother, Dustin, sitting on his lap.

Back at his place in town, he took out his phone to text

Matty. He needed to know what she was up to, maybe invite her over for a few hours.

But then he hesitated as he stared down at her number. "Maybe not," he said aloud and dropped the phone on the kitchen counter.

Really, he might be getting a little out of hand with this Matty thing. They couldn't spend every free minute together. They both had their own lives, after all.

He picked up the phone again—and then set it down. No. He wouldn't try to get a hold of her.

Then again, if she reached out to him, great. He would love to spend the rest of his Sunday with her.

But Matty didn't reach out. Which was fine. Good, really. Like him, she'd probably realized they needed to give it a break.

And why was he making such a big damn deal about it anyway? Why was he stewing over it like he somehow had a serious problem?

He needed to stop that. She was his friend and he cared a lot about her. And he would see her any damn time it worked for both of them.

Or not...

Matty didn't call Monday, either.

That evening, he picked up Sylvia at six thirty. She answered the door wearing a snug wool dress and high-heeled boots. "There's my guy." And then she was suddenly in his arms, lifting her mouth for a kiss.

He pulled her close, acutely aware of how slim she was and of her scent, which seemed heavier, somehow, spicier than he'd found it before.

When the kiss ended, she rested her hands on his shoulders and beamed up at him. "I missed you."

"I missed you, too," he parroted back to her and felt like a phony.

What was wrong with him? She'd been gone a few days, yet he felt like they'd lost touch somehow, like he hardly knew her.

"Come in." She stepped back for him to enter. "I'll just grab my coat…" A minute later they were walking out the door together. She tucked her hand in the crook of his arm. "Let's walk over, shall we?"

"You bet."

They set off for Arlington's Steakhouse, where her favorite table by the window was waiting for them. He ordered them a nice bottle of wine. After the shared appetizer they agreed on Angus filets, medium rare, seared to perfection, for the main course.

Sylvia filled the silence with endless chatter—about tax season and the long day she would have at her office tomorrow. About her trip to Denver and her sister who could be so needy and annoyed her no end but had a good heart, really.

He thought how pretty she was. A nice woman who worked hard at her accounting business. Sylvia would make a good future partner in life.

They walked back to her place holding hands. He knew she would invite him in when they reached her door, and for no logical reason whatsoever, he felt like he was having some kind of existential crisis over that.

She was his girl. They were exclusive. He'd been neglecting her lately, and he should spend the night with her. He needed to make it up to her for not checking in with her, not returning her calls.

But he didn't know if he could bring himself to do that.

She pulled him inside—and her phone rang in her shoulder bag. "What now?" She took out the phone.

It's Carrie... She mouthed her sister's name as she put the phone to her ear. "Hey, I just..." Silence. Then, "Settle down. It's okay... Yes, I hear you, I do. Listen, just hold on for a minute, okay?"

She muted the phone and looked up at him mournfully. "There's an issue. She can't find her keys, and she's freaking out about it..."

Ridiculously relieved, he reassured her, "It's okay. You have an early day tomorrow anyway, right?"

She made a sad face. "I *will* make it up to you."

"Not a problem." They shared a quick peck of a kiss. "I'll call you tomorrow."

"You better." And she put the phone to her ear again.

He ran down the steps and hurried home before Carrie could find her keys and give Sylvia a chance to summon him back.

Later, alone in his own bed, he wondered what, exactly, was wrong with him. The last thing he should be feeling was relief that he wouldn't be having sex with his girlfriend tonight.

By morning, he'd convinced himself that he'd made a big deal over nothing. He didn't have to feel like a bad boyfriend because he'd left without making love to his girl. On the contrary, Sylvia hadn't stopped him when he'd said he was leaving. She'd been focused on her sister, and he was just in the way.

He called Sylvia from the office. They talked briefly. He learned that after forty-five minutes of suggesting possible places where Carrie might have left her keys, Sylvia's sister had found them in a porcelain vase on the mantel.

"...and I have a call I need to take," she said with a sigh. "Ethan, I will get back to you as soon as I can find a spare minute."

He had court that day and was with a client before the judge when Sylvia called back, so her call went to voicemail. He didn't even notice it until he checked his messages as he was about to head home late that afternoon. He called her. She didn't pick up.

He waited for the voicemail prompt and said, "Sorry I missed you this morning. I had court. And now I've missed you again. I'll try later..."

At home, he was staring into the fridge, trying to decide what to thaw out for dinner when his phone buzzed in his pocket. He pulled it out and saw he had a text from Matty.

Any chance you're free for dinner? My treat. I was thinking Carmelita's.

He called her right back. "I love Carmelita's. It's like you read my mind."

She laughed. He grinned at the sound. There was no laugh like Matty's laugh, open-mouthed, kind of cackly, wild and free. "Meet you there?" she asked. "Ten minutes?"

"You're on."

She was waiting in a booth when he arrived at the cozy Mexican restaurant. He hung his coat by the door and went to her. She stood to greet him wearing that beautiful smile. He kissed her cheek, breathed in her fresh, sweet scent and then sat across from her.

The owner came right over. They decided to share an

order of chicken quesadillas along with another of beef fajitas. As they dug into the quesadillas he asked what she'd been up to since very early Sunday morning.

"Not a whole lot," she grumbled. "I went to see my cousin again. Something really is off there between her and Billy—but I still don't know what's wrong, and she's not talking. She just keeps hinting that Billy is way out of line."

"It is odd that she won't really give you any information about what's going on."

"It's worse than odd. It's really getting to me. I'm worried about her." Matty nibbled a wedge of cheese-filled tortilla. "At least my cousin's kids are great. I baked imaginary cookies down in the playroom with the three-year-old twins, and then on Sunday, I played whiffle ball in my mom's backyard with Will and Troy, who are now—wait for it—nine and six respectively."

"Weren't they in diapers just yesterday?"

Matty confirmed that they definitely were. And then she announced, "Here's the exciting news. My mom finally agreed to let me start helping out at the bookstore. I actually worked today, and it almost made me feel like a productive member of society again."

"Good for you."

"Oh! And I got a call yesterday from Starr. We're meeting tomorrow morning at the Perfect Bean."

"I heard she interviews all her victims there."

She laughed that terrific, wild laugh again. "I think you might be a little bit intimidated by your own big sister."

"Nah. I'm just joking around. Starr's the best."

Suddenly, Matty looked kind of forlorn.

He pushed his beer out of the way and leaned closer to her across the table. "What's wrong? You okay?"

She nodded. "Just, you know, hormones, I guess. I've had very little morning sickness, but sometimes I do get kind of glum—all of a sudden, you know? Out of nowhere..."

He didn't like the sound of that. "But you're all right?"

"Of course."

"Have you seen a doctor yet, here in town?"

She looked at him sideways. "Ethan. I've been here for what, one full week on Thursday? So no, I don't have a doctor here in town yet."

"You need to call Doctor..." He frowned and then nodded. "Hayes. That's his name. Doctor Hayes. He took over when Doc Crandall retired. You remember Piper, my cousin Jason's wife...?"

"Of course. The librarian. I grew up in town, too, you know."

"Piper went to Dr. Hayes for both of her pregnancies. She claims he's the best."

"Jason's wife talks to you about her ob-gyn?"

He shrugged. "Not really. I just remember Piper mentioned Dr. Hayes at some family get-together. She said he's kind and smart and takes her questions and concerns seriously." Ethan waited. Because he wanted to be sure she got herself a doctor sooner rather than later.

"You're staring at me," she accused. "What'd I do now?"

"Not a thing. Say you'll call Dr. Hayes."

Matty put up both hands. "Okay, I'll call him." Before she could change her mind, Ethan whipped out his phone. "What are you doing?" she demanded.

"Looking up Dr. Hayes online—ah, there he is. Texting you now..."

Her phone buzzed. She checked the screen. "Got it."

Her expression softened. "Thanks. For the number. And for looking out for me."

"Always."

Now she was leaning in, too. "Also, well…" She seemed to run out of words.

"What? Talk. Tell me…"

"Ethan, about you and me…"

He felt a tug of alarm. *You and me.* It sounded so…intimate, somehow. He wasn't sure how to react.

But then she went on, "You have to tell me if I'm being too clingy. If I'm monopolizing you, I want you to say so. I mean, I do know that you have your own life to live."

He wanted to reach for her then, to pull her close, rub her back, remind her that she never had to be alone, not really. That he would always be there for her—but he kept his hands to himself. Talk about getting too intimate… "You are not monopolizing me," he said. "I love hanging out with you."

"Same," she said softly. "Always."

"And wait a minute—is this why I haven't heard from you since I walked you home last Saturday night?"

She let out an exasperated little sigh. "Technically, it was Sunday morning and this is only Tuesday. It's not like I ghosted you. But yeah. I was giving you some space."

"Well, stop. I mean that."

"Are you sure?"

"Absolutely."

"You asked for it." She wrinkled her nose at him. "Now you'll be seeing way more of me than could possibly be good for you."

"I'll be the judge of that."

She picked up another wedge of cheesy tortilla. "Here's a question." She took a bite.

He sipped his beer. "Hit me with it."

"First, let me start with how much I love my parents. They're wonderful."

"Okay…"

"But already I'm thinking I can't live at my mom's house and spend all day working with her, too. We're just too much alike, Mom and me. I want to start looking for a place. Something right here in town—close in, I mean. So I'm not far from the bookstore."

"You plan to rent?"

"If I can't find anything I like, yeah. But I have the money to buy. I put my North Hollywood duplex on the market in January. It sold the first week. I can afford a house of my own."

"You need a Realtor?" He was thinking of Nicole.

She must have read his mind. "I was thinking maybe Nicole, your law partner's wife?"

"Great idea." He pulled out his wallet and gave her one of the business cards Nicole was always handing out to everyone she met.

Matty read, "'Bravo Realty.'"

"Yeah, Ty set Nicole up with her office before they were divorced. She goes by her married name now. But she kept the Bravo name on the door, partly because she gets a lot of business from both Ty and Cash." Cash Bravo was Ty's dad. The two of them bought and sold a lot of property. They were always closing one major deal or another. "Surprisingly, Nicole and Ty get along pretty well now that they're both happily married to other people. Do you want me to have her reach out to you?"

"Nope." Matty looked at him so patiently. "I think I can manage to pick up the phone all by myself and give her a call."

Chapter Four

Matty had to practically wrestle the check away from Ethan. In the end, he finally gave in and let her pay for dinner.

It was almost eight when they left the restaurant. Like the nights they'd spent together last week, time had raced by. He walked her to her parents' house and waited by the front gate until she let herself inside.

She said good-night to her folks and went on up to her room. Since she'd moved home, hanging out with Ethan was her favorite thing to do.

He liked being with her, too. He'd made that very clear. She just needed to remember not to go overboard about it. Ethan had his own life, including a serious girlfriend, one he'd been dating for more than a year. From now on, Matty intended to respect certain boundaries. She would not be asking him to get together night after night.

In her late forties now, Starr Bravo Tisdale was as Matty remembered her, stunningly gorgeous with thick black hair and violet eyes. She was as down-to-earth as she was beautiful.

They laughed through lunch. Matty told stories of her adventures as a travel writer. Starr said she'd never been really happy until she married Beau Tisdale. They'd been together for more than twenty-five years now.

An hour into the interview that felt more like a much-needed visit with a longtime friend, Starr asked, "So you came home because you've always planned to take over Cloud Peak Books someday?"

Matty considered the question—and then answered honestly. "Oh, hell no. Until recently, I never really thought about what might happen when my mom was ready to retire. I guess I thought she would sell the store—or just shut it down if she couldn't find a buyer."

Starr's gorgeous eyes widened. "Shut down Cloud Peak Books? That would be a crime. It's practically an institution. My oldest, Lizzie, used to spend almost as much time there as at the library. I thought she was going to hyperventilate when she walked in one day to browse the shelves and found Sarah J. Maas signing stock."

Matty was nodding. "I know. It would be a shame to have to close down."

"But now that won't happen. Because you've come home to take over."

That made Matty chuckle. "Right. Tell that to my mom. She wants to retire—and yet..."

"I understand. It can be hard to let go of something you built yourself, something that you're proud of. Something that contributes so much to the community."

"You're right." Matty said the words softly. "Mom loves that store. And it shows."

Starr tipped her head to the side and asked, "So what made you decide to come home and manage the family store when you could be flying to fabulous places and writing about your travels?"

Matty considered her reply for several seconds. And then she decided to simply tell the truth. "I've been considering coming home for a while now. My mom does want to retire, to spend more time with my dad, to travel, all that. I'd never seriously considered what would happen as my parents got older. But the past few years, I've been thinking about the future a lot. I love the bookstore almost as much as my mom does. The idea of coming home started to feel like a possibility for me. And then I got pregnant."

Starr sat back in her chair. "Well. Congratulations."

"Thank you. I got pregnant, and everything got crystal clear. Suddenly I was thinking about home all the time. So I talked with my folks and they were thrilled with the idea of having me close again—me and their grandchild. And my mom is pleased to know that when she retires, I'll be there to carry on at the store."

Starr was nodding. There were questions in her eyes. Personal ones. But she kept them to herself.

Matty did like Ethan's sister. A lot. She found she wanted to say more. So she did. "At this point, I'm fourteen weeks along. The father is not in the picture. I really *want* this baby, and I want this baby to have what I had, a hometown upbringing with family nearby. I want to be there, every day, for my baby."

"A baby." Starr was grinning—and then the grin faded. "I never would have guessed."

Matty laughed. "In a few weeks, you won't have to guess." She pushed her chair back enough to frame her hands around her barely there baby bump. "See?"

"Oh, yeah." Starr leaned closer across the small café table. "I'm guessing Ethan already knows everything you've told me."

"You're guessing right."

Starr said, "Well, don't worry. As I explained to my brother before I strong-armed him into approaching you about this interview, my focus will be on the story of how you loved your career and now you're ready for a whole new chapter in your life, including taking over the family store. I won't be mentioning your pregnancy in my article."

Matty shrugged. "And here I was thinking you could make the announcement for me."

Starr put up both hands. "No way. That's *your* job."

It was good, Matty thought, to be back home, where people knew way too much about her. Ethan's sister had known Gabe, too—pretty much everyone in town had. Matty remembered Starr taking her hand in the reception line at Gabe's funeral. Those violet eyes had gleamed with barely held-back tears—tears for Matty, for the husband she'd lost.

"It's a lot about Gabe, too," Matty said. "I mean, about losing Gabe. Losing Gabe changed me in a deep way. I started realizing I wanted to come home. My life as it used to be just didn't work without Gabe in it. I needed something different. The baby coming only made it all the more clear to me that I was ready for a change."

Starr managed to get her interview with Matty into the next issue of the *Clarion*. It came out just a day after their meeting at the Perfect Bean. It was beautiful. Starr used everything Matty had told her—except the news about the baby.

Matty's mom and dad both teared up as they read it together over their morning coffee. "That Starr," said Matty's mom with a discrete little sniffle. "She keeps the *Clarion* going with articles like this. Small-town papers are folding like lawn chairs nowadays, but the *Clarion* is still going strong because Starr Tisdale knows what people want and gives it to them."

Matty's dad slanted her mom a look over the wire rims of his glasses. "And what people want is...?"

"Hopeful stories," replied Simone. "Stories of people who get through the tough times, figure out what they want and go after it—and hometown stories, too. That's what this is. Even better, it's a *homecoming* story. Those are the best."

Matty watched her parents across the breakfast table and thought how grateful she was to have been raised by them. Even if her mom did have a tendency to get on her last nerve now and then.

It was a busy Thursday at Cloud Peak Books. People came in to tell Matty how much they loved reading about why she'd moved home. There was general agreement that she'd made the right choice. Who would want to live out there in Los Angeles when you could spend your days in the shadow of the Bighorns where the pronghorn antelope run free?

Her mom had always bought several copies of the life-style, nature and travel magazines that contained articles Matty had written. That day they sold out of those. Matty signed every one of them.

"I read your interview in the *Clarion*," Ethan remarked that evening at his house as they ate slow-cooker pot roast. "It's terrific."

"I thought so, too. Starr did a great job."

"Yep." He was looking at her kind of thoughtfully.

"What?" she demanded. "Say it."

"There's no mention of the baby."

"And this bothers you somehow?"

"No."

"Then…?"

"I'm just curious. Did you tell her?"

She grinned then. "You bet I did. She said she wouldn't print it because it was my job to tell people I was having a baby. I really like your sister."

"Me, too. She's a powerhouse. But sometimes she scares me. I never know what she'll do next."

"Ethan, as your big sister, it's kind of her job to keep you on your toes."

"Is that what you call it?" He gave her a wry look. She grinned wider.

On the end of the kitchen counter, his phone buzzed. He didn't get up to check it. Matty wondered if that might be Sylvia and felt instantly guilty. She kept reminding herself that she really should give Ethan more space.

But somehow, almost every day, either Ethan called her or she called him. They would get to talking. They would chatter away at each other until someone or something interrupted them. And before they hung up, he would ask her over and all her best intentions would go winging out the nearest window. She couldn't say yes fast enough.

Inevitably, they ended up spending the whole evening cooking and streaming movies and talking about everything from their shared past to all the things they wanted to do in the future.

He was watching her. "What?"

"What do you mean, what?"

"You've got a look. Something's bothering you."

Did she really want to talk about monopolizing his time—again? If he didn't want to be monopolized, well, he should just stop calling her. She did know how to take a hint.

"Matty, just tell me."

She didn't tell him. Instead she changed the subject to the big decision she'd made just that day. "There's a house for rent on Spruce Street. A cute little bungalow. It's all freshly painted with old-timey tile in the kitchen and bathroom. It's got a bedroom for me and one for the baby. There's even a small bonus room in back off the kitchen where I can set up an office, just in case at some point I might ever get going on that novel I keep promising myself I'll write one of these days."

"Did you call Nicole?"

"I keep meaning to, but no." She pushed her plate away. "Buying a house takes time. When I finally find the one I want to own, then it's a month at least until closing. And right now I'm focused on the bookstore and the baby.

"I mean, my folks are wonderful. But I'm used to having my own space, and when I saw that For Rent in front of that little house, I just knew it was going to be the right thing for right now. I called the owner early this morning and she met me there for a walk-through before I went to the bookstore…"

He was watching her face so closely. "You love it."

"Well, yeah—I mean, as I said, for now. The rent is so reasonable. I can sign a year's lease tomorrow and move in next week. A few months before the lease is up, I'll be ready to start looking for a house of my own."

"Sounds to me like you have a plan."

She folded her arms. "Would you mind telling my mom that for me?"

He pushed back his chair and held out a hand. "Come here."

She got up and went to him. He wrapped those warm arms around her. Against her better judgment, she snuggled in close. "What?" she grumbled into his soft chamois shirt.

"Let me guess—you told your mom you want to move, and she tried to talk you out of it?"

Matty pulled back enough to look up at him. "She's protective. She loves me. All that. She keeps saying there's plenty of room at the house and they love having me there. And I love them and… Oh, Ethan. You're so lucky to have siblings. It's hard to be the only child."

He faked a heavy sigh. "I can imagine. The pressure."

"Do not mock my sad state of only-hood."

"Hey." He cradled her face between those big hands. It felt good. His palms were warm and comforting against her cheeks. "Rent that bungalow on Spruce Street."

She held his gaze. "Yeah?"

"Yeah."

"So all right, then. I'm doing it."

"That's the spirit."

"Brew me a nice decaf, Ethan. I'm in the mood to celebrate."

The next day during breakfast, she told her parents that she was taking the little house on Spruce Street.

Her mom got right to work trying to talk her out of it. "Sweetheart, there is no need for you to rent a place. We have plenty of room here."

"I love you guys," she said—and meant it with all her heart, "but I'm used to being independent. I need my own space."

"Well, I think you need your family close by even more."

"That's true. And you *are* close by, just blocks away. If I need you, all I have to do is call—and vice versa. It's going to be great, Mom. You'll see."

"Just take a little longer to think it over. Just consider staying here…"

Matty held firm. "It's so cute, Mom. You'll love it, too. I called the owner just a few minutes ago. She says I can sign the lease this morning and start moving my things in as soon as the payment clears at the bank."

Her mom began, "I just think you should…" But her dad leaned close and whispered something in her mom's ear. Simone huffed out a breath. "Oh, all right, Neal." She glared at Matty's dad. "Fine. It's not my decision." She turned a wistful smile on Matty. "Congratulations on your new place."

"Thank you, Mom."

Her dad gave Matty a tender smile. "We'll miss having you to ourselves."

Simone huffed again. "We certainly will." But then her face softened. "We love you, Matilda Joslyn." Her mom had named Matty after Matilda Joslyn Gage, an American writer, freethinker and activist, a frontline suffragette and fighter for the abolition of slavery and the rights of Native Americans—not to mention the mother-in-law of the guy who wrote *The Wonderful Wizard of Oz.*

Matty felt kind of misty-eyed. "I love *you* guys. So much!"

They all three pushed their chairs back at the same time and moved in for a family hug.

At eleven that morning, Matty signed the lease on the Spruce Street bungalow and then arranged for electronic payment of her first and last month plus the cleaning deposit. She also set it up so the rent would be paid automatically every month.

Out on the street, a cold wind was blowing. It had started to snow. She climbed in her Jeep, turned on the engine to get the heater going and called Ethan.

The call went to voicemail.

When the beep sounded to leave a message, she announced, "I did it! I rented that little house. Reach out when you get a chance."

Her phone lit up with Ethan's call as she rolled into her parking space behind the bookstore.

She turned off the Jeep and picked up. "I'm so excited!" she crowed.

"Congratulations. Come over tonight. Six. We'll cook something delicious, and you can have a big decaf to celebrate your new place."

She groaned. "Is it pitiful that a mug of decaf is now my party drink of choice?"

"Oh, hell no."

"Thank you for your support—and are you sure about tonight?"

"Of course. Why?"

Because he did have a girlfriend and Matty really ought to stop monopolizing his evenings.

And she would. Soon. Just not tonight.

Still, she made herself remind him, "Well, I thought maybe it was date night or something."

"It's tax season," he replied as though that explained everything. "Six?"

She debated whether or not to mention Sylvia by name—

and instantly chickened out. "See you then," she chirped brightly.

That evening, she showed up with a bagful of groceries and a highly rated bottle of wine—which she wouldn't even be drinking.

"You shouldn't have," he said, ushering her in as she handed him the wine.

"Please. It's my celebration, and you deserve a nice Chardonnay."

He gave her his most gorgeous grin. "Well, I am pretty amazing, now that you mention it."

They cooked *murgh makhani* together. The dish, which they used to cook often back in LA, was also known as butter chicken. It was rich and creamy, seasoned with a spice blend from India called garam masala, along with ginger, garlic, lemon, turmeric and a whole lot of cream.

The food was amazing. They congratulated each other on yet another perfect meal.

She stayed past midnight and almost let him convince her that she might as well just take the guest room. But no. So far, she'd only slept over that first night. It seemed like a line she needed *not* to cross again. Plus, she was opening the bookstore in the morning. She held firm and went back to her parents' house.

Saturday was a pleasure. She ran the store alone, just her and the cats until noon when Colin came in. The day went by at the speed of light. It was nice to be in charge, not to have her mom constantly reminding her of things she already knew.

Colin left at four. She closed up at five with Ethan on her mind. She wanted to call him, find out how he was doing.

Which was completely ridiculous. She knew how he was doing—just fine. And she'd promised herself she would leave him alone tonight.

He called just as she climbed into her Jeep. She hit the phone icon at the speed of light. "What's up?"

Of course, he wanted her to come over.

And of course, she went.

That night as they cooked, they played songs from back in the day—"Can't Feel My Face," "Shut Up and Dance," "Uptown Funk" and "The Heart Wants What It Wants." After they'd eaten and cleaned up the kitchen, they just kept on ordering up the old tunes, calling out the titles so Alexa would play them. They laughed as they remembered when they'd first heard each song, and also when they argued over which song was playing when this or that happened. Along with Gabe, they'd been the rebels of their senior class at Medicine Creek High—at least when it came to music. The three of them were less country, more funk, R&B and soul.

They were arguing over which Beyoncé song had been Gabe's favorite when he told Alexa to play "Texas Hold 'Em."

She said, "Now, there's my kind of country. We can definitely do a line dance to this. I'll teach you…"

They did their best, but they weren't going to be giving the TikTokers any competition. Finally, he caught her hand and pulled her in. They whirled around, kind of two-stepping but not really, faking it for all they were worth.

They were laughing together. She felt so good, safe and happy and very comfortable in the strong circle of his arms.

He twirled her under his arm, catching her hand and then swinging her out, pulling her back in again. She moved in close. They spun in a circle—and she saw a pretty brunette standing in the wide arch that led to the front door.

Matty blinked and almost stumbled. The woman was staring at Matty and Ethan in what could only be called sheer disbelief.

Sylvia, Matty thought. *This must be Sylvia.*

By then, Ethan had seen her, too. "Sylvia! Hey…" He still had hold of Matty's hand. Gently, she pulled her fingers free of his grip.

For an awful, awkward moment they all three stood frozen in place.

Sylvia broke the silence. "I rang the doorbell, but you didn't hear it, I guess."

Ethan said, "Alexa, shut up."

The music stopped. Sylvia continued woodenly, "I could hear you both laughing from out on the porch. The door was unlocked, so I just came on in."

"Good!" Ethan lurched to life. He went to her and kissed her cheek.

Sylvia blinked up at him like someone waking from a trance. "I take it this is the famous Matty Gage Hunt?"

"Yes!" Ethan piled on the false enthusiasm. "This is Matty."

"Hey," said Matty, smiling way too wide, feeling excruciatingly guilty though she'd done nothing wrong.

Or had she…?

Sylvia nodded and said coldly, "Ethan never mentioned how pretty you are."

Ethan said, "Here. Let me take your coat."

"No." Sylvia jerked away from his touch. "I…can't stay. Nice to meet you, Matty. But I…" Her sudden forced smile seemed made of glass. "I really have to go…" And with that, she whirled and marched back out the door, pulling it shut good and hard behind her.

Matty heard swift footsteps descending the porch steps. A car door slammed. The engine turned over and the car drove away. Through all that, Matty and Ethan just stood there, unmoving, staring at the spot where Sylvia had been.

"You need to go after her," Matty said into the awful silence.

Ethan blinked several times in rapid succession. He seemed disoriented, like someone shaken suddenly awake from a deep sleep. "Right…"

Matty turned for the door. "Call me?" She grabbed her coat and purse off the hook.

"Of course."

She wanted to go to him, hold him, reassure him that everything would work out with his girlfriend. But how could she do that? She had no idea what would happen next between Sylvia and him.

In the end, she let out a soft cry of sympathy. "Oh, Ethan. She did not look happy. I'm so sorry."

"There is nothing for you to be sorry about." He seemed to mean that. "I'll go right over there now. I'll talk to her, work things out."

She forced a smile. "Okay, then." For a suspended moment, they stood there staring bleakly at each other. Finally, she said, "Bye, then."

At his nod, she went out the door, shutting it quietly behind her.

Chapter Five

At Sylvia's house, Ethan rang the bell and waited. When she didn't appear, he considered his options and poked the doorbell again.

That time, Sylvia pulled the door open so fast, he knew she'd been standing right there on the other side of it. She'd shed her coat and taken off her shoes. They stared at each other. Her face betrayed nothing. He had no idea where to begin.

Syliva said tightly, "Now I'm starting to understand why our relationship never went anywhere..." She stepped back. "No need to give the neighbors a show. You'd better come in."

He trailed after her to the living room. "Have a seat," she instructed.

He took the nearest chair and sat forward in it. "Sylvia, I..."

She cut him off by showing him the hand. "It doesn't matter what you say. I get it now. I mean, I should have put two and two together months ago. I knew there was something—or rather, some*one*."

"What are you getting at? There's no one."

"You're...not available, Ethan. You never were."

"That's not true." The words tasted like a lie on his tongue. He pushed them out anyway.

"Please." Sylvia wasn't buying. "Now that I've finally seen you with her, it's so painfully obvious. You're in love with your dead friend's widow."

He felt as though she'd hauled off and slapped his face. "You're mistaken." He made himself speak quietly.

"No, I'm not."

"Sylvia. You are completely off base."

"Give me a break," she scoffed. "I saw the way you looked at her. You have never looked at me that way."

Wrong, he thought angrily. With effort, he continued in an even, reasonable tone, "I have no clue what you're talking about." Okay, that was partly a lie.

He did have a clue. Eight years ago, he *had* believed himself to be in love with Matty. But that was all in the past. Matty never knew how he felt back then and neither did Gabe.

It was a crush, that's all. An impossible and completely one-sided attraction—an attraction that had faded away naturally over time. He and Matty were friends now, close friends, as they should be, as they'd always been.

And nothing more.

"Matty's my friend," he insisted. "I care for her. I think the world of her. But I am *not* in love with her."

Sylvia stared at him. She was shaking her head, her eyes full of hurt and fury, her mouth pinched tight. "You're lying to yourself—I mean, if you really believe what you just said, you're lying to yourself *and* to me."

"No. You don't understand. It's not like that."

"Ethan. Please. It is exactly like that. And believe me, I

do finally understand. You've wasted my time. You've kept me on the hook for months."

Had he?

He drew a slow breath and let it out with care. Because, really, she did have a point. A sick wave of shame washed through him at his own stubborn thick-headedness. He thought of Monday night, of how relieved he'd been when her sister called and he realized that he could go home without taking her to bed first.

Who did he think he was kidding? Sylvia was right about one thing—it really wasn't going anywhere between the two of them. And right now, he needed to stop selling what she wasn't even buying.

"We're done," she said, her voice gentler now, her mouth softer, not as pinched as before. "Oh, Ethan. We are so done. I think you know that."

He stood. "All right, then."

She shook her head slowly. "It's so strange." A single tear broke free and slid down her cheek. "After that awfulness at your house, I drove home knowing it was over, and I thought about how long we've been together. I thought how I ought to get my things from your place..." Her voice trailed off. She drew a sharp breath. "And then I realized, *What things?*"

"Sylvia, I—"

"Don't. Please. Just let me finish—I mean, come on, Ethan. Think about it. I have nothing to collect from your house, and there's nothing—not so much as a toothbrush— here at my house that belongs to you. I've never just hung out at your place the way Matty Hunt obviously does. You and me, we were never that close."

Ethan actively despised himself at that moment. She

made it seem as though they'd only been marking time with each other—and, well, it looked like she was right.

"I want you to go now," she said.

What could he say but "All right." He turned for the door.

Back at his house, Ethan poured himself a double whiskey and turned on the fireplace. He stared into the cheery flames and knew himself to be a complete jerk—and not because he'd cheated on Sylvia. He hadn't.

His hopeless crush on Matty had ended years ago. There was only friendship between them now. Still, he would rather hang out with Matty than anyone. They'd always had a real connection. Given a choice between getting together with Sylvia and spending an evening with Matty…

Being with Matty won, hands down.

He should have broken it off with Sylvia months ago. He could see that so damn clearly now. He'd screwed up in a big way by not facing the truth, by letting himself simply drift along in a relationship that was never going to be much of anything.

And right this minute, who did he want to talk to about that?

Matty, of course.

She'd asked him to call her, and he'd said that he would. She would come right over—he knew that. All he had to do was ask. He could tell her what a mess he'd made, get it all off his chest, admit what a fool he'd been, how blind. How wrong.

However, there was no way to tell her everything without revealing that Sylvia believed he was in love with Matty. He didn't want to get into that with Matty, not now.

Probably not ever.

* * *

Matty hardly slept that night.

She waited for Ethan to call and let her know what had happened with Sylvia. If it hadn't gone well and he wanted to talk, Matty would be there for him. She would help any way that she could.

But the hours went by and he never called. She reminded herself that his not calling was a good thing, that he and Sylvia must have patched things up.

Should she call him and find out for sure?

No, she decided. She really didn't want to butt in.

She must have dropped off finally. When she woke up, daylight crept in between the curtains. She grabbed her phone and checked messages.

Nothing. Ethan had not gotten in touch.

And that's a good thing, she reminded herself. He'd probably spent the night at Sylvia's. They'd worked things out and all was well.

Matty groaned, flopped back against her pillow and pulled the covers over her head. Because, *ugh.* Getting to know Sylvia now was bound to be awkward.

And she had only herself to blame for that, the way she'd sought Ethan out night after night, all the while telling herself she wasn't going to do that.

But no matter. They would get past this. One way or another, she would find a way to make peace with Ethan's girlfriend.

Downstairs, her mom sat at the table, her reading glasses perched at the end of her nose, doing the *New York Times* Sunday crossword puzzle. Her dad was flipping pancakes at the cooktop. She sat down to eat with them.

"You got home early last night," her mom remarked after taking a thoughtful sip of her coffee.

Matty felt a totally unreasonable spurt of annoyance—completely unjustified annoyance. Because it was only the truth, a perfectly innocent remark. Too bad it served to remind her all over again that Ethan hadn't called and that his girlfriend probably hated her now.

She looked at her mother and her mom stared back at her.

"What'd I do?" asked Simone.

"Not a thing, Mom. Not a thing." Matty stuffed a big bite of pancake into her mouth.

Her mom and her dad shared one of those looks—the kind with a whole conversation in it. Matty read what they were thinking on their faces. Her mom was about to follow up, ask another of her *harmless* little questions. Her dad gazed steadily at her mom, his expression clearly communicating, *Sweetheart, let it go.*

To Matty's relief, her mom did let it go—in favor of asking Matty what her plans were for today. The bookstore was closed Sundays, so she didn't have to work.

Matty thought of her cousin. "I'm going to call Heather. Maybe we can go for coffee or something."

"Great idea," her mom said with enthusiasm—because her mom loved her and was only trying to be helpful and supportive.

Objectively speaking, Matty knew herself to be the classic only child. Adored by both parents, she felt alternately smothered with love—and regretful that she couldn't stop resenting the care and concern they lavished on her every chance they got.

After breakfast, she called Heather, who said she could

get Billy to watch the kids for an hour or two. They agreed to meet for lunch at Henry's Diner.

Matty got to Henry's before her cousin.

The diner looked as homey and welcoming as ever, with green vinyl booths and a long counter, the vinyl-cushioned stools bolted to the floor. A cook she didn't recognize stood behind the service window, and a server she'd never met appeared with a menu and a red plastic glass of ice water.

"Hi," said the server with a big, cheerful smile. "I'm Linda. Anyone joining you today?"

Matty explained that her cousin would be there soon. She was about to ask after Sadie McBride Bravo and her parents, Henry and Mona, who had owned and run the diner for as long as Matty could remember. But right then, Heather walked in and it was all about what to eat and drink.

Five minutes later, Linda had taken their order and delivered them each a Sprite.

Heather sipped her Sprite. "I'm so glad you called. Billy's home today." She said her husband's name with an angry twist of her lips. "He's driving me crazy. I've been alone with the kids for most of the week. I was trying to come up with some reason to sneak out for a while—and then you called. Ta-da! Matty to the rescue." Before Matty could probe for specifics about the situation with Billy, Heather added, "So how're you feeling?" She went right on, not waiting for an answer. "Oh! When you came over last, I meant to recommend my new doctor to you."

"Dr. Levi Hayes, maybe?"

Heather beamed. "That's him! How did you know?"

"Ethan heard good things about him and gave me his

number. I have my first appointment with him coming up Tuesday."

"Look at you, taking care of business in all the major ways. I even heard a rumor that you'd rented a house."

"Oh, really? Let me guess—my mom told Aunt Leonie, and she called you with all the family gossip…"

"Exactly. My mom says Aunt Simone is sad to see you move out."

"Yeah, well, what can I say? My mom is wonderful and my dad is the best. But it was time, you know?"

Heather waved a hand. "Please. No need to explain. I get it, Mat. I do. No grown-up woman needs to live in her mother's house."

"Well said." Matty raised her Sprite.

Heather tapped the plastic glass with hers. "To a home of your own."

"Thank you."

"*And…*" Heather smirked. "My mother reports that *your* mother shared that you and Ethan have been spending a lot of time together…"

Matty really did not want to get into the situation with Ethan. Not now. Maybe not ever. After last night, it was all too fresh and awful. She played it off. "Yeah, it's been great to catch up with him, you know?"

Linda appeared with their grilled-chicken Cobb salads and hot rolls.

As soon as the server moved on, Matty got busy leaving the subject of Ethan behind. "How are my nieces and nephews?"

Heather rolled her eyes so far back in her head it was a wonder she didn't fall out of the booth. "The twins want a kitten—correction, they *each* want a kitten, but they're willing to share one if I give them no other choice. Will wants a cell phone—and Troy wants whatever his older brother is hoping for. So far, I'm holding the line on all four of them. It's a big job, and I could crumple any day now."

"I feel your pain."

"No, you don't." Heather faked an evil grin. "But you will, starting about six months from now."

"And Billy…?"

Heather suddenly got all interested in her salad. She forked up a bite of grilled chicken. "He's fine," she said darkly and stabbed at a lettuce leaf.

Matty pounced on the opening, leaning in, speaking softly. "What's the problem between you and Billy? Come on. Talk to me…"

"I told you the other day." Heather spoke in a low voice, as though sharing nuclear secrets.

Matty said carefully, "Well, I got that you're not getting along, but…"

Heather groaned. "He wants everything to change. I don't. It's as simple as that."

"Change how?"

"He wants me go work for the business—not right away, but in a couple of years, as soon as the twins start kindergarten. He says we have big bills coming up in the future and we need to start putting money away for stuff like braces and college."

That didn't sound unreasonable. "Well, with the twins in school, you *will* have a little leeway, time-wise, right?"

Heather froze with her fork halfway to her mouth. Very slowly, she set the fork down without eating the half wedge of hard-boiled egg she's speared onto the end of it. "Mat. I am a full-time mom. That is my job. That was the deal when Billy and I got married—that I would stay home and be there for our kids the way my mom was there for me and my brothers growing up. These days, some people act like motherhood isn't really a full-time job. Wrong. Because it is, Matty—for me anyway. I'm good at it, and I'm proud that I'm there for my children twenty-four seven."

"Oh, honey. I only meant—"

"I don't want to hear it, okay? I love my job, Matty. It's demanding and it's full-time, and it's my husband's job to find some other way than hiring me to bring in extra cash."

Matty felt like she'd stepped on a landmine. She soothed, "Hey. I understand. I do."

"Oh, do you? Really?" Heather kept her voice low, but her fury was palpable. "I don't think so. Talk to me when your baby is nine and wants a cell phone. My babies are growing up so fast I feel like I miss them already. I can't even tell you how frustrating this is for me. And frankly, I don't need you taking Billy's side in this."

"But Heather, I'm not taking Billy's—"

"Stop," Heather hissed. "No more. I mean it, Mat. This is not the time and it sure isn't the place."

They finished their salads in a heavy, cold silence. When the server came back, they split the check as they always did and walked out together.

It was another gray day, and the wind was blowing. They walked a few steps together and then stopped on the sidewalk.

Matty tried one more time to smooth things over. "Heather, I'm sorry if I—"

"Never mind," her cousin said flatly as she reached for a hug. They wrapped their arms around each other. "See you soon." Heather sighed as she turned for her Suburban.

Matty had walked over from her parents' house. She zipped up her coat, stuck her hands into her pockets and started back the way she'd come. But she wasn't ready to go home yet—and she had her keys in her pocket, including the one to the bookstore.

She went there instead of home, letting herself in the back door, where the cats greeted her. Xo Cat came running. She rolled to her back and wiggled around, grabbing for Matty's hand as Matty petted her. Edmund appeared a moment later. He was calm and sweet as always—a very big boy who weighed fifteen pounds. He purred and nuzzled her hand as she gave him long strokes from the top of his sleek black head to the end of his tail.

Matty turned up the heat a bit and went out to the front of the store with the cats following along behind. She wandered between the shelves and circled the display tables, very much aware of what a great job her mom had done here—and also imagining the changes she hoped to make eventually.

In the future, after her mom got used to having a partner in the store, Matty wanted to find ways to collaborate more regularly with the Medicine Creek Library and the local schools. She wanted Cloud Peak Books to set up author visits at the schools—and provide books for those events. She wanted to organize book fairs and educational initiatives. She hoped to forge connections with local teachers and school administrative staff by offering special discounts and teacher nights.

And they really needed a permanent coffee nook in the front of the store, she thought as she brewed herself a cup of chamomile tea in the back room. Her mom always offered refreshments when she held events and signings. But why not offer them every day? People stayed longer if they had something to sip.

Matty took her tea out front and settled in a fat armchair near the register. Edmund jumped up to stand guard on the back of the chair. Xo Cat claimed Matty's lap. Both cats were purring. Matty smiled at the comforting sounds.

But thoughts of last night and of her lunch just now with Heather kept dragging her down.

She tried to take heart when it came to her cousin. At least today Heather had been a little more forthcoming about her issues with Billy.

As for what had happened last night at Ethan's house, Matty cringed just thinking about it. She'd kept promising herself to give Ethan some space—and then she'd done no such thing. She should have known it would all blown up in her face.

Now Ethan was avoiding her, and she had no idea what to do about that. It seemed to her that she'd only make the problem worse if she tracked him down. What would she even say to him? It was too late for apologies. And what if he said he couldn't hang out with her anymore, that Sylvia didn't trust her?

That just might break her heart.

Xo Cat reached up and gently patted her face.

Matty pouted down at the cat. "I messed up. I was needy and clingy, and Ethan tried to be nice to me. If I've lost him as a friend over this, I will never forgive myself—Xo Cat, today is one of those days when I feel like I just can't do anything right."

Behind her, Edmund stretched out along the chair back. His furry warmth soothed her. She told herself it would be all right, that Ethan would reach out to her soon.

But he didn't reach out, not that afternoon or in the evening. Matty went to bed feeling pretty low. At least she slept fairly well—mostly because she was exhausted from not sleeping the night before.

On Monday her mom had morning errands to run. Matty opened the store by herself for the first time since moving home. That cheered her up a bit. She rearranged a few of the displays and tried to predict how her mom would react as she reminded herself that Simone Gage was a supremely reasonable woman.

If Simone wanted them back the way they'd been, she would say so upfront. Then they could discuss it. But whatever happened, it was a baby step in the direction of Matty taking charge.

Her mom came in at ten thirty. She entered through the back and joined Matty at the counter. "How's it going?"

"What can I tell you? It's Monday and it's been quiet."

Simone leaned close and Matty smelled roses. "You've been messing with my displays."

Matty turned and looked directly at her mom. "So what do you think?"

Simone grinned then. "Good work."

The two simple words lifted Matty's flagging spirits. "I was hoping you would approve."

"Well, I do. They look great."

Around noon, the sun came out and more customers appeared. At a quarter of one, Matty's mom was back in the history section helping out sweet and ancient Mr. Smith, who was writing a book about his experiences as a torpedoman in the Pacific on the USS *Suwannee* during World War II. Matty stood at the register ringing up a sale.

The bell over the door rang. It was Sylvia O'Grady, in

a tight knee-length black wool dress, a coat to match and fancy boots, her long brown hair sleek and smooth to her shoulders. She marched toward Matty with fury in her dark eyes.

By rote, Matty handed over the receipt and pushed the bag of books across the counter. "There you go," she said to her customer with a determined smile. "Happy reading."

The customer nodded and turned for the door.

Sylvia kept coming. She zipped around the man waiting to have his purchase rung up. Once she'd cut in front of him, she glanced back over her shoulder and said silkily, "This'll just take a minute."

Matty wanted to run for the back door. But she held her ground. She tried really hard to look calm, even welcoming. "Hello, Sylvia. How are—"

"Please," Sylvia interrupted. And then she scoffed. "I wasn't going to come here. I didn't plan to say a word to you. I was going to keep my dignity and take the high road. Because I am a nice person, a *calm* person. I am a professional person who is respected in this town, not some fancy writer from Los Angeles who suddenly decides to move back home and take over the family store. Oh, no. Uh-uh. I am not you. Not on your life. But you know what?"

Matty gulped. "Uh, Sylvia, I think that you're..." Her mind went completely blank.

Sylvia leaned closer across the counter. "Screw all that." She tossed that head of perfect hair.

Matty said, "Listen, let me help this gentleman right there behind you, and then you and I can—"

"You and I are doing nothing, Ms. Matty Gage Hunt. I just came in to tell you that you have my blessing."

Matty blinked, confused. "I'm sorry, I don't...?"

"Stop talking. Just listen," Sylvia muttered through clenched teeth. "Did he tell you I dumped his ass?"

What? Sylvia and Ethan were through? "Oh, no! Sylvia, I—"

"Do. Not. Speak. I'm not finished—and you know what? Whether he told you already or not, yes, I did dump his ass. So now you can go for it. You can pull out all the stops. Knock yourself out. I want nothing to do with him. He is all yours."

"Sylvia, I honestly don't know where you got the idea that I—"

"What did I just tell you? Don't talk to me. I don't want to see those lips of yours moving. You're just wasting your breath because I have zero interest in anything you might have to say."

About then, Matty realized that keeping quiet was probably her best bet. So she shut her mouth, folded her arms across her chest—and waited for Sylvia to either wind down or leave.

For an endless chain of excruciating seconds, they simply stared at each other. And then, without another word, Sylvia spun on her heel and made for the door, which she flung wide and slammed shut behind her as she stormed out.

Chapter Six

"Yikes," said the man Sylvia had elbowed aside to get to Matty. "That was intense."

No kidding. And now everyone in town would know that Sylvia had dumped Ethan and it was all Matty's fault.

"You okay?" asked the customer.

Matty drew herself up. "I am just fine. And I'm sorry you had to wait." Matty held out her hand. He set down a hardcover copy of the latest thriller in the Joe Pickett series by CJ Box. Box was big in Medicine Creek—understandably so. He wrote books you couldn't put down, many of them set in Wyoming.

The bookstore was pin-drop quiet as Matty rang up the sale. By the time she handed the customer his receipt, her mom was at her side.

"How about a break?" Simone asked softly.

Matty shut her eyes and took a slow, deep breath. "Yes, please."

"Take as long as you need."

"Thanks, Mom. I think I'll go for a walk—or maybe a drive. It's pretty cold out."

"Whatever you think." Her mom wrapped an arm around her, gave her a gentle squeeze and then let go.

"Just, uh, call me if you—"

"I will, Matilda. Now, go on."

A minute later, Matty grabbed her coat and purse from the peg by the back door and went out into the parking lot where the sky had clouded over again and sleet was spitting down out of the sky.

Her Jeep waited right where she'd left it, a few feet away. She got in and headed for Ethan's law office, which wasn't all that far. She easily could have walked, even in the blustery weather.

But she felt so exposed after what had happened in the bookstore, like if she walked down Main Street, passersby would stop and gawk and point at her.

There she goes. Matty Hunt. She used to be someone who knew where she was going. Not anymore. She got pregnant by accident, gave up everything she'd worked for and ran back to her hometown like her hair was on fire. Now she's broken up her good friend Ethan's longtime relationship with that nice accountant woman, Sylvia O'Grady. That Matty Hunt—what outlandish stunt will she pull next?

She found a parking space around the corner from Ethan's office and sat there for a minute behind the wheel reminding herself that she really ought to call him before barging in on him at his place of business. It was the middle of the workday, after all. Exactly the wrong time to bother him. He was probably in a meeting or maybe out with a client for lunch. Really, she should wait. Call him this evening...

She got out of the car anyway. Rounding the corner onto Main Street, she entered the law offices of Stahl and Bravo as Ethan and his law partner, Gavin Stahl, were going out.

It was almost comical. She spotted Ethan at the exact moment that he realized it was her coming in the door.

Simultaneously, they froze in mid-step and gawked at each other.

"Matty!" he said.

"You're busy," she muttered. "Look, I'll just…"

"Hold on." He caught her hand as she tried to whirl and head back out.

"No, really. I'm sorry. I'll call you, or you can—"

"I'll catch up," he said to the other man. "Matty and I need to talk."

"Take your time." With an easy smile and a nod in her direction, Gavin eased around the two of them and went out the door.

Ethan still had hold of her hand. "Come on into my office."

She went reluctantly—which was ridiculous. Hadn't she driven over here hoping she might get a few minutes with him?

He ushered her in ahead of him. "Have a seat," he offered, shutting the door and nodding toward the sofa and two chairs a few feet away.

All her life choices flashed before her eyes. In retrospect, so many of them seemed all wrong. "Really, I—"

"Here." He moved in behind her, slid her coat off her shoulders and carried it to a closet a few feet away. She watched as he hung up her coat and then his. When he turned back to her, he asked, "Are you okay?"

"Not really."

He came back to her and took her hand again. "Come on…" She trailed along behind him to one of the chairs in the sitting area. "Sit down." As she sank into the chair, he offered, "Want decaf or something?"

She shook her head. "Nothing, thanks. I'm just here to apologize."

"For...?"

"Sylvia came into the bookstore about fifteen minutes ago. She says she dumped you."

"That's right, she did. Saturday night."

"Right after she walked in on us dancing at your place?"

"Yeah."

Matty pressed her palms together and stuck her hands between her knees. "Oh, Ethan. I was purposely leaving you alone, thinking you needed quality time with her. But instead you got dumped, and I haven't been there for you. Why didn't you reach out to me?"

He looked away. "I was going to call you, Matty. I honestly was..."

"But you didn't. After all you've done for me—when Gabe died and now, since I've been back home—I would like to think that someday I might get a chance to return the favor, that if you need a friend, I'm the one you would turn to."

He still wasn't looking at her. "It's not your fault. I've just been feeling a little down about everything, that's all."

"I am so sorry. You miss her, right? You want her back."

"I didn't say that."

"Ethan." She pulled her hands from between her knees and straightened her spine. "Look at me." When he finally shifted his gaze to her, she said, "I will talk to her. I will make her see that she has it all wrong. I'll explain our history together, that you feel obligated to look after me because of your lifelong friendship with Gabe. I'll let her know that yes, I was taking total advantage of you, self-ishly hogging your attention. But she's got it all wrong if she thinks I was somehow trying to move in on her guy..."

Did she sound the least bit convincing? Doubtful. No matter how innocent her intentions, she'd come between Ethan and Sylvia simply by taking up pretty much all his free time. That made her the last person Sylvia O'Grady was likely to listen to. But so what? Matty owed it to Ethan to do what she could. "Ethan, I mean it. I will make her see."

Ethan shook his head. "No, you won't. Don't even try."

"But I want to help."

"Matty. Don't help. Please." Was he trying not to laugh?

"Ethan Bravo." She glared at him. "This is not funny."

"Yeah, it is," he replied. His broad shoulders were shak-ing. "It's funny, and you know it."

She waited for him to get control of himself before she said, "I'm so pleased to be a source of amusement for you."

"Aw..." He got up, went around the low table and held down a hand. "Come on. Get up here."

"Hmph." She went ahead and gave him her hand. He pulled her up and wrapped those long arms around her. With a sigh, she sagged against him. "I just want to help." She tipped her head up so she could look into his eyes. "But really, I don't get it."

"Get what?"

"I mean, okay, you hadn't been spending a lot of time with her lately. And yeah, I was a lot to blame for that. And then she walked in and caught us dancing together—and that's what I don't get."

"What do you mean?"

"I mean, it was just that. Dancing. Laughing. With all

our clothes on. You weren't cheating on her, and that should have been obvious. You were just hanging out with an old friend—which is what you told her that night, when you were alone, right?" He was frowning. She asked again, "Ethan, am I right?"

Slowly, he nodded. "Yeah."

"So I'm not even sure why she broke up with you. What happened Saturday night, her showing up and finding us dancing together, that's the kind of thing that can be explained pretty simply. You could have told her about the baby, said you felt obligated to look out for me in my, er, time of trial, because Gabe was your best friend, that there was nothing for her to be upset about. And then she could have said she feels neglected or whatever. And you could have promised to spend less time with your dead best friend's needy widow—but that didn't happen. Instead she dumped you. I just don't get that. And I still feel it's at last partly my fault."

"Matty." He pressed his big, warm palm to the side of her face. His touch felt so good, comforting and steadying, too. "Listen to me—it is not your fault. It's true I wasn't spending enough time with Sylvia, but that wasn't because of you. It was because it wasn't working, what I had with her. It hasn't been working for a long time. I promise you it's not your fault that Sylvia dumped me."

"I still feel bad about it."

"Don't. Sylvia and I just got in a rut, that's all. We were…comfortable for each other. But it wasn't going anywhere. Your coming home, the time we've been spending together—time I wasn't spending with her—that made it more obvious that Sylvia and I were not working out. But believe me, the end *was* coming." What he said made a sad kind of sense.

"You're sure?"

"Absolutely. Stop blaming yourself. Saturday night, after she left, I realized that she was right to break it off with me. It was going nowhere, and ending it was the right move."

"I wish you'd called me Saturday, that you'd given me a chance to be there for *you* for a change."

"I just needed some time, Matty."

"To…lick your wounds in private?"

"More or less, yeah."

"I get that. But what about now? Are you okay now?"

He smoothed a hand down her hair, and she melted inside—because he was such a good guy and such a wonderful friend. "Yeah. Better every day."

"Well, I still feel awful. I need to make it up to you somehow."

"There's nothing to make up for. We're good, I promise you."

"I'm cooking you dinner. Tonight. And since I don't have a place of my own, it'll have to be at your house."

"Hey." He was grinning now, looking like he didn't have a care in the world. "Works for me."

That night, Matty cooked Ethan one of his favorites—spiced lamb with shaved carrots.

Ethan let her do everything—partly because she insisted. But mostly because he liked it when she cooked for him. What was not to like? She was so damn good at it. She always seemed happy in the kitchen, and she loved to share what she cooked.

That night, she told him she had her first appointment with Dr. Hayes the next day.

"I'll go with you," he said.

"It's just a routine first visit. I'll manage it on my own."

"You sure?"

"Positive. Pass the pita bread."

He took some for himself and then handed it over. "I'll expect a full report."

"I've already been to my doctor in LA. It's a checkup, that's all. *Bor-ing.*"

"What about the first ultrasound?"

"I had that back in Los Angeles. Dr. Hayes will sched-ule me for the second one. It'll be sometime next month."

"Will you let me come to that, be with you for it?"

"Why?"

"Because you need someone with you in all this. Is your mother going, or your cousin?"

"Ethan, I'm all grown up. I'll go by myself."

"You should have somebody. Let it be me."

She set down her fork. "It's really sweet of you to offer."

He wasn't finished. "And what about your…what do they call them? Your birth coach? You know you need one of those."

She had a look—unsure. But hopeful, too. He decided right then that he was not giving up until she let him do what her baby's father should be doing. "You're serious?" she asked in a hushed little voice.

He nodded. "It should be me. Look at it this way—you'd be doing me a favor."

"How so?"

"We need to get realistic here. At the rate I'm going, I'll never have kids of my own."

"Oh, Ethan. Don't talk like that. You're only thirty-one."

He faked a sad face. "Thirty-one, still single. Probably never getting married. I've accepted that now."

"Thirty-one is not that old. I mean, *I'm* thirty-one, too."

"You're just proving my point. You were with Gabe forever, a happy couple. I've never really had that. Maybe I never will."

"Now you're making me sad."

"Don't be sad, Matilda. Be my friend."

"Always."

"And do me a favor—let me be there for you and the baby."

"You're already there for me and the baby."

He tore off a piece of pita bread and dredged it in the lamb and sauce. "Just think about it, okay?"

She was quiet. He had no idea what might be going through her head. In the end, she said, "Yeah. I will. I'll think about it."

He forked up more delicious lamb. "Can't ask for more."

The next night, Ethan found her waiting at his door when he got home from the office. She had a big bag of groceries in her arms, and she grinned at him as he came up the steps. "I thought you'd never get home." It was barely forty degrees out, and the wind was blowing. Her nose and cheeks were cherry red.

"That does it," he said as he unlocked the door and ushered her in ahead of him. "You need a key. I can't have you sitting out there, freezing on the front porch waiting for me to come home." He hung up his coat.

Without a word, she slipped off her boots. Then, still

wearing her coat, she went on through to the kitchen island and set down the bag of groceries.

He followed her over there. "You're cooking again? That's not fair. You cooked last night."

"Noted," she said over her shoulder as she went back to the entry to hang up her coat. As she reentered the great room, she gave him a wink. "You get to help."

"Of course I'm helping—I'll be right back." He headed for his office to get a spare key from the safe.

When he returned to the kitchen, she waved a package wrapped in butcher paper at him. "The chicken breasts were big and juicy looking. I was thinking pesto chicken bruschetta."

"Works for me." He went to her, took the package from her hand and set it on the island. "Here." He put the key in her palm and folded her fingers over it.

She held up the key and shook it at him. "You should think this through. I could end up taking total advantage, wandering in and out of here at all hours of the day and night."

He shrugged. "You mean just like you do now?"

"Smartass." She picked up the wrapped chicken breasts again and hefted them as though she planned to lob them at his head.

He laughed. "Put those down before you hurt somebody."

They washed their hands and got to work. As they cooked, he got a mini report on her visit to Dr. Hayes that morning. Her next ultrasound was scheduled for the third Wednesday in April. He didn't push to be there for her.

Sometime in the next few weeks, he would bring it up again. And if she still said she wanted to do that alone, so be it. Matty was always bound to make her own choices, and he respected that.

But he would be disappointed if she turned him down. He wanted to be there for her—and for her baby.

When they sat down at the table to eat she said, playing it casual for all she was worth, "By the way, my first, last and deposit on the bungalow cleared the bank." Before he could congratulate her, she held up a key ring and twirled it on her finger. "I not only have a key to your house—I now have one to mine." Her sweet face glowed with happiness.

He shoved back his chair, marched to her side and pulled her up into a hug. "Congratulations." He breathed in her scent of oranges and tropical flowers.

"Thank you. I'm so happy." She pulled back to beam up at him. "I really am."

"When are you moving in?"

"All this week. My mom's giving me tomorrow through Saturday off from the bookstore, and my dad is helping move all my stuff. My plan is that Saturday night will be my first night in my own place again."

"I'll pitch in, help your dad load up the furniture and haul it all into your new place." He was already rearranging his calendar in his head. It would be tight, but he should be able to juggle some things around.

"I know that face." She narrowed those blue eyes at him. "You're booked work-wise, and you're thinking of what you'll need to reschedule."

"So?"

"So, you work hard and you don't have time to be hauling my stuff around. It's okay. My dad and I, we've got this—Heather and Billy are pitching in, too. And don't forget their boys and the twins…"

"Right. The twins are what, three?"

"Yep. Hard workers, those girls."

"I mean it, Matty. I want to help." He realized he might actually be pouting.

She reached up with both hands, clasped his shoulders and gave them a squeeze. "You *can* help. I would love to have your help. On Saturday, if you're free."

"But—"

"Shh." She put the pads of two soft fingertips to his lips. Her skin was cool. He smelled lemons, tart and fresh. And he remembered watching her earlier as she squeezed the lemon for the bruschetta sauce, remembered how she'd glanced up when he spoke to her and that cute little dimple had tucked itself into her cheek…

Out of nowhere, heat rushed up the back of his neck. His breath got trapped inside his chest. He stared at her soft pink lips, imagined bending forward, kissing the tip of her nose—and then taking her mouth in a slow, deep kiss…

"No *but*s," she said sternly. "You're not taking off from work to help me. But please come over Saturday if you're free."

He thought, *Breathe, you fool*. And he did. One slow, even breath. And then another.

Fine. He was fine. Whatever that was a minute ago, it was over. As if it had never been.

"Ethan?" She gazed up at him, the smooth skin between her eyebrows scrunched up. "You okay?"

"Of course. Why?"

"For a moment there, you seemed a little… I don't know, stunned, maybe?"

He managed a reasonably credible chuckle. "Yeah, well.

I can't believe you're going to do most of the moving without me."

"Don't worry. It won't be easy, but somehow, me, my dad
and my cousin and crew will get it done—so, Saturday?"

"Just try to keep me away."

Matty and her dad got to work first thing Wednesday
morning. Billy showed up an hour later.

Tall and muscular, with dark hair and eyes, Billy Dolan
was a sweetheart. Matty greeted him with a hug.

He smiled down at her warmly. "Matty, I have to say.
It's great to have you back home. It really is."

Staring up at him, she couldn't help thinking of her
cousin, couldn't help wondering, *How could anyone stay
angry with this man?* The guy was not only patient and
sweet, he was also always ready to pitch in wherever he
might be needed.

By that evening, the two men had everything moved
from her parents' garage to the bungalow. Matty didn't do
much, really. Her dad and Billy wouldn't allow her to help
move any of the heavy stuff—which included most of the
boxes and all of the furniture.

Thursday was more of the same. She couldn't lift or
carry, so her job was embarrassingly easy—she told the
men where everything went, and they carried the furniture
and boxes into the various rooms.

Billy left at a little after five. Her mom appeared at six.
Simone had brought takeout from Henry's. The three of
them—Matty, her mom and her dad—sat at the oval dinner
table Matty and Gabe had bought together for their North
Hollywood duplex.

When her parents got up to go, Matty hung back. "I'm

just going to start putting things away here in the kitchen," she said. When her mom made a pained face, she added. "I promise you, Mom, no heavy lifting."

Her mom was not appeased. "You're having a baby, and you've worked all day."

"Pointing, Mom. That's what I did all day. I told Dad and Billy what to put where. They did all the work."

Her mom wasn't going for it. "Matilda, it's enough."

"But I just want to—"

"Come home with us. Please." Her mom spoke gently now.

Okay, maybe she was a little bit tired. She went back with them.

Ethan called at seven thirty. She reported on the progress they'd made at the bungalow. "Tomorrow Heather's coming with Billy. So there will be four of us—not that I'm much help. I'm not allowed to lift anything over ten pounds."

"Good," Ethan said.

"What do you mean, good? It's not good to be useless. I don't like it at all."

"You're not useless." He said it soothingly.

"Don't be nice to me," she grumbled. "I know I'm being unreasonable."

"Your words, not mine."

She wished he was going to be there tomorrow. "Is it weird that I kind of miss you?"

"Very weird. But no problem. Just say the word and I'll be over tomorrow to help."

"No way. Go to work, Ethan. And by that I mean your regular job. Saturday—you are helping me on Saturday."

"Yes, ma'am."

They nattered on together about nothing in particular for

another half hour or so. When they finally said goodbye,
she dropped her phone on the nightstand, snuggled down
under the covers and went right to sleep.

Friday morning, like the day before, it was Matty, her
dad and Billy at the bungalow. The two men spent four
hours or so putting Matty's bed together and arranging
rugs and furniture under her supervision. By the time they
broke for lunch, the rugs were down and every room had
all the furniture right where she wanted it—well, except
for the baby's room. There was nothing to put in there. Yet.

Her dad had errands to run, so he left at a little before
two. For an hour or so, Billy helped Matty out with cleaning
and stocking the kitchen. They set out her small appliances,
and he hung her spice rack on the inside of a cabinet door.

Then Heather showed up with all four kids. Very little
work got done after that. Matty gave her cousin and the
kids a quick tour of her new home.

The boys followed along dutifully. The twins were adorable as always. For them, everything was a new discovery.

"Pretty!" Claire announced at the sight of the bright-col-
ored quilt Matty had bought in Morocco a few years before.

"I like your new house!" exclaimed Elissa, throwing
her arms wide.

Heather had brought a snack. They all gathered around
the table for that.

Matty loved having them there. Too bad the tension between Heather and Billy was thick and toxic as a nox-
ious gas. They hardly looked at each other, and they talked
around each other. Once Matty caught Billy looking at
Heather. He seemed both sad and angry—and he turned
away instantly when his wife glanced in his direction.

What's going on with you guys? Matty longed to ask. But she knew that neither of them would welcome the question. And besides, it wasn't the kind of thing she wanted to get into with the kids sitting right there munching apple slices and mini pretzels, sipping happily at juice boxes.

The snack vanished in record time. By then, the children were bored. Heather gathered them up and herded them to her Suburban. Matty and Billy followed them out and waved as Heather pulled away from the curb.

Once the car disappeared around the next corner, Billy said kind of glumly, "I guess I ought to get going, too."

Matty wondered for half a second if he and the rest of the family were still living in the same house. "Billy, are you...?"

"Don't ask me," he cut her off in a pleading tone. "Okay?"

"All right."

"Just...talk to Heather."

"I will."

He was watching her face. "You have no clue what the problem is, do you?"

"Um, not really."

"I think it would be good if she would, you know, open up to you."

"I understand." No, she didn't. But what else could she say? The hurt-puppy look in his eyes broke her heart.

Back inside, he gathered up his tools. "If you need me tomorrow, I can come in the morning."

"Nah. Everything else, I can pretty much handle. And if I need help, I'll can call my dad. Also, Ethan's coming over to give me a hand, so I think I'm in good shape."

"Okay, then. But all you have to do is call."

"Thank you, Billy. You are the best."

Once he was gone, she organized the kitchen drawers and filled the ice trays in the fridge. Then she hung a few pictures and set out a few personal treasures, things collected during her travels, home decor from the North Hollywood duplex that she hadn't been able to part with.

She ended up standing in the doorway to the empty baby's room, smiling dreamily to herself as she imagined how it might look with a cute crib, a nice changing area and a comfy chair where she could rock her child to sleep.

When Ethan called that night, she told him proudly that she had the bungalow under control. "Thanks to Billy and my dad, there's nothing left to do but put stuff away in drawers and cabinets and set out more knickknacks. I can handle all that myself."

"You're done?" He sounded disappointed.

"Ethan. It's a good thing. You don't have to spend your Saturday moving my furniture around."

"I want to help. You have to have *something* for me to do. I have a drill, you know. And a cordless electric screwdriver. I'm amazing at hanging window coverings."

She laughed. "The house has blinds throughout…but yeah, there's always something—that's true."

"Exactly. You need me. You know you do. I'll meet you at your new place at nine tomorrow morning and bring my power tools."

She wanted to reach through the phone and hug him good and tight. She really could manage the rest on her own. But he was Ethan, after all. That meant he was bound to help out no matter what. "As if I'm going to argue with an offer like that."

"See you at nine, then."

* * *

The next morning, when she arrived at the bungalow, she found him waiting out in front wearing jeans, a Henley and a canvas coat. He was leaning against the driver's door of his fancy crew cab.

She pulled her Jeep in next to him and jumped out. "I am thrilled to announce that I've brought over the rest of my stuff from my parents' house. Tonight I'm sleeping in my own place." She'd also brought sandwich fixings for lunch.

He helped her carry everything inside and then went back out to get his tools from the lockbox in the bed of his truck.

They spent the morning doing all the small things—arranging more of her pictures and table decor in the living room, putting up the shower curtain and hanging decorative shelves on the empty wall in the kitchen.

At noon, they broke for lunch. As they wolfed down grilled ham-and-cheese sandwiches, she announced, "Enough for today. I need to do some serious grocery shopping. You are free to go. For now. But come back at six and I'll cook you dinner."

Did she know he would refuse to go?

Maybe. A little. And she didn't argue very hard when he insisted on taking her shopping so he could carry all the grocery bags for her. After all, she had to stock her kitchen and there were bound to be a lot of bags.

But the real benefit of having his help was that everything was more fun with Ethan there. They shopped for a long time, and he never once seemed bored or ready to call it quits.

He took her down to Buffalo first and they went to the Family Dollar Store, where they argued about silly things—

which cheese grater was better quality, and did she really need a lemon zester right now? Back in Medicine Creek at Big Country Grocery, they took their time choosing ingredients for dinner along with the produce and staples she hadn't picked up down in Buffalo.

It was after five when they finally pulled into her driveway again. He switched off the engine and turned to her. "Let's take the groceries in, put away the perishables and go out to eat."

She really did want to cook him a nice meal in her new home. "Let's cook. Please."

He grinned. "So now I'm going to be allowed to help with dinner?"

"Well, I have to admit that everything is easier when we're working together."

"And more fun," he added.

"So true."

"All right, then. Let's get after it."

They carried everything in, stuck the bags of non-food items out on the little screened porch next to the bonus room in back and started putting the food and staples away. The process went pretty quickly considering how much she'd bought.

But then she grabbed a five-pound bag of unbleached flour and turned for the cabinets to the right of the sink. She took one step—and the bottom of the bag gave way.

With a grunt of surprise, she tried to get her hands underneath the bag in order to turn it upside down so no more would spill out. She managed to get it turned over.

And the other end of the bag gave way.

Flour exploded everywhere—including all over every inch of her—down her front, all over her arms, hands, legs and feet. It was in her hair and eyes. It even got into her nose and she sneezed.

Ethan, at the refrigerator, shut the door and turned around. "What the hell?" He started for her.

She put out a hand. "Stop. No need for both of us to be covered in flour."

He said, "I'll...grab the broom."

She stood very still. It seemed dangerous to move. "The broom and dust pan are out on the screen porch. You'll need the shop vac, too. It's in the closet in the baby's room."

He looked her up and down. "Just stay there. I'll take care of it."

"Thank you. Because I really do need a shower." Carefully, trying not to send the white dust flying, she brushed flour from her hair, her shoulders and her arms. Then, moving very slowly, she lifted one foot and then the other, backing out of the dry puddle of white dust that had formed all around her when the bag exploded.

By then, Ethan had retrieved the broom. "Go ahead," he said. "Clean up. I'll deal with the mess."

There was flour on the table, the chairs, the counter, in the sink. Everywhere. "I'll help with the mess first."

"Go."

"It'll be quicker if I help."

He huffed out a breath. "Have it your way."

She took a minute to brush off more flour. Then she grabbed the broom and dust pan. He went off to get the shop vac.

Twenty minutes later, things were looking a lot better. The table, fridge and range still carried a light dusting of flour, but the worst of it was swept away.

Ethan said, "Now go. I'll finish here."

She went—through the arch to the living area and then into the tiny rectangle of hallway that led to the two bedrooms and the bathroom. Ducking into her room first, she shut the door and eased off her shearling boots. Next, she peeled off her clothes and rolled them up to shake out and wash later. In the kitchen, she heard the shop vac start up again.

Thank God for Ethan. Best. Friend. Ever.

She stood there by her bed, stark naked and grinning. Because Ethan Bravo really was the world's best friend...

The shop vac shut off. She needed to get moving, rinse off the flour and get back to work.

After grabbing her overnight case from where she'd left it on the end of the bed, she scampered naked into the bathroom, shut the door and twisted the privacy lock.

In the mirror over the sink, her hair had a dusting of white. There was flour in her eyebrows, too. But it could have been worse, she reminded herself. Yes, it had been a long day and then a flour bomb had exploded in her kitchen. But her bathroom had a shower curtain and she'd had the foresight that morning to hang up clean towels and set out her bath products.

Shoving back the curtain, she reached in to turn on the shower. The weirdest thing happened then. From the corner of her eye, she saw something skitter across the vintage turquoise tiles. As she assured herself that the skittering thing was just her overactive imagination, a giant spider landed, *plop*, on the back of her hand.

All rational thought fled. She flicked the spider into the air, threw her head back and let out a scream so loud and piercing, it scared her even worse than the spider had. Leaping back from the tub, she dropped to the toilet seat— and screamed again.

* * *

At the sound of Matty's terrified scream, Ethan dropped the wet rag he'd been using to wipe down the fridge. He was just turning into the hallway that led to the bedrooms and bath when she screamed again.

It was two steps to the bathroom door. He grabbed the knob and turned it—but of course, she'd locked it. He tapped on the door. "Matty! Are you all right?"

"Just a minute!" she screeched.

Two seconds later, the door swung open. Matty stared at him, eyes big as dinner plates, a towel tucked around herself. "Omigod, Ethan!"

He took her by the arms and pulled her close. She huddled into him. "You're shaking," he said. She looked up at him, blue eyes stunned. He asked, "What happened?"

She went on tiptoe and whispered, as though sharing a terrifying secret, "There's a spider in here. It could be anywhere. We have to go."

"What kind of spider?"

She groaned. "A big one."

He pulled her out into the miniscule hallway with him. "Where is it?"

Clutching her towel, she backed off a step. She was shaking all over. He honestly had never seen her eyes that wide. "I was turning on the water, and it jumped off the tile under the window and landed on my hand. I freaked and threw it off."

"So...tub area?"

She pressed her lips together, white-knuckled her towel and nodded. "Probably." She shuddered. "Spiders...they scare the crap out of me."

"I'll find it," he said with a lot more confidence than he

felt. She could have thrown it just about anywhere. It could be scuttling down the hallway by now—or dangling from the ceiling, about to drop into her flour-dusted hair. But he didn't say that. "Don't worry."

He turned back toward the tub, took another step—and spotted something on the tiled window ledge. "I think I see it." He leaned in. "Yep. Looks like a common house spider. Nothing to be—"

"Wait!" She grabbed his arm and yanked him back toward the open door to the hallway—and then let out a squeak of surprise as she almost lost hold of her towel. "Don't hurt it!" she commanded, tucking the towel back in.

"Matty." He spoke her name reproachfully. "It's a spider, and you hate them."

"Yeah, so? That doesn't mean I want it dead. Even icky, gross spiders have a right to a full, rich life." Her eyes shone with determination to protect the spider *and* make certain it was removed from her house.

He had to bite the inside of his cheek to keep from laughing at her sheer intensity. "I'll try," he said mildly.

She hitched up her chin. "I hate spiders, but that doesn't mean I want you to murder one for me."

He turned to look at the spider again. It was still there. "Trust me," he said.

"I do," she replied.

The spider did that skittery thing they were so creepily good at. It was now three inches to the left of its earlier position. It still had all its legs and could zip off up the wall and dart across the ceiling any given second now. Better to deal with it sooner than later. "No screen on the window," he noted with a glance back at Matty.

"I'm aware." With one hand still securing the towel, she

used the index finger of the other to point at the fixture in the ceiling. "At least there's a working exhaust fan in here. I'm making a list of stuff that needs fixing, and I…"

Before she could finish, he stepped into the tub, slid the window wide and brushed the spider out with the side of his hand. "There you go." He slid the window shut and engaged the latch. "Spidey is unharmed and no longer living in your house."

"Thank you!" She let out a laugh that verged on a sob. "Oh, Ethan, it's childish, I know. But they creep me out and I hate them—and I don't want them hurt."

He stepped out of the shower and turned to face her.

She was right there, an inch away now, still sprinkled with flour—her hair, her eyebrows and eyelashes, the slopes of her silky shoulders. She was clutching her towel, sort of swaying toward him.

He did the natural thing. He opened his arms. She stepped right into them with a soft, happy sigh.

Now he was holding her, their eyes locked on each other in some strange, suspended moment where who they were—Gabe's wife and Gabe's best friend—was somehow busted wide open, falling away, splintered to pieces.

Left behind in scattered shards.

Now there was only the two of them, Matty and Ethan.

Alone. Here. Together.

She stared up at him, eyes dewy, cheeks pink, body soft and smooth, full and curvy, dusted in flour—everything he'd always wanted. Everything he'd always known was never meant for him.

Except…

Well, right now, she showed no inclination to pull away

as he'd always known she would if this moment ever really happened.

Instead, she melted into him. She plastered her body along the length of his.

"Ethan..." So soft and hopeful, she lifted her face to him and breathed his name as her mouth touched his. "I'm so glad. That you're here, right here. Right now."

Heat exploded through him.

And then they were kissing...

Him and Matty.

Kissing...

It was a wild kiss, wet and open and hungry and frantic—the kind of kiss he used to despise himself for dreaming of back in the day, a forbidden kiss, a kiss that could never happen, a kiss so needy and desperate and real...

He took her shoulders and broke the hold of her soft, warm lips. "Matty?" He asked her name in sheer disbelief, with a yearning he kept trying with all his considerable will and self-control to hide.

"Ethan..." She lifted her arms then and wrapped them around his neck.

The towel plopped to the tiles at their feet.

For Matty, that perfect kiss they'd just shared had started out as sheer gratitude—that he'd gotten rid of the spider without killing it. Sheer gratitude that he was here and he was her friend and she could trust him and count on him.

Sheer gratitude that he'd made moving home so much better than she'd ever dared to dream it might be. Sheer gratitude that after three sad years of feeling like half of herself had gone missing forever, she could finally believe again that someone really *got* her, that she had a true friend and she could tell her friend anything. He wouldn't judge her and he wouldn't let her down.

With Ethan, she would never get that awful feeling that she'd had with Ted—that she'd been tricked somehow, that she'd thought she'd known him—but she didn't. Not really. That she'd believed he was trustworthy—but he wasn't, not in the least.

Uh-uh. No. That awful sense of deepest disappointment would never happen. Not with Ethan.

She could trust Ethan with her life. Trust him and know that he fully deserved her trust.

"Damn," he said, rough and low, his eyes more amber than green right now.

They stared at each other. She was holding her breath.

This was all-new territory. Who knew where they went from here?

She didn't.

She only knew that she wanted this—this moment, naked, with Ethan. And she knew that he did, too. She could read him so well. She could see his desire shining in his eyes.

"Matty...?"

She breathed out and breathed in again as she looked down at her body, at her breasts that were even fuller than they used to be, at the sweet bump her tiny baby made, held safe in her belly. Everything was changing.

Who knew how it would all end up?

She certainly didn't. She'd had no advance knowledge that this moment with him would ever happen. That she would be here in this too-small bathroom of her thoroughly charming and slightly rundown rented bungalow—naked. With Ethan.

Her nakedness, the kiss they'd just shared—all that seemed so inevitable right now. But still, she never would have guessed it could happen. Not until today, not until right now.

Until today, they were locked into their long-established roles—Gabe's girl. And Gabe's best friend.

"Matty, I'm—"

She reached up and touched his lips—to feel their heat and softness *and* to silence him. "Don't say you're sorry," she pleaded in a whisper.

His lips moved against her fingertips. "But I'm—"

"Don't," she insisted as she surged up again and pressed her mouth to his.

The rest was sure, swift, glorious perfection.

He hoisted her onto the tiny section of counter next to the sink. She spread her legs wide and unhooked his belt. Kissing him madly, she undid his fly and shoved his jeans down right along with his boxer briefs.

She held him and kissed him some more as the heat between them licked higher. Taking him into her hand, she stroked his hard, thick length as he groaned into her open mouth.

And when she took him inside her—well, it was tight. At first. But she went on kissing him, deeper and hotter, went on rocking against him, insistent and bold.

Until her body relaxed and let him in.

Then it got frantic. He moved within her, hard and deep. She cried his name as she came.

And she didn't stop there. She kept right on rocking against him, her ankles hooked at his waist, taking him deeper, until he lost all control. Throwing his head back, groaning her name, he went over the edge.

She sagged against the mirror, pulling him with her, kissing him slow and lazy, wrecked in the best kind of way. Sex with Ethan?

Yes, please! The man was amazing. She felt more satisfied, relaxed and fulfilled than she had in such a long, long time. By slow degrees, she returned to some semblance of reality.

"Ethan," she whispered. "Oh, Ethan. Oh, my, my..." Smiling softly up at him, she stroked the back of his neck and then threaded her fingers up into his thick hair as she realized that he hadn't smiled back.

Her own pleasure in the moment faltered. Something had gone wrong.

"Ethan?" She blinked up at him and began to understand that he didn't share her lovely feeling of sweetly shattered contentment.

Too carefully, he pulled away. He was still wearing his shirt, the sleeves shoved up to his elbows. His pants were in a wad down at his ankles. His was so pale, with two spots of vivid color on his cheekbones.

"Are you okay?" she whispered.

He stared down at her, but he wasn't really looking at her. He seemed stunned, frozen in place.

Still, she smiled up at him and waited for him to say something, to tell her what, exactly, was going through that brain of his.

But he said nothing. And that tormented look on his face? She just didn't get it. He seemed...guilty, somehow—like he'd committed some crime.

"Ethan, what's the matter?"

He still didn't speak. Gently, he took her hands and helped her down from the counter.

"Ethan?"

The moment she was on her feet, he let go of her to pull up his jeans and boxer briefs—and then, holding his pants in place with both hands, he backed into the hallway.

"I know what you're thinking," he whispered. "I understand."

"What? Ethan, I don't—"

"Listen. It never happened, okay?"

"But Ethan, it *did* happen and I'm not the least—"

"I am so damn sorry, Matty. So sorry. I really am."

"Sorry? There is absolutely no reason for you to feel—"

"I can't, okay?" He fastened the jeans. The muscles of his hard forearms worked as he buckled his belt.

"Ethan, you can't *what*?"

"I just, well, right now, I really have to go."

"But if you would only…"

"Please, Matty." He put up a hand. "Not now. I'll call you, I will." And then, without another word, he turned and left her there.

She was still standing in the bathroom doorway, stricken, bewildered, wearing nothing but a light coating of flour, as she heard the front door close behind him.

Chapter Seven

Ethan didn't come back—and he didn't call, either.

Over and over again that night, as Matty finished cleaning up the kitchen, put the rest of her purchases away and fixed herself a solitary dinner, she kept pausing, frowning—and then reaching for her phone. She wanted to call him so bad. The pain of his leaving like that was physical. She burned to make it right between them.

But he'd seemed so...disconnected when he walked out. She didn't have to be a therapist to get that he probably needed time to process what had happened between them.

And hey, so did she.

Because having sex with Ethan? Now, that was a whole other level of *new and different.*

Have I ever even imagined such a thing? she asked herself as she locked up and turned off the lights.

Yeah. A little. She nodded at her reflection in the bathroom mirror as she brushed her teeth.

How could she help but imagine having sex with Ethan? Especially lately, since she'd come home. Ethan was a fine-looking man, after all. And smart and funny and protective of the people he cared about. Ethan had it all going on. Any woman with a pulse would find him attractive.

She spit out the toothpaste and rinsed her mouth, remembering the years in LA, how he used to go out with so many women. None of them hung around all that long, but they all seemed really gone on him while it lasted. Sometimes she used to wonder what manly mojo he had that the ladies couldn't get enough of.

Sighing, she stared at her reflection in the mirror. Her cheeks were flushed and her eyes were dilated, heavy-lidded. After tonight, she no longer had to wonder what Ethan had that women couldn't get enough of.

I had sex with Ethan...

Just thinking about it made her breath get all tangled up in her throat. Never in her life had she thought tonight could happen.

After all, she'd always been Gabe's girl.

Back in the day, she couldn't even have imagined getting anything going with Ethan. He would never have betrayed Gabe that way. And neither would she.

When she had Gabe, her thoughts of other men were just passing fantasies, brief indulgences of her own sexual curiosity. Gabe was the owner of her heart and the center of her world.

No man could compare to her man. Gabe was almost as tall as Ethan, with dark hair and obsidian eyes. Gabe always looked at her like she was so special. She never doubted that she was the only one for him.

As he'd been the only one for her.

She used to feel so blessed, to have found her one and only in middle school. Too bad she'd lost him forever at the age of twenty-eight.

Life could be so cruel. She stared into her own eyes in the slightly cloudy bathroom mirror, acutely aware that it was her first night in her little bungalow—and her thoughts were all sad ones.

In bed, she cried a little. But then she put her hand to the soft swell of her belly and reminded herself that no matter how messed up things got, at least she was back in her own bed again. And she might have lost her husband, but she had her baby to think about now and that made her smile.

As for Ethan, he would be fine, she reassured herself. He just needed to get over the shock of having sex with his best friend's wife.

On Sunday, he didn't call. She reasoned that he still hadn't gotten over what had happened in the bathroom. She kept herself from contacting him because she knew that sometimes a woman just had to leave it alone and give a guy his space.

That morning, she puttered around her house. Then at noon, she met Heather for lunch at the Stagecoach Grill while Billy watched the kids at home.

During lunch, Heather made repeated references to Billy's supposed failings—how he didn't take her needs seriously and he never *listened* when she talked to him. How he wanted things *his* way because, as far as he was concerned, *his* way was the *only* way.

Twice Matty asked for specific examples of these complaints. Both times Heather waved a hand and muttered that Matty just didn't understand.

Matty was getting pretty tired of Heather's vague, bitter complaints. Worse, she hated watching her cousin suffer—especially while getting zero real information about what the problem actually was.

By halfway through her club sandwich, after Heather

had blown her off twice, Matty decided it was past time to push harder for an explanation.

"Heather, I'm so sorry that things aren't good between you and Billy. But it's been weeks now and you haven't really told me anything about what Billy actually did to drive a wedge between the two of you. I still have no idea what the problem is."

Heather leaned across their small table and spoke intently in a heated whisper. "I don't want to talk about my private life in a *restaurant*."

Matty whispered right back, "But you *are* talking about your private life. That's *all* you've talked about since we sat down. You've got nothing but bad things to say about your husband—and no explanation of what he's done to make you so furious at him."

Heather accused, "You refuse to understand."

"That's not true. I want to understand." Matty whispered back in a purposely soothing tone. "And okay, let's not talk about it here. Let's finish up and go to my house."

Heather scoffed. "I have a thousand things on my to-do list today. I can't just hang out at your place and cry on your shoulder."

By then, Matty wanted to grab her and shake her. "You're being unreasonable."

"Too bad. I just can't get into it with you right now."

If you can't get into it, why do you keep bringing it up? Matty thought but somehow kept herself from saying out loud. Instead, she gritted her teeth and asked very softly, "When, then?"

"Not today…"

"Listen, if you can't talk to me about it, maybe a family therapist could—"

"Stop!" Heather commanded in a hissing whisper. "I don't need some shrink to tell me how to live my life."

"But I just think if you—"

"I said, I don't want to talk about it anymore. Drop it, Mat. I mean it."

They finished their lunch in chilly silence, and Matty went home feeling awful about everything.

That evening, Matty had her parents over for a home-cooked dinner. It went well. Her mom was on her best behavior, complimenting Matty's herb-crusted roast chicken and impressed with how quickly Matty had pulled her little place together. Her dad was sweet as ever. He said he was proud of the way she'd thrown herself right into making a new life here in town.

"And we're grateful to have you home," her mom said and then quickly added, "Not that we ever *expected* you to move back home."

"We always wanted you to have the life you dreamed of." Her dad's voice was rough with emotion.

It was one of those moments, infinitely sweet. Matty looked at her mom and then her dad and thought herself the luckiest woman alive to be born to good people who only wanted the very best for her.

"I love you both," she said. "So much…"

By then, all three of them were looking pretty choked up.

Matty got up and gave them each hug. When they settled back down at the table, she considered confiding in them about the situation with Heather.

But what would she say? Heather had told her so little.

And it would probably just cause trouble if she shared what she did know with other members of the family. Especially considering that the family as a group prided themselves on their happy marriages—Simone and Neal, Matty and Gabe, Leonie and Darryl and all three of their happily married children. Including Heather and Billy.

Her mom was still talking about how great the bungalow looked. Then she added wistfully, "We miss having you at the house with us, though."

Her dad jumped right in with, "But we get it. A grown woman with a little one on the way needs her own home."

Matty's mom sighed. "Yes, I suppose so…"

Then her dad asked, "So how's Ethan doing? We haven't seen him a while."

"He was here all day yesterday helping me finish up in all the rooms. Then he took me shopping for hours."

Her mom quoted, "'In the sweetness of friendship let there be laughter. For in the dew of little things the heart finds its morning and is refreshed.'" Simone smiled her most beatific smile. "Khalil Gibran."

"That's beautiful," Matty said. "And Ethan really is the best. He's so helpful and kind." Too bad he'd freaked out and run out on her after they had wild sex on the bathroom counter…

"Are you feeling all right, sweetheart?" Her mom patted her arm. "Your cheeks are flushed."

"A bit tired, I guess." She pretended to hide a yawn. "I'll get to bed early tonight and be fresh and ready for work tomorrow…"

She did get to bed early, but she didn't sleep all that well. She wanted to call Ethan, to give him a very large piece of her mind for not even calling after he'd promised he would.

But she didn't call. Because now she was getting a little bit pissed off at him and she wanted to be calm when she finally tracked him down.

Tuesday came. And Wednesday and Thursday.

As for Ethan, he never called. He didn't stop by the bookstore. He didn't zip her a text explaining that he was fine and just needed more time before he reached out to her.

Friday and Saturday blew by. Sunday, too.

By Monday, she was done waiting. And she wasn't angry anymore.

In fact, she was kind of worried. She felt that she'd messed up. That she'd put off reaching out to him for much too long. Whatever was going on in his head at this point, they needed to talk it out and get things back on track between them.

That morning before she drove over to the bookstore, she brought him up on her phone and almost hit the call icon. But then she realized that she might lose her ever-loving mind if he refused to pick up. The thought of leaving a voicemail in a situation like this was just too completely nerve-racking—not to mention pitiful.

An hour later at work, she'd just finished ringing up a sale when her mom came up behind her and whispered in her ear, "Take an hour. Or two. As long as you need. Whatever's bothering you, take a break and find a way to work it out."

"Oh, Mom..." Matty turned and grabbed her mother in a hard, tight hug. "I love you."

"Love you too—now get out of here."

Matty went out the back door and started walking—straight to Stahl and Bravo, Attorneys at Law. She had no idea if Ethan would even be there right now. She knew he often had meetings other places and that some days he spent in court.

She took a chance anyway. If he wasn't available, well, at least she'd tried. And later, she could try again.

The woman at the desk near the door looked up and smiled at her as she entered. "Hello. How can I help you?"

Before she could answer, Ethan's law partner came at her, hand outstretched. "Matty Hunt, how are you?"

"Hi, Gavin. I'm well, thanks. I was, um, hoping I might catch Ethan, if he's here?"

"You're in luck. Follow me." He led her down a hallway with doors to either side and tapped on the one with Ethan's name on it.

"It's open!" Ethan called from inside.

Gavin pushed the door wide, stepped aside and gestured at Matty, who was right behind him. "Guess who stopped by."

Ethan looked up from his laptop. "Matty. Hey." It wasn't the most enthusiastic greeting she'd ever received.

She thought about that other time she'd shown up here without warning, two weeks ago after Sylvia ambushed her at the bookstore. She'd barged right in that day, too, like she had every right to track him down anytime, anywhere.

Yeah, he was being something of a jerk not to call her or somehow let her know that he was all right. But showing up without warning at his workplace...

She needed to stop doing that.

"You know what?" she said. "I can see that you're busy. I'm sorry to bust in like this. Just, um, give me a call when you get a chance, okay?"

With a quick "Thank you" for Gavin, she turned and headed back the way she'd come. She walked fast and made it all the way to the receptionist's desk before Ethan caught up with her.

"Matty. Hold on."

She drew a slow breath and turned to face him. "Sorry." Hiking her chin high, she pasted on a tight smile. "I shouldn't be interrupting you at work. Just call me, okay?" She turned to go.

He spoke from behind her. "You're not interrupting me."

Halting in mid-step, she stared at the door that led to the street, painfully aware that her face was flaming. And his receptionist had to be wondering what her problem was. "No, really," she said to the door. "It's okay."

"Please." He spoke quietly. Firmly. At least he didn't try to touch her. She couldn't bear that right now. "Come on back."

She swallowed. Hard. And then made herself turn around and look at him. "Are you sure?"

"Positive." His eyes were tender. She felt murderous at this moment, vulnerable. Her nerves were scraped raw. He gestured back toward his office. "Please…"

Had she ever in her life felt like more of a fool?

No way—but wait. Of course she had. That day she'd walked in on Ted plowing another woman in her bed.

"Fine," she grumbled miserably.

He reached out his hand. Against her better judgment, she took it.

When they turned into the short hallway, Gavin was nowhere in sight. Which was great. One less person to be embarrassed in front of.

Ethan led her into his office, where he shut the door and gestured at the seating area. She trudged over there and dropped into a chair. He sat on the arm of the sofa.

Silence. They stared at each other.

And now that she had a minute to really look at him, he

looked awful, all guilty and concerned, with dark shadows under his beautiful eyes. "I'm sorry, Matilda. I honestly am."

She believed him. And she did feel bad for him, for his obvious distress over...what, exactly? She wasn't sure.

So on second thought, maybe she didn't feel all that bad for him after all. "Sorry for what happened in the bathroom?" she asked sourly. "Or for the way you promised to call me when you left me standing there naked—and then didn't call? At all. Leaving me with nothing but crickets from you for more than a week..."

"Everything." His voice was bleak. "I'm sorry about all of it. I truly am."

"Well, I'm sorry, too—about the way you disappeared on me. But as for what happened in the bathroom? No. Uh-uh. Sorry, *not* sorry in the least. What happened in the bathroom was beautiful and real—or it was for me anyway." She waited for him to drive the knife deeper, to remind her so gently that they were good friends and nothing more.

"You mean that?" He almost looked hopeful all of a sudden.

She quelled the urge to grab him and hug him. He did not deserve a hug from her right now. "I have a lot of flaws, but lying isn't one of them. So yeah. I mean that."

"I just... Come on, Matty. You've always been Gabe's girl. I would never put a move on you. But I did. It's hard for me to deal with—that I did."

She shook her head and glanced away.

"Listen," he said gently. "I *know* he's been dead for three years. I know you've moved on, that you've lived with someone else, that you're pregnant and it's not Gabe's baby. I *know* you're not Gabe's girl anymore. But the habits of half a lifetime are sometimes damn hard to break."

"I understand. But it happened. We had sex, you and me. I wanted it. I *enjoyed* it. I hope you did, too."

His jaw was set, his expression bleak. She knew he was going to say something that would wreck her. "Oh, yeah." He sounded tortured and appalled. She braced for rejection. But then he added, "I enjoyed it, all right. I enjoyed it a whole hell of a lot. In fact, *enjoyed* is in no way a strong enough word for how damn good it was."

Relief poured through her, sweet as a long, cool drink of water on a blistering summer day.

Okay, he didn't sound happy that he'd liked making love with her. But at least he'd admitted that it was good for him, too. "Really?"

He looked right in her eyes again. "Really."

She was breathing easier as she reminded him, "We're both adults and we're both single. You did not betray your best friend. Can we please move on now?"

He studied her face. "You sure you're not pissed off at me for stepping over the line?"

"We just agreed that Gabe is gone. That line you're talking about does not exist anymore."

He almost smiled. "When you say it like that, it makes total sense."

"Because it's the truth. I hate that he died, but he did. We can't bring him back. All we can do is remember him with love and make the most of our lives as they are now."

"Yeah, but..." He hung his head.

"Ethan. What? Will you please just say whatever's going through that mind of yours?"

"Well, Matty. We didn't even use a condom. I wasn't

gentle. I grabbed you and jumped all over you. I feel like such a douchebag. I can't believe you're even talking to me right now."

"I was there, too," she said. "It was perfect—until the part where you ran off on me. As for the condom, you might have noticed that I'm already pregnant, so that's not an issue. And you'd better believe I got tested after what happened with Sleazeball Ted. You won't be catching any STIs from me."

"Same." He seemed more relaxed now. Finally. "Sylvia said the pill made her bloated, and the implant she tried gave her cramps. We always used condoms."

Matty observed, "So here we are, saying what we should have said before I jumped you in the bathroom."

"True." He stuck his hands in his pockets. "And the jumping? It was mutual." He slanted her a look full of heat and desire. "It was good, Matilda. Really, really good."

"Well." Her chest felt tight in a lovely sort of way. She drew a slow, deep breath. "Okay, then." She definitely felt better about everything now. "Allow me to summarize."

His eyes were heavy lidded. "Please do."

"You need to call when you say you will. Sex in the bathroom was terrific. For both of us. As it turns out, it's okay that we didn't use a condom. And given that Gabe is no longer in the land of the living, there is no way you betrayed your best friend."

The corner of his fine mouth twitched in the beginnings of a real smile. "Agreed. On all counts."

"Whew." She made a show of wiping her brow. "Finally."

He stood and held down his hand. She put hers in it, and he pulled her to her feet. "I missed you," he said, soft and low and oh, so sincerely. "So much…"

That did it. She threw her arms around him and buried her face in his crisp white shirtfront. "And I missed *you*. Desperately." Tipping her head back, she instructed, "Do not disappear on me again."

"I won't."

"Promise?"

"I promise, Matilda."

"Good. Because it really hurt me that you did that."

He ran the back of his finger over the curve of her cheekbone. The simple touch felt like heaven. "I am so sorry," he said. "I won't do that again."

She whispered, "Apology accepted."

He said, "Come to my place this evening. I'll cook."

"Yes," she replied. "I'll be there."

"Feeling better?" her mom asked when she breezed into the bookstore a few minutes later.

"Very much so, thank you."

"The Ingram order came in while you were out."

"Yay!"

"You want to handle the displays?"

"Oh, yes, I do."

She spent the rest of the day ringing up sales, arranging the book displays, packing up orders, breaking down boxes—with Xo Cat assisting by climbing in and out of the waiting boxes and rolling to her back, batting at Matty's hand until she paused in her work to deliver a belly scratch—and then zipping off across the back-room floor completely without warning. Edmund mostly took on a more supervisory position. He climbed to high shelves and watched the goings-on from above. Later, he got the zoomies, startling random customers when he leapt out at them from under display tables.

Matty left work that day smiling. She went home, showered, dressed in nice jeans and a snug sweater and spent way more time than necessary perfecting her winged eyeliner. Because she felt good about everything this evening and looking her best made her feel even better.

Also, those moments between her and Ethan in the bathroom nine days before were never far from her thoughts. Naked, with Ethan, she'd felt sexy, excited, happy, safe, respected and cared for.

She wanted more of that.

She hoped that he did, too.

When Ethan answered the door, he found Matty looking like a million bucks and holding out a bottle of Pinot Noir.

"I brought this with me from LA to give to you. As you're well aware, it'll be a while before I'm drinking wine again." She took his hand and put the bottle in it. "Enjoy."

He admired the label. "It's a good one—and you really should save it for some time after the baby's born."

She waved a hand. "No. It's for you. And something smells wonderful—not to mention familiar."

He ushered her in. "Truffled risotto with mushrooms and parmesan."

"Yum. That brings back good memories." It was a dish he'd cooked often when they lived in Los Feliz.

In the kitchen, he opened the wine and poured himself a glass. She accepted a flute of sparkling cider, and he served the meal. Now that they'd cleared the air about what had happened in her bathroom, the conversation flowed easily between them. They caught up with each other again after the time apart.

Damn. It was so good to be with her. The days and nights when he couldn't bring himself to face her had been pretty bad. He'd spent extra hours at the office just to avoid coming home to his empty house.

But thanks to her, they'd worked it out. And the world was once again a great place to be.

She was all excited about having her own house now. "It's just what I was aching for, you know? My folks are the best, but I need my own space."

Things were going well at the bookstore, she said. And she still didn't know what was happening between Heather and Billy. "Billy says to talk to Heather. And Heather always has a reason why she just can't talk about it now."

"Eventually she'll open up."

"But how long is it going to be until *eventually*? They've been on the outs with each other since before I moved home. And it only seems to be getting worse. I don't understand it."

"And I don't know what to tell you."

"What *can* you tell me? It's my cousin who needs to start talking…"

By the time they'd cleared the table and moved into the living area, he was inching up on the important conversation he kept meaning to have with her. They sat on the sofa together.

She leaned her head on his shoulder. "Ethan, I…" She sounded so serious—and also unsure of how to continue.

He had his arm around her already, and her strange tone had him holding her closer. "What's the matter? You can tell me."

She glanced up at him. "I hope so..."

Was it something bad? "Matty, what? Tell me. Is it the baby...?"

She drew a sharp breath. "The baby? What do you mean?"

"I mean is the baby...all right?"

Her eyes softened. "Ethan, don't worry." She patted the barely perceptible new roundness at her waist. "The baby is just fine."

"Then what?"

"It's about the sex." She said it in a tiny, embarrassed little voice. And now she had her head tipped down like she was too shy to look at him.

Matilda, too shy...?

That was just wrong. Matilda was never shy. She always said what she meant, just put it right out there.

With a light touch beneath her chin, he tipped her face up and teased, "*The* sex? Isn't sex just...sex?"

She let out a frustrated little growl. "As a matter of fact, yes, sometimes sex is just sex. But I'm speaking specifically of you and me. And *the* sex we had in my bathroom..." She seemed so determined and serious.

He nodded. "Ah. *That* sex."

"Exactly. That was not *just* sex." Her cheeks had flushed pink. It was kind of adorable. She grumbled, "You did say it was good for you, too."

It had been very good for him, too. Spectacularly so. Though he fully intended never to go there again, he was nonetheless having a little bit of trouble putting that evening behind him. "I did, yeah. I said it was good, and I meant what I said."

"Ethan, I..." She threw up both hands and plopped them back down in her lap again. "Gah. This is all just so awkward. I don't even know how to start." She shifted so that she was facing him. "It's like this…"

Okay, now she was looking way too intense. "Matty, what is it?"

Before he could finish, she grabbed him by the shoulders, yanked him close and kissed him—hard.

Resist! he thought frantically. He should resist and he knew that.

But he couldn't. Because her mouth tasted so damn good and she smelled like heaven.

All his best intentions?

They vanished, melted like snow in the warmth of spring sunlight. He kissed her right back.

Her mouth softened beneath his, and she sighed. The kiss went on and on, and that was just fine with him. That was pretty much perfect.

Yeah, he'd promised himself he would not make another move on her.

But right now, with his lips on hers and his arms wrapped around her, he had no intention of stopping—he didn't think he could even if he tried.

He licked her bottom lip. She moaned and opened for him.

He gathered her even closer.

See, this was the problem. Though he'd promised himself not to go there again, well, how was he supposed to keep that promise when she grabbed him and kissed him?

After all, he reasoned, she *had* made the first move. It seemed fair to assume that she was kissing him on purpose. Plus, how could he possibly resist her when she felt absolutely perfect in his arms?

For a sweet span of minutes, he relearned all the delicious secrets beyond her parted lips.

When she pulled back, she said breathlessly, "That. I want more of that."

His brain had gone on a brief vacation. He struggled to understand. "Uh, kissing? You want more kissing?"

"Most definitely. Kissing and touching and, well, everything. All of it. What I'm getting at, Ethan, is that I've been thinking..."

Was she thinking what he thought she was thinking?

He hoped so. Because what had happened in her bathroom was more than a *little* problem if he was going to finally get honest with himself.

It was a major problem.

Trying *not* to think about how much he wanted to do it again was driving him a little bit out of his mind.

Was she saying that she wanted more, too?

He gulped. "You said you've been thinking. Thinking what?"

"Well, the way things are looking right now, I'm not all that likely to have sex with another person until at least a couple of years after the baby's born. There's just too much going on to find some stranger and come to an arrangement with the guy."

What the hell? "An arrangement?"

She wrinkled her pretty nose at him. "Ethan, keep up. For sex. I mean, it's not like I want a relationship. I've had true love and it was wonderful, and frankly, it almost killed me when Gabe died. I can't go there again. I don't want love. I'm not up for that. But I do want a sex life. And how do I go about getting one? That's the question.

"I have no interest in giving Tinder another try—or

Bumble or AdultFriendFinder or any of those other hookup sites. And I certainly don't want to actually date anybody. I can't be going on *dates*, you know? I also can't be hooking up with strangers on the street—I mean, where would I even find a suitable stranger? I grew up in this town. If I haven't met a guy already, somebody I know has.

"I don't even think I'm mentally equipped to pick up a complete stranger. Ted was, essentially, a stranger. We both know how that turned out." She pressed her hand to her belly again. "Ethan, I'm starting to show. In about twenty-three weeks, my life will be all about taking care of my baby and running the bookstore. By then, I won't have time for a sex life. As for you, right now you're single..." She paused and then frowned. "I mean it *is* over with Sylvia, and there's no one else, right?"

He made an absurd strangled sound as he gave her another nod. "Right." And then he shook his head. "No one."

"See? It's perfect. You're single. I'm single." Matty kept pitching, and by now, he was pretty much positive where the pitch was going to land. "Ethan, I'm just a mess of hormones. And you said yourself you liked having sex with me. Plus, I trust you. I truly do. You're my closest friend— you really are. So I was wondering if you might consider the idea of you and me and a lot of sex?"

"Ah," he said very quietly. Because even though he'd known that was coming, to hear her say it right out loud somehow shocked him to the core.

And she wasn't done. "I'm thinking it would be you and me in an exclusive hookup situation until I'm too big to do that anymore—or until you meet somebody or until one of us is just ready to move on. It would be a strictly private arrangement, just between us. We can both go into it knowing it's only for now, knowing that it's not meant to last. It just would be two people enjoying each other for as long as it works for both of us."

She paused for a slow breath. "So. That's it. That's my, er, proposal. Now I want you to think about it—and let me know. And Ethan, please, whatever decide, you have to stop avoiding me. Because you are my best friend and I love you."

Before he could muster up a reply, she pressed two soft fingers to his lips. "Shh. Think about it. And let me know."

Chapter Eight

As if he could think about anything else.

That night was another sleepless one as he stewed over what he should do. All the next day was a struggle, to keep his mind on his work and the needs of his clients when all he could think about was the taste of Matty's mouth and the sounds she'd made when he was inside her—and how easily taking her up on her offer could result in disaster.

When he left the courthouse in Buffalo at a little after five that evening, he still had no idea what he would do. And he had no business knocking on her door until he'd decided what to say to her. His plan was to go straight home and stay there.

But he didn't go home. At five thirty, he was pulling to a stop in front of her bungalow. As he rushed up the walk, she came out the front door in jeans and a sweater, with thick pink socks on her feet.

He walked even faster, taking the porch steps two at a time.

The look on her face—so happy, so hopeful.

She let out a soft cry as he reached for her. His hands at her waist, he scooped her right off her feet. She wrapped her arms around his neck and kissed him as he carried her inside. Holding onto her with one arm, his mouth locked with hers, he shoved the door shut behind them.

That kiss.

It was perfect—just like every kiss he'd shared with her so far. He spun her around right there by the door, kissing her like a starving man, just eating her up.

When he finally stopped mauling her sweet mouth and let her feet touch the floor again, she stared up at him with dazed eyes and a glowing smile. "So, then." She was breathless. "That's a yes?"

All the things that could—and probably would—go wrong spun in a loop through his brain. "It could blow up our friendship."

"No." She shook her head adamantly. "We're solid. We'll be fine."

"One of us could want out and the other not be ready yet."

"Ethan." She reached up, clasped his shoulder. "We will work it out. You'll see. We will talk it over, communicate. Be honest with each other."

He bent for a quick kiss—and then couldn't pull away. They stood there by the door, their arms wrapped tight around each other, kissing endlessly, pulling back for a moment just to look in each other's eyes—and then crashing back together, kissing some more.

Finally, with a low, throaty laugh, she clasped his shoulders and held him away. "So you're still not decided, huh?" Her cheeks were flushed, her eyes sapphire bright.

Not decided? Please. There really was only one answer he could possibly give her. "Yes, I have decided. Please let me be your pre-baby fling."

She threw back her head with a wild, joyful laugh. And

then she just looked at him, her breathing kind of shaky. "It will be fine," she whispered. "It will be wonderful."

"I have no doubt."

She took hold of his coat. He let her slide it off his shoulders and hang it in the tiny closet by the door.

When she turned to him again, he said, "Before we get carried away…"

"What? You look so serious." She caught her lower lip between her teeth. "Is something wrong? Ethan, just tell me."

"Nothing's wrong. But there is something else I keep wanting to settle."

"Tell me. We'll deal with it." She stared up at him, her breathing hectic, her eyes gleaming so bright.

"I still want to be your birth coach. Will you let me? And what about that ultrasound? Let me come to that."

She tipped her head to the side, studying him. "Is it that important to you?"

"You're damn right it is—and we did agree to talk some more about it…"

"Yeah, we did. I remember."

"I keep trying to choose the right time to get into it. This is probably not it. But well, it's a happy moment and maybe that will work in my favor. Is that shameless of me—to use this hot thing going on between us to make sure I get to be there for you when the baby comes? You bet. Matty, I want to be there. I want to help out."

"Are you sure, Ethan?"

"Absolutely. Whatever happens with this pre-baby fling we've just agreed to, I will still be your friend, Matilda. Always, no matter what."

Her eyes glistened. One tear escaped and trickled down

her cheek. She sniffled and swiped it away. "I was going to ask Heather..."

"Oh, hell no. She's got four kids, and she and Billy are having problems. Give the poor woman a break. She can throw you your baby shower so she won't feel left out."

"If you do this, there will be prenatal and childbirth classes up at the hospital in Sheridan," she warned. He knew she intended to sound stern, and he found it completely adorable that her voice wobbled as she tried to be tough. "The good news is the classes I'm thinking of will be pretty basic and there will only be a few. Those will happen in June, and you will be expected to go with me."

"And I *will* go with you. I promise you."

"What if you have a court date you can't miss?"

"Gavin and I will work it out. He's having a baby, too, you know. I'll be there for him. He'll be there for me."

"Oh, Ethan..."

He was grinning now. "I know that look on your face. That look means yes."

"Thank you—and yes, I would love for you to be my birth coach."

He grabbed her close, spun her around and then claimed another slow, scorching-hot kiss. That time, when they paused for a breath, he scooped her up against his chest, carried her to her bedroom and set her on her feet beside the bed.

Clothes went flying. In the blink of an eye, they were both naked. He took her down to the bed. When she tried to wrap those fine thighs around him, he resisted.

But only to make it last longer.

Lifting up on an elbow, he pressed her down onto her back and ran his eager hand along the center of her, between those soft breasts and lower, pausing at the new roundness of her belly.

She gazed up at him, eyes dreamy now, mouth impossibly soft. "Taking it slow, are we?"

"I'm damn well going to try. All bets are off as to how well I'll succeed, though." He bent close to nip at her plump lower lip. "Already I'm growing very impatient..."

He let his hand glide upward again over the velvety terrain of her sweet body. Capturing one breast, he flicked the rosy-brown nipple and bent close to suck on it. She moaned his name.

Matty, he thought. *Matty here. Now. Naked in my arms...*

No moment had ever been quite this perfect. He wanted it to stretch right on out into forever.

It couldn't. It wouldn't. She'd made that very clear.

And so be it. He had right now with her, and he intended to make the most of every touch, every sweet, perfect kiss.

He stroked his hand down her body again. "Open..."

She took his meaning, spreading her legs for him, revealing herself beneath the neatly trimmed dark-gold patch of curls. He scattered kisses as he moved down her body—on the side slope of her other breast, the crest of her hip bone. In that place below her navel where her baby was growing.

When he eased between her open thighs, she lifted them over his shoulders.

She tasted of heaven. He kissed her endlessly, stroking her with his fingers as she tossed her head on the pillow. He could have stayed right there, kissing her, licking her, eating her right up, for hours.

But she was eager and ready, and it didn't take her long at all. She cried out as she came.

And then she was reaching down, urging him upward,

guiding him to straddle her. "Over," she commanded and rolled.

He went with her, and suddenly, he was on his back and she was bending over him, taking him in her hand, stroking him slowly. When she licked his hard length, he came way too close to losing it.

She laughed at his long, drawn-out groan.

"That's right," he mock-grumbled. "Torture me."

"You got it." She licked the tip—and then she opened her mouth and surrounded him with soft heat and slick wetness.

He gripped the bright bedcover in either fist as he groaned out her name.

Impossible. Him and Matty. Never would he have believed this could happen. He'd accepted for years that it never would.

But now here they were, naked together.

Life could be so astonishing. Sometimes the impossible actually did come true.

He whisper-groaned, "You have to stop that. I'll lose it completely."

She paused and released him just long enough to give him a saucy wink. "That's kind of the point." And she took him into her mouth again.

"Not this time," he managed on a drawn-out moan. And then he reached down and clasped her waist. "Get up here. I mean it, Matilda. Don't screw with me." She laughed around his aching erection, and he knew he would go over the edge. Yet somehow, barely, he held it together.

She gave him one last, long lick that had him gritting his teeth to keep from losing it all over her. By then he had her under the arms and was pulling her up so they were face-to-face.

"Ethan." She bent close and licked at his lower lip. "You are so hot."

He managed a grin, but it took serious effort. "Right…"

She wasn't finished. "I mean, I always knew that objectively. You're very good looking and also easy to be around. And women love you—not just me. But pretty much all women. They're drawn to you. You're hot *and* approachable. But it's a whole other experience to be up close and personal in this way with you. Honestly, it's amazing." Now she was whispering, like she had some secret that she needed to keep under wraps. "I don't know if I'll ever get enough."

He caught her gorgeous face between his hands. "You are messing with me."

"Uh-uh. No way. Honest truth, I could become an Ethan Bravo junkie. I could end up just following you around, begging you for one more time…"

"Do not make me laugh. It will ruin the mood."

"Oh, no. Impossible. This mood is unkillable."

"Yeah?"

"Yeah…"

"Well, okay, then." He kissed her. She kissed him back, forgetting to razz him, getting lost just as he was in the heat that kept building between them. He groaned at the taste of her. And then she reached down between their bodies. "That's it," he whispered against her parted lips as she guided him where they both needed him to be.

It was still a tight fit, but this time she was primed for him. She moaned into his mouth as she sank down onto him. "Ethan. Oh, yes…"

He held her hips and rocked up into her. She caught the rhythm, and they were rolling together on a sweet, hot sea of pure pleasure. It went on and on. He wished it might never end.

But apparently she had other plans. She whispered on a ragged breath, "I'm...so close..."

He kissed her more urgently. He rocked up into her harder, deeper.

He wrapped his hands around the twin globes of her bottom and started helping her along, bucking up into her as he pulled her down tight.

It worked. "Ethan! Oh, Ethan..."

"Yeah." He kissed the word onto her open mouth. "Now, Matty. Come now..."

And she did, letting out a deep, eager moan as her climax rolled through her and her body pulsed around him. When she hit the crest, he pulled her down tightly against him.

And then he was losing it, too. His own finish barreled through him, a fireball of heat and need rolling out along his limbs. The world expanded, whirled away and then flowed back into him again as he pulsed deep inside her.

A few minutes later, as his breathing evened out, he bit her earlobe. "Matty..." It came out in a low, needful rumble.

She tucked her head under his chin. "Mm..."

His breath stirred her tangled hair. "I think you might have killed me."

She kissed the bulge of his shoulder. "I try."

"I think I want to be you," Heather muttered sulkily.

It was two weeks since Matty and Ethan had made their friends-with-benefits agreement. Since then, they'd spent every night together, either at her house or his. He planned to be with her at her second ultrasound next week. Matty was loving the way things were working out.

But as for this lunch date at Arlington's Steakhouse with her cousin?

Not quite so much. Matty still didn't know the real story behind Heather's ongoing unhappiness. Today, Claire and Elissa were at a playdate. Heather didn't have to pick them up until two. It was now twelve thirty.

Heather fiddled with her chef's salad, spearing up a slice of cucumber and nibbling the edge of it. "You're literally glowing, you know that? It's a little bit disgusting. Mostly because I'm jealous of you, Mat—so happily pregnant, with Aunt Simone and Uncle Neal doting on you and Ethan at your side. Before you know it, you'll be a mom with a little one in your arms." She stared off into space, her expression bleak. "Enjoy every moment. I'm telling you—they grow up way too fast."

By then, Matty was seriously considering pretending that her mom had texted her to get back to the bookstore ASAP.

Heather sighed. "I mean, you are something else, Mat. The way you're working it…pure genius. You always were the smart one. For years, you lived your dream, galivanting all over the world, writing about fabulous places. I know, it was unbearable, when you lost Gabe. And then there was that creep, Ted. But here you are, coming back from all that awfulness. Now you get to have a baby who is all your own. And not only that, but you also have Ethan Bravo at your service, your bestie and your booty call…"

Why, Matty wondered, had she told Heather that she and Ethan were having a fling? It had just slipped out last week when Heather had dropped by the bookstore.

Her cousin had noticed right away that something was different about Matty. "Look at you," Heather had whispered. "You look *good.* Your skin. Your hair. Everything about you is just…more. Ultra. You look so happy. Something's going on." She'd grabbed Matty by the arm and dragged her into the back room. "Tell me. You know you want to."

And Matty had told her. Big mistake. Because lately, with Heather, all personal information was at risk of being weaponized.

"Frankly," Matty said coolly, "that was nothing short of passive-aggressive, what you just said." And this lunch date? It was going downhill fast. "What is going on with you?"

Heather ate a wedge of hard-boiled egg and ignored Matty's question. "Yep. I mean, Ethan's hot *and* he's your dearest friend. He's all excited to be your birth coach. And when you don't want him around, all you have to do is go home alone to your own house and shut the door."

At that point, Matty was just weary enough of Heather's attitude to add fuel to her bitter fire. "I don't want to go to my house alone," Matty said with her sweetest smile. "And I don't. Ethan and I like to spend our nights together."

"Oh, good Lord in heaven." Heather knocked back a big gulp of iced tea. "I really thought you were playing it smart."

Matty speared a cherry tomato and took her time eating it before replying, "Fine. I'll bite. You thought I *was* playing it smart? Meaning you were wrong and I'm not so smart, after all?"

"Well, yeah. Because now I'm starting to worry that before you know it, he'll be asking you to marry him—and you'll be saying yes."

Matty buttered a dinner roll. "That's not going to happen. True, Ethan and I are close. We are friends and we are lovers. But we're not getting married. It's not like that."

Heather mic-dropped her fork onto her plate, sat back and folded her arms across her chest. "Oh, honey. Just you wait. He will ask, and eventually you will give in and say yes."

"Wrong. Ethan's never been married. He's not a marrying kind of man."

"What does that even mean? People say stuff like that, but it's crap. Every man's a marrying man once the right woman comes along."

"What are you talking about?"

"As if you don't know. Word around town was that he was going to marry that accountant. But then *you* came home. And here we are, the accountant totally out of the picture, and you and Ethan spending every night in bed together. Here we are with him taking you to your ultrasound appointment, signing up to be your birth coach. No guy does stuff like that unless he's put a ring on it—or is planning to do so."

Now Matty was really getting pissed off. "Heather, I love you with the power of a thousand suns, but that's just not true."

Heather smirked. "Want to bet on it?"

"Please. You sound like a child. Of course I don't want to bet on whether or not Ethan going to ask me to marry him. He's not ever doing any such thing. That's just not who we are together."

"Take the bet, then. A hundred bucks says he proposes before the baby's born."

Matty groaned. "Honestly, where do you come up with this stuff?"

"I have eyes and ears, Mat. It's not rocket science. He

dumped the accountant because he wants to be with you, and eventually he'll be dropping to one knee and presenting you with a big-ass diamond ring."

"Wrong."

"Bet me."

"I will do no such thing."

Heather laughed. "Because you know I'm right."

"No. Uh-uh. *You* don't know what you're talking about. For your information, he did not dump Sylvia. She dumped *him.*"

Heather ate a strip of julienned turkey. "But *why* did she dump him? Oh, wait! Let me guess. Because he was spending every spare moment with *you.*"

"I have no idea why I keep arguing with you about this. There's no getting through to you once you've made up your mind."

Heather leaned in, eager and grinning gleefully. "Because you know I'm right."

"I don't know any such thing." Matty made a real effort to look on the bright side. "At least you're smiling and cackling away for a change. It's nice to see you in a better mood."

Heather tipped her nose toward the ceiling. "I am not, nor have I ever been, a cackler." She cackled some more.

Matty gazed at her cousin across the table and thought how much she loved her. They could drive each other up the wall, but they were sisters at the core. Always had been. "It's good to see you cackling." Her voice was softer now.

Heather put on her frostiest expression. "Do not push me." But then she sighed. Her eyes were so sad all of a sudden. "You really annoy me, Mat. And I am so glad you're home."

"Me, too." And then Matty asked, very quietly, for what

seemed like the hundredth time, "Really, Heather. What's gone wrong between you and Billy?"

Heather looked away and shook her head.

The glass doors slid wide. Ethan and Matty walked out into the hospital parking lot without saying a word. They were quiet when they got into his crew cab, settling into their seats with barely a sound.

He sat back and stared out the windshield at the front of the hospital, at the blue sky above it and the few white wisps of cloud floating around up there.

"Ethan."

He turned to her. "Yeah?"

"Thanks for coming with me."

He chuckled. "Thanks for letting me. Took me a while to convince you."

"Yeah, well. I hesitated to take advantage of you."

"But you get now that you really should take advantage of me at every opportunity. Because that's what I'm here for."

"Thank you. I mean that."

He nodded. "You have the memory stick?" She held it up. "Excellent," he said.

"I can't wait to look at the pictures all over again." Her mouth was softly parted, her eyes so bright. Damn, she was beautiful. "A girl," she whispered, more to herself than to him. Then she smiled right at him. "I thought I wasn't going to want to know. But then I did. Not because I care either way. Just... It all feels more real now." She sighed. "Oh, Ethan. Those perfect hands. Those adorable little feet. It was so much different than the first ultrasound. In that, all I saw was a tiny, pulsing spot in a dark tunnel. Now she really does look like a baby."

"That's what babies do—grow."

She reached for his hand. He wove his fingers with hers. "I am so happy." She whispered the words, like a secret between them.

"It's a good day."

"The best." She gazed out the windshield. A slight frown creased the smooth skin between her eyebrows.

He asked gently, "What is it?"

"I was just thinking of my cousin, remembering back nine years ago, when Heather had Will. Gabe and I flew home a week or so after the birth. I went straight to Heather's house. She was sitting on the sofa, nursing Will, big piles of laundry on either side of her. They were renting that little house out on Tucker Road then. No dishwasher. The sink was overflowing with dirty dishes. And Heather was just sitting on the sofa, blissed out, nursing her new baby boy. She was so happy then. She's always been happy— with Billy, with her kids, with everything about her life. But now…"

Ethan squeezed her hand. "So things are still rocky between her and Billy?"

Matty turned those big blue eyes on him. "She's miserable. She's angry at Billy all the time. She won't say why, though. She won't tell me what's wrong. She never explains what he did that has her so upset. She won't get near why she's so fed up with him. She just keeps telling me that it's all Billy's fault."

"And Billy…?"

"Mostly Billy just seems sad. Defeated, you know? He would never look at another woman. That guy worships the ground my cousin walks on. He would do anything for her. But right now, they are not on the same page about something. I can't tell if he has no clue how to make things right between them or if he's done something she can't forgive him for or…" She blew out a hard breath. "I don't know, Ethan. I just don't know."

"So, do you think he even knows what's going on with her?"

"I'm not sure about any of this, but my guess would be yes, he knows what she's not happy about."

"So then, whatever it is, he's not willing to try to fix it?"

"Ethan, maybe he doesn't even know how to fix it— hey, I'm just shooting in the dark here. She won't talk. *He* won't talk. But it's really starting to feel to me like they're headed for…" She hesitated.

"Say it."

"Fine. I'm thinking a separation, at least."

That shocked him. "Heather and Billy Dolan? No. Never going to happen."

"Yeah, well. I used to think that, too. But lately…" She wrapped her other hand around their joined ones. "Ethan, I want to *do* something. To help them somehow, shake things up enough that maybe they'll start talking to each other again."

"You really think you can get them talking if they can't—or won't—do it for themselves?"

"Maybe not. But I really would like to try."

"How?"

She narrowed her eyes at him. "You have to promise not to judge."

"Judge what?"

"I'm just saying that I have no idea if my plan will do any good at all."

"Matilda. The plan. Tell me."

"Well, I was thinking I would invite them over to my place for dinner, sort of a housewarming party, a way to thank them for helping me move. It would be you, me, Heather and Billy. I'll ask my mom to watch the kids. Maybe if it's just the four of us, we can get them talking, get them to start opening up about what's going on with them."

All he could think of to say to that idea was "Whoa."

She wrinkled her nose at him. "Didn't I just ask you not to judge?"

"I'm not judging."

"Ethan, have you seen your face? Judgy. Just tell me what you're thinking."

"All right. To me, it sounds like an ambush."

She cast a glance up at the headliner, as though seeking advice from above. "Frankly, Ethan, right at this moment I can't think of anything else to try."

"I have a question."

She sent him a grumpy look. "Of course you do."

"Did you tell your cousin that you and I are now more than friends?"

Her soft cheeks flushed hot pink. "Um. Yeah. And I know we agreed not to tell people, but Heather and I have been telling each other our secrets since we were old enough to talk. I don't know how to keep a secret from her."

"I knew it." And did he really care that she'd told Heather? No. "It's okay. I just want us to be on the same page about this stuff."

"I understand." She reached across the console and gave his forearm a squeeze. "Honestly, the more I think about it, the more I just don't care who knows that you and I are having a thing. Tell whoever you want to tell—or don't tell anyone. It's up to you."

Warmth spread through him that they didn't have be a secret anymore. "Agreed."

"Now," she said, "back to my suggestion. It's not an ambush. We're just going to provide a nonthreatening space where Heather and Billy might be willing to confide in us."

He still didn't like it. "I'm not judging, I'm just thinking of all the ways a plan like that can go horribly wrong—and what about your dad?"

"Huh? What about him?"

"Matty, I thought he was right there with you, getting stuff done every day of that week you moved."

"Not *every* day—but yes, he was terrific. And what does my dad have to do with my plan?"

"Well, given all the work he did, Neal should definitely be invited to your thank-you housewarming dinner, wouldn't you say?"

"Ethan."

"Well, shouldn't he?"

Now she stared resolutely out the windshield even though nothing was going on out there. "No, my father should not be invited."

"Why not?"

"You know why not. Because the dinner is just a pretense, an opportunity to invite my cousin and her husband to open up in a safe environment."

"A *pretense*. See, there's your problem. The least you can do is be honest with Heather when you invite her, don't you think?"

"Now you're just being sarcastic."

"Think about it. Your cousin hasn't told you what's going on between her and Billy, though you've tried several times to get her to talk about it and you're supposedly the one she shares her secrets with. Billy hasn't told you, either. Shouldn't that be a clue that they won't welcome you trying to *open them up*?"

She put up both hands and patted the air between them. "Okay, okay. My plan is not perfect. But Ethan, I have to do *something*."

Do you really? he thought. But what he said was "I get that. But…maybe not this?"

"Then *what*?"

Too bad he had nothing.

And she read him like a large-print book. "You've got nothing," she said. "So please don't try to stop me from doing whatever I can to help them."

"But what if it blows up in our faces?"

"I'm willing to take that chance. The worst that can happen is Heather gets pissed at me for butting in where I have no business going."

"There. Did you hear yourself? You just said you would be butting in where you have no business going."

"But it will be okay. Heather will get over that. Eventually."

"Just listen to yourself. You know she won't like this yet you're doing it anyway."

"I really do think it's time to shake things up a little with her and Billy."

"I don't know…"

"Well, I do."

"Matty, if you could just be honest with Heather when you invite her? Tell her upfront that you're only inviting her and Billy and me. And if you're going to start pushing them to get honest about their problems, you'd better warn her ahead of time."

"If I do that, she won't come."

"Exactly. You're planning an ambush, and that's a bad idea."

At least she took a moment to consider his argument. Finally she challenged, "I'm serious, Ethan. I'm not willing to sit on my hands and do nothing at all. Those two love each other. They always have. It breaks my heart to watch them falling apart."

"I get that. Just don't ambush them. Please."

"If you have another approach, you'd better share it with me now."

He didn't, not really. But he knew he had to come up with something or Operation Ambush would be put into motion.

"Well?" she demanded.

"I'm thinking, I'm thinking…"

She looked out the side window, studied her fingernails and huffed out more than one impatient breath. "Come on, Ethan. At this rate, they'll be divorced before we get out of this parking lot."

"All right. How about this? Just tone it down a little."

"In what way?"

"Invite your cousin to dinner, tell her it's a thank-you dinner for how much Billy helped with your move. Say it will be a quiet evening, just the four of us, a friendly, relaxing night out with people she can trust. And then deliver on your promise. Keep things easy and lowkey and don't push too much."

"And that's going to help *how?*"

"It's an opportunity for them to have a nice night out together. Maybe they'll start talking about what's not working between them. Or maybe they won't. Either way, that's up to them."

Matty frowned out the window some more. He waited for her to shoot his idea down. But she surprised him. "Okay, fine. You might have something there."

"Hallelujah."

She bopped him on the shoulder. "Look. I see what you're saying, and you do have a point. An intervention is probably not the way to go. I don't want to traumatize them. It should be baby steps. I'll say it will be just the four of us having a nice evening together—and that's what it will be. No big deal. How about that?"

"You're serious?"

"Of course I'm serious."

"You're going to offer a nice evening, and you're not going to try to save their marriage over dinner or anything?"

"Ethan. I promise. Baby steps. Because you made a good point and I agree with you. If the four of us can have a nice evening together, well, that's a step in the right direction for them, isn't it?"

He had no idea about that. But at least she'd given up her plan to pull a Dr. Phil on her unsuspecting cousin.

"I don't know if that's such a good idea," said Heather when Matty dropped in at her house an hour later to invite her and Billy to dinner on Friday night. "I mean, it's sweet of you to think of us. But you know how it is with us lately…"

Downstairs, one of the twins let out a happy laugh as the other little girl started singing "The Wheels on the Bus." A moment later, they were both singing.

Heather groaned. "They love that song. Do you know

how many verses there are? A lot. And I swear to you on my mother's vintage Spode Christmas dishes that my daughters know them all…"

Matty listened through a couple of verses. "They're so cute."

"Oh, yeah. But trust me. It doesn't take all that many times through before you start to hate 'The Wheels on the Bus.'"

Matty brought the subject back around to dinner at her house. "So. What do you say? Come on. It will be fun. Just the four of us. I'll make lasagna, and everybody can have Chianti but me."

Heather still looked doubtful. "I would have to find a sitter."

"Handled. Mom says she can do it."

"You already asked Aunt Simone?"

"I did. She said yes without missing a beat. You know how much she loves her great-nieces-and-nephews."

Heather was silent.

Downstairs, the girls were still singing. "Mommies on the bus say don't do that, don't do that, don't do that…"

"Just say yes," Matty coaxed.

Heather glanced out the big windows that overlooked the deck. "All right."

"Yay!"

"Don't get excited. I mean, I'll ask Billy. But the way things are going with us lately, he'll probably come up with some made-up reason he can't be there."

Matty brushed a hand down her cousin's arm in a reassuring caress. "Are you okay?"

"Meh. I've been better."

"You ready to talk about it?"

Heather scowled. "Please don't start."

"But if you—"

"Mat. No."

"Okay, okay. I'm not going to push."

"Good."

"But please tell Billy how much I appreciate his help with the move and say that I really hope he will come."

"Yeah, sure." Heather gave her a wistful little smile. "Maybe a nice dinner with you and Ethan will help. I can't see how. But you never know…"

Friday evening started out pretty well.

Heather and Billy came in smiling. Wine was poured. Matty gave her guests a quick tour of her mostly furnished bungalow. Both Heather and Billy said how great everything looked.

When they got to the empty baby's room, Heather said, "This reminds me that we need to get going on the baby shower."

They discussed potential dates for the big event. Heather said, "I'm calling Aunt Simone tomorrow. It never hurts to have plenty of time to plan."

A few minutes later, they gathered around the kitchen table. Matty brought out the antipasto. It was then that the evening began to go horribly wrong.

It started innocently enough with Heather praising the antipasto platter. "This is beautiful, Matty."

"Don't thank me. I made the lasagna, but this platter is all Ethan's doing."

"Well, it's fabulous," Heather declared. "So good." She popped an olive into her mouth and reached for a cube of cheese. "I love that you cook, Ethan." She sent Billy an icy little smile. "More men should learn their way around the kitchen."

Billy didn't bite, but he didn't look happy, either. He raised his glass of wine. "It's killer good, Ethan," he said.

Ethan played it off. "It's meat and cheese on a plate with garnishes, but thank you."

Heather wouldn't quit. "I just love that you make the effort, you know? Too many men take things like meal preparation and childcare for granted."

Billy stiffened—and then he struck back. "Yeah, and some women just keep pushing until a man gives up and heads for the door."

Heather gasped and whispered, "Honestly, there is no hope for you."

"Cut it out," Billy whispered right back, adding, with more volume, "A nice evening, Heather. Isn't that what you said?"

By then, Matty was thinking she might as well have staged that intervention—and that at this point, she ought to just pivot and go there after all.

But Ethan was watching her. When she frowned at him, he shook his head. With a hard sigh, she made an effort to stick with the program. "Here's to you, Billy—and Ethan, you, too." She raised her glass of sparkling water. "No way could I have pulled this place together in a week without the two of you."

Both men nodded and smiled—Ethan kind of stiffly, Billy with sheer frustration in his eyes.

"Really," said Heather to Matty. "You and Ethan are so cute. And so romantic. Billy used to be romantic, too." She drank a big gulp of Chianti. "Not anymore, though.

Not with me anyway. I guess it was bound to happen, that I would eventually become old news..."

Billy just sat there. Matty had never seen him look so miserable.

She glanced pleadingly at Ethan. Because they had to do something here. Didn't they?

Ethan stared back at her, his green eyes bleak. Apparently he had no clue what to do, either.

Matty seriously considered going rogue about then. Really, her intervention idea made a lot more sense than Heather laying waste and the rest of them pretending desperately that this was just a nice little dinner between friends.

What had gone wrong in Heather's marriage, Matty kept asking herself. What had Billy done that Heather couldn't seem to forgive him for?

"I just can't take it anymore," Heather cried on a soft little sob. She stared straight at Matty now, big brown eyes begging for support.

That did it.

Matty turned to Billy and waded in on her cousin's behalf. "Look at her, Billy. She really is hurting." Billy just sat there, face grim, shoulders hunched, a portrait in misery.

Ethan said, "Matty, I think we should..."

Matty stopped him with a quick shake of her head—and pressed on. "Billy, please just be honest. Just face up to whatever you did. Admit what happened, whatever it was, and—"

"Stop, Matty," Billy said quietly.

"But I—"

"Please stop." Billy shook his head with a sad little smile. "You don't have a clue what's really going on here, do you?"

Heather huffed out a hard breath. "Don't you dare start in on my cousin."

Billy ignored her. "Matty." His voice was low and gentle. "*Do* you know what's going on here?"

Matty kind of wanted to sink right through the floor at that point. "Well, not really. But I—"

"Hold on." Billy turned to his wife. Heather stared at him defiantly. "Are you serious here?" he demanded. "She's your cousin who is the same as a sister to you, and you still haven't told her the truth?"

Heather scoffed and looked away.

Billy slid his napkin in at the side of his plate and stood. "When are you going to get honest?" he asked his wife.

Heather said nothing, and Billy added, "You need to tell your cousin what the real problem is." With another regretful smile for Matty, he pushed in his chair. "Thanks for trying." He started walking.

Heather burst into tears as the front door closed behind him.

Chapter Nine

"Come on, honey. This way…" Matty pulled her sobbing cousin up out of the chair and into her arms. Heather clung to her, still crying, as Matty led her into the living area and guided down onto the sofa. She stroked Heather's hair and rubbed her back as Heather sobbed like she'd never stop.

Ethan approached silently and set a box of tissues on the coffee table. When Matty glanced up at him, he tipped his head toward the door. She gave him a nod and mouthed, *Thank you.* And then he left, too.

After several minutes of soft words, gentle pats and long hugs, Heather's sobs wound down to sniffles and sad little sighs.

For a while, they just sat there with their arms around each other. And then, finally, Heather began to talk.

"I want another baby," she said in a desperate whisper. "I want another little one so bad…"

"And Billy doesn't?"

"No. He wants…more time, he says."

"Time to…?"

"Time with me. Time when I'm not wrapped up with taking care of a baby. He says four kids is plenty. He talks about Little League and basketball and gymnastics, how he wants to be there for each of the kids, to help them do all the things a kid might want to do growing up. And he goes on about college and how much it costs and how he's going to see to it that his kids have options. He says if we keep having babies then the kids we have already won't get the attention they deserve and there won't be a whole lot left for the new ones, either. He makes me feel so guilty, Matty."

"Oh, honey…" Matty pulled her close again and rubbed her back some more.

"He says he feels like he doesn't even know me anymore, that he works long hours running the business and I'm all about the kids all the time. He says when the long day is over and the kids are in bed, the only thing the two of us are good for is to zone out in front of the bedroom flat screen for an hour before passing out from sheer exhaustion. He says we need to work on being just us again—just Heather and Billy—and he says that's never going to happen if I'm buried in diapers and run ragged dealing with colic and midnight feedings all over again."

Matty hugged her cousin even closer. She didn't know what to say. Now that Heather had finally come out with it, Matty could see Billy's side of the issue every bit as clearly as she saw her cousin's desperate longing to hold a new baby in her arms.

"You know what I hate the most?" Heather asked in a tiny voice.

"Tell me."

"I hate that everything he says is right. I hate that so damn much. Because Matty, I want the best for our kids, too, and Billy makes it seem like I don't, and… Well, I'm just so *angry* at him. In my heart, all I can think is that he's selfish and unfeeling. I mean, I just want another little one

to love. Will and Troy are busy with boy things. And now
the twins are getting so independent. They're talking nonstop, getting into everything and constantly telling me, *No,
Mommy! I want to do it myself!* I miss having a tiny one in
my arms all the time. It's who I am—it's what makes me
feel happy and okay with the world. How is that so awful?"

"It's not awful. It's beautiful. It really is."

Huddled against Matty, Heather looked up sharply and
accused with an angry sniffle, "But you still see Billy's
point, right?"

"Oh, Heather…"

"Don't *Oh, Heather* me. I can see what's written right
there on your face. Just say it. Just tell me what you really think."

Still, Matty hesitated.

Until Heather whispered furiously, "Just tell me!"

Matty gave in and answered reluctantly, "Well, did you
ever think that it might be time for you to find new ways
to…be okay?"

"New ways to *be okay*?" Heather narrowed her swollen,
tear-damp eyes. "What does that even mean?"

"It means you've been raising young children for almost
a decade now. It's what you know and what you're comfortable with."

"Excuse me?' Heather jerked away. "Like it's easy or
something, is that what you're telling me?"

"No, Heather. That is not what I'm saying."

"Could have fooled me."

Gently, Matty stroked a hand down Heather's thick dark
hair. "What I'm saying is Will and Troy and Claire and
Elissa…their needs are changing, and that's going to put a
whole new set of demands on you. I'm saying—"

"That you're on Billy's side, *that's* what you're saying."

"No. I'm on *your* side, Heather. I truly am and I always will be."

Heather groaned and slapped Matty's hand away. "Please. You are trying to tell me I should do what Billy wants, and that is not being on my side."

"What I'm telling you is that your growing children are going to keep needing you for years more, just in different ways than they do now. And honey, there's only so much of you to go around."

"Oh, please. A lot of women have more than four children."

"Yes, they do. And somehow they cope with it all. And I admire that so much, but that doesn't mean *you* have to do it."

"Have you listened to a single word I've said, Mat? It's not that I *have* to do it. I *want* to do it. And you may be pregnant, but so far you have zero experience with what it's like to raise a kid."

"I realize that."

"Then listen to me when I tell you I can take care of the children I have and cope with a new baby, too."

"I know that you can—truly I do." Still, she kept hoping that her cousin might at least consider Billy's side of the argument. "But there's so much to take into account here…not the least of which is you and Billy and your relationship, the love and the time you need to give to each other in order to keep your marriage strong."

Heather's eyes gleamed with angry fire. "Just to be clear here, you *are* siding with Billy."

"No. That's not true. I am always on your side. And that means I want you to have the life that you love *and* the man that you love. Yes, you're furious at him now. I understand that. But you and Billy, you have so much. You are so good together—you always have been. Please don't throw all that away."

"But I'm not! It's him. It's Billy. *He's* the one who's decided that the life we've shared for all these years suddenly has to change." Heather was crying again, fat tears sliding down her flushed cheeks.

"Come on. Come back here." Matty opened her arms again.

Heather glared at her. Matty picked up the tissue box and held it out. With a low moan, Heather grabbed a handful of tissues.

"Come here," Matty offered again.

That did it. Heather surrendered and let Matty hold her. For a while, Heather cried and Matty rocked her.

When the tears trickled down to nothing again, Matty took her cousin's flushed face between her hands. "Listen. Please."

"What?"

"We both know that Billy's a good guy."

Heather pulled back, dabbed at her eyes and admitted grudgingly, "Yeah. So?"

"So, I have to tell you from my own personal and painful experience that if, God forbid, you should lose the good man you've got, you might have to learn the hard way that there are a lot of jerks out there just waiting for a chance to break a woman's heart."

Heather gulped. Her big dark eyes were sympathetic now. "You're talking about Ted."

"Oh, yes, I am. And Billy's no Ted. According to you, your husband's main goal here is to get more time with you. Just consider that. Consider the good things you have with him. Will you find that again if you two can't work it out? You and Billy, you really love each other. Don't throw away the man you love who is also a wonderful father to your children."

"I'm not throwing Billy away! Matty, it's *him*. It's Billy. He just doesn't listen. He doesn't understand."

"But I think if you—"

"One more baby!" Heather cut Matty off on a sob. "That's all I want. And I really don't think that's too much to ask."

"You seem preoccupied," said Simone on Saturday afternoon as she, Matty and Colin were pushing display tables toward the outer edges of the floor to make room for rows of chairs, a book-signing table and a podium.

Matty thought of Heather, who had been way too silent last night when Matty drove her home. "I'm fine."

"Translation—you don't want to talk about it."

Matty laughed. "Love you, Mom."

"I'm here if you need me."

"And I do appreciate that."

They started setting up chairs just as Xo Cat jumped onto the signing table. She misjudged the landing and sent a tall stack of books sliding to the floor.

"I'll get her." Matty reached for her just as she leapt again, sending a second stack of books over the edge.

The cat landed on the podium with a self-satisfied "Reow..."

"Come here, you..." Matty scooped the wily tuxedo cat up in her arms and buried her face briefly in Xo Cat's ruff of silky fur before setting her down on the floor a few feet away. "Now, behave," she instructed as the cat, looking way too pleased with herself, strutted away.

An hour later the store was ready for the event.

At five, Matty's dad showed up with takeout. The four of them—her dad, her mom, Matty and Colin—ate standing up as they finished preparing for the author's talk and signing scheduled for seven.

LT Bowers wrote murder mysteries, many of them set in Wyoming. In her mid-sixties, she was plump and pretty with white hair and a great sense of humor. By the time she stepped up behind the podium to talk about her newest release, every chair was filled. For almost an hour, she entertained her readers with great stories about her current release and her life as a writer. Then she answered a lot of questions, signed books and visited with her fans.

The event, unsurprisingly, went long. The store didn't close until ten that night.

At ten-thirty, when Matty pulled into her one-car driveway, Ethan rose from the front steps.

She jumped from the car and ran to his arms. "Hi."

He wrapped her up close in his warm embrace and lowered his mouth to hers.

When they came up for air, he kissed the tip of her nose and said, "You didn't reach out last night. I couldn't decide whether that was good news or bad."

She put her hand to the side of his face, felt the rough scratch of new stubble, thought how handsome he was, how much she wanted him—and how much she'd grown to count on him.

Was that bad, to be so wrapped up in him?

It didn't feel bad.

Yet sometimes she wondered if they'd become too... involved.

He peered down at her, eyes narrowed, like he was trying to see inside her head. "What? Talk to me."

"Let's go in."

With a shrug, he stepped aside, and she opened the door.

"Hungry?" she asked as they shed their boots and hung up their jackets.

"I had something at home. You?"

"We had takeout before the signing tonight."

He caught her hand, reeled her in close and kissed her again. It felt so good, his arms around her, his warm lips on hers...

When he started walking backward, she kept her mouth fused to his and mirrored his steps. In her bedroom, they shed their clothes and fell across the bed all wrapped around each other.

Her everyday worries melted away, leaving her easy and pliant, yearning only for the next touch, the next long, hungry kiss. When he rose up above her, she wrapped her legs around him, opening to him eagerly.

The rest was frantic and hot and fast and so sweet.

Afterward, she used the bathroom first. Then he went in, and she turned down the bed.

When he returned to the bedroom, she was sitting on the edge of the bed, thinking about Heather and Billy, hoping they would come through this rough patch together.

Ethan sat down beside her and took her hand. She realized about then that neither of them had bothered to put on any clothes. Lately, it just felt perfectly natural to be naked with him.

"So," he said. "Did you get anywhere with Heather after I left last night?"

"I did finally find out what's going on between her and Billy."

"Really? That's great."

She threaded her fingers with his and looked up to meet his eyes. "I'm going to tell you what she said, but it's in confidence."

"You're saying she doesn't want you to tell me?"

"I don't know. She didn't swear me to secrecy. But I didn't ask permission to talk it over with you, either. I probably should have, but I was afraid she would say no and I kind of want your input. So you can never tell anyone what I'm about to say, or I will have to kill you."

"Understood."

"Don't judge her—or Billy, for that matter."

He held her gaze, his eyes serious and steady. "Never."

She thought again how much he meant to her. How hard it was going to be for her when this gorgeous, perfect fling of theirs ended. Would their friendship survive?

Of course. It would have to. She wouldn't have it any other way, and neither would he. Their friendship mattered a lot to both of them.

"Let's get under the covers," she said.

"Good idea."

Once they were settled, with the covers over them and her head on his shoulder, she repeated everything she could remember of the conversation she'd had with her cousin the night before, ending with, "So Heather wants another baby desperately, and Billy doesn't. He wants them to move on to the next phase of their lives. He wants them to focus on the kids they already have—and on each other. He says they don't have enough time together, just the two of them. For her, it's another baby, period. Nothing else will do."

He made a thoughtful sound. "You think he might give in eventually and agree to have one more child?"

"I doubt it. Heather can be relentless. If Billy was going to change his mind, I think it would have happened by now." Matty tipped her head back to look in his eyes. "She's so hurt, Ethan. I don't think she even sees that Billy's hurting, too. They used to be so close, and now they live in the same house and they're a million miles apart. I don't know what to do."

"What *can* you do? Be there when she needs you. Tell her the truth as you see it."

She rolled to her stomach and braced up on her elbows. "Yeah, well. I want to be a hundred percent on her side, you know?"

"But you're not?"

"Hmm." She whispered sheepishly, "No… I mean, if Billy wanted more kids, too, more power to them. But he doesn't. And they have four already. I get where he's coming from. He loves her and he wants more of her attention. Is that so much to ask?"

"Does your cousin know how you feel?"

"Of course. We often slept in the same crib when we were babies. We peed in the same wading pool and fought over whose Barbie was cuter. All she needs to do is look at my face and she knows how I feel about any given subject. So no matter how many times I reassure her I'm on her side, she knows where I stand. And she is not happy with me. Can I blame her? Not really."

Ethan brushed a kiss at her temple. "You feel what you feel."

"Yep. Babies grow up and get their own lives. But a good husband should be forever. I don't want her to lose Billy, and I'm afraid that just might happen. And when it comes to couples having babies, it seems pretty obvious to me that both partners have to be up for it. If one of them is not on board, there's bound to be trouble…" She thought of Ted then and let out a small, unhappy sound.

"What's the matter?" Ethan asked.

"It's just…here I am proclaiming my noble beliefs about couples having babies—and look at my own situation. Ted made it brutally clear that he wants nothing to do with this baby."

"That's all on him. You know that, Matty."

"Yeah. You're right. And I'm actually glad Ted feels that way. I just hope and pray that he never changes his mind. Is that fair to the baby? Probably not."

She rolled to her back, tucked the covers up under her arms and rested her hand on the swell of her belly. Twenty weeks along, she thought. Halfway there. Her pregnancy was flying by at the speed of light. "I've been wondering…"

"Yeah?" he asked in a rough whisper.

"Well, as a lawyer, can you tell me if there's some way Ted can…relinquish paternity? Is there a possibility that if he did want out, we could make a legally binding agreement to that effect?"

He braced on an elbow and idly traced a finger down her cheek, over her jaw and along the side of her throat. She loved that—the way he touched her, the feel of his warm fingertips brushing her skin.

But then he said, "The short answer is no. Ted can't just relinquish paternity and turn over all rights to you."

She made a sad face and faked a pitiful whine. "No?

Just like that? Ted can walk away for as long as he wants to and then show up out of nowhere, demand to meet his child—and the law will back him up?"

"In most cases, yes."

"But not always, then?"

"Matty, there are two ways a father can give up his rights."

She reached up, slid her hand around the back of his neck and pulled him close for a quick, firm kiss. Then she settled back down on her pillow again. "Explain."

"No father can legally relinquish paternity except to an adoption or by order of a judge for abandonment. No matter how bad a guy Ted might be, no matter how completely absent he is from your baby's life, judges don't like to terminate a parent's rights and responsibilities unless there's another parent waiting in the wings. That's why stepparent adoptions are usually successful in cases where the biological parent is willing to give up all rights."

"And that means...?"

"Your best bet is to marry someone who wants to be a dad to your baby and then look into a stepparent adoption."

"Yeah, well. That's not going to happen."

"Matty, you never know..."

"Yes, I do know. I'm not getting married again."

He bent close. The kiss they shared then was long and slow and achingly sweet. When he finally retreated to his own pillow, she sighed in equal parts pleasure and contentment.

"If you never get married again," he said, "most likely Ted will always have a claim on your baby should he ever want to exercise it."

"Ugh. That is not what I was hoping to hear."

"I know. But there's good news…"

"Tell me."

"If you sue him for child support, you'll win that suit hands down."

"I don't want to sue Ted. I would honestly love it if I never have to see or hear from him again."

"And maybe you won't. From what you've told me, Ted only wants exactly what you want."

"Yeah, but as the years go by, he may have second thoughts."

"It does happen."

"Exactly." She sighed. "Plus, well, as the baby gets older, she's bound to ask questions. I'm not looking forward to that. I don't even know what I should say to her."

"The truth is always a good start."

"Yeah, right. And chances are she'll want to meet him someday. I just hope we don't have to deal with him until she's older. Because Ted showing up out of nowhere in a few years claiming he suddenly wants to be a dad? I'm going to have a really hard time being civil with him if that happens."

"Hey," he said, so softly. And then he lowered his mouth to hers in the lightest, sweetest brush of a kiss. "Don't ask for trouble."

"Yeah, well. I don't trust him, not one bit. My little girl doesn't need a dad like Ted."

"Matty."

"What?"

"Wait till the bad stuff actually happens before you get all worked up about it."

"I just want him out of my life and my baby's life."

"And he is."

"But for how long?"

He bent close again. "Sorry, Matilda. In this situation, there are no guarantees."

"I don't want to talk about it," Heather said flatly when she opened her front door and found Matty standing on the step.

It was the third Monday in May. A full month had passed since the disastrous double-date dinner at Matty's bungalow. All that time, Matty had been calling and texting her cousin every few days and getting nowhere. Heather always had a reason she couldn't meet for lunch or come over to Matty's.

So today, Matty had come to her. "I brought takeout from Henry's." She held up the big, brown grease-spotted bag.

Heather hitched up her chin. "I said I don't want to talk about it."

"Talk about what?" Matty tried to look innocent.

"You know what," Heather accused.

"Fair enough. We won't talk about it. I have to be back at the bookstore in an hour. Let's eat. I got enough for you, me and the girls. Henry's has junior burgers now, just right for Claire and Elissa."

"The girls are at Grandma Lily's." Lily Dolan was Billy's mom. "It's just me and Meredith."

The golden retriever edged in between Heather and the doorframe and gazed up at Matty with big amber eyes. Matty gave her a pat on the head and said, "Great. Let's eat."

"I mean it. I don't even want to *think* about it."

"Think about what?" Matty faked a confused expression.

"Har-har. Very funny."

"Are you going to let me in or not?"

"Hmm..." Heather folded her arms and made a show of thinking it over.

Matty groaned. "Oh, come on. It's been weeks. I miss you."

"Fine." Heather stepped back at last. "Let's have a burger." She led Matty to the kitchen. "Sit."

Matty pulled out a chair at the little table that looked out on the front steps. She set the bag down. "I didn't bring drinks."

"I have apple juice or ginger ale."

"The juice would be great."

Heather got down two plates, filled a couple of glasses with juice and then joined Matty at the table. Meredith flopped down in the middle of the kitchen floor.

There was a deep silence as they munched on the burgers.

Heather lasted about three endless minutes before she said grudgingly, "Good burgers."

"It's Henry's, after all."

"How are things at the bookstore?" Heather frowned as she stuffed a pickle slice back into her bun.

"Things are actually pretty great at the bookstore."

Her cousin glanced up, surprised. "Really?"

"Really. Mom and I are working things out. She's letting go more, letting me take more initiative. And since I moved to my own place, it's easier between her and me anyway. We do better without the constant contact, if you know what I mean. She's the best, but sometimes she hovers."

Heather seemed wistful now. "You were always the independent one. Not me. I miss my mom so much. She was always here to rely on. She used to come over at least a couple times a week. But now she's off in Florida. I'm lucky if I get to see her three or four times a year." She set down her burger.

Matty reached over and laid her hand over her cousin's. "My mom mentioned that Aunt Leonie and Uncle Darryl are coming to stay with you for a couple of weeks this summer."

"Not till July. That seems like forever..." Heather let out a hard breath and picked up the burger again. "I'm kind of resentful, you know, that she left. And she's probably not moving back. She and Dad love it in Sarasota. Really, think about it—everybody's gone. Junior. Vern. Kaylee and Jessica." Junior and Vern were Heather's older brothers. Kaylee and Jessica were their wives. "I also miss my nieces and nephews," she said. "I'm glad you came home finally. But still, I feel kind of deserted by my family, you know?"

Matty had the distinct impression that whatever she said next would be all wrong. She tried anyway. Leaning in she offered softly, "I know you miss them. I get that it's hard."

Heather slid her a bleak glance. "Yeah, well. I love you, Mat, but you *don't* get it, not really. How could you? Your mom's still here. And you never had any siblings to lose."

Ouch, thought Matty. She really would have liked to have had a sister or brother of her own—and Heather knew it, too.

"Sorry," Heather offered reluctantly. "That was kind of mean and I'm trying not to be mean, I really am."

"Apology accepted." Matty got to work on her burger as she tried to come up with a diplomatic way to suggest that Heather consider talking to a marriage-and-family therapist.

Because what else could she offer? Matty felt at a loss. She had no idea how to help her cousin unpack all that obvious frustration and resentment.

Heather sent her another unhappy glance. "Go ahead. Ask. You know you want to."

Did Matty want to? Not at this point. "You said you wouldn't talk about it. Let's just leave it alone and have our lunch, shall we?"

"Oh, I don't think so. Just ask me, why don't you? Ask me how it's going between me and Billy."

"Heather, I don't want to—"

"Bad, Matty. That's how it's going. He hardly speaks to me. And that's fine. I don't want to talk to him anyway. He's sleeping on the futon in the playroom downstairs, in case you were wondering."

Matty dropped her burger onto her plate. "I was trying really hard not to wonder. But now that you've said it, I'll bite. Why, Heather? Why is Billy sleeping in the playroom?"

"He's mad at me."

Billy was the least angry person Matty knew. "Why is Billy mad at you?"

Heather tipped her chin high and announced with defiant pride, "Because I took matters into my own hands and went off my birth control without telling him."

Chapter Ten

"She didn't," said Ethan in sheer disbelief.

"Oh, but she did," Matty replied.

"What did you do then?"

They were at his house, in his bed after dinner and a long, sweet interval of perfect lovemaking. She wanted to reach for him again, pull him close, get swept away in the incomparable feel of his hands on her skin.

But really, she could use his input on the Heather situation. "Ethan, I honestly intended to eat my burger and keep my mouth shut. I swear to you, that was my plan."

"Uh-huh. And what did you actually do?"

"Well, I did manage to keep quiet for a little while. But Heather wouldn't stop talking about how she set out to trick Billy into giving her another baby. She said that I didn't have to look so disapproving, that *he'd* been talking about getting a vasectomy and if he could do that, why was it so very wrong for her to seduce her own husband?"

"Well, that's...not encouraging," Ethan said grimly.

"No. It's not—but she did admit that her plan hadn't worked because when she starting getting cozy with him he got suspicious. He confronted her, said he didn't get why suddenly she was all hot for him when they were still barely speaking. Heather told me that she refused to dignify that question with an answer."

"Let me guess. Then Billy checked the medicine cabinet?"

"Yep. He figured out that she'd stopped taking her birth control pills. That's when he moved to the futon."

"So she never actually went through with her plan?"

"No. And she was furious about that because—her words—'Now, he's never going to give me another chance get pregnant'"

"Oh, Matilda. This is bad."

"My thoughts exactly."

He felt for her hand and wove their fingers together on top of the covers. "How will Billy ever trust her again?"

"That's a great question. Too bad I have no answer for it."

"What did you say to her?"

"I was a little hard on her."

He squeezed her hand. "Tell me."

She turned her head on the pillow. His eyes were waiting. They shared a smile. She was twenty-five weeks along, inching up on her third trimester and obviously pregnant now. Even fully dressed, her belly led the way wherever she went—and this pre-baby fling of theirs?

Still going strong. He gave no sign he was ready to end it.

As for Matty, she hoped they could keep spending every night together right up to the day she had to head for the hospital.

"Tell me what you said to her," he coaxed for the second time.

"Fine—you asked for it. I said that she'd betrayed her marriage vows, that trust is the most important thing between life partners. I said that tampering with her birth control without telling her partner falls under the heading of reproductive coercion and it is no more acceptable when a woman does it than when a man does. Finally, I said that I understood completely why Billy was now sleeping on the futon."

"Wow, Matilda. You didn't pull any punches."

"No, I did not."

"And how did she take it?"

"Not well. In fact, she asked me to leave."

Ethan wrapped those strong arms around her and kissed the top of her head.

She cuddled in nice and close. He smelled so good, so clean and manly. "She's been avoiding me for weeks. And now she's just going to avoid me some more. I've called her twice since I left her house today in hopes of smoothing things over."

"And?"

"Straight to voicemail. I feel really crappy about what I said, even if it was the truth as I see it. All I did was put more distance between her and me. Now she won't even pick up the phone when I call."

"Give it time. What you said was pretty harsh."

"Hey!" She wriggled in his hold. "So what if you're right? You're supposed to be on *my* side—and what about poor Billy? How's Billy ever going to trust her again after she tried to trick him into getting her pregnant?"

"Settle down." He kissed her, a quick brush of his lips against hers. "I *am* on your side. And I hear you, I do. What you said *was* harsh, but you needed to say it because she needed to hear it from someone other than Billy."

"Exactly. I just hate that she feels so alone. Her parents and her brothers moved away, and all the nieces and nephews went with them. Heather lives to be surrounded by family, and she feels deserted by hers. She's angry at Billy and now at me, too. In a way, I get why she's desperate to have more babies. If she can have a lot of kids, the odds increase that at least some of them will stay in town when they grow up."

"I really think she'll come around."

"I hope so."

Matty gave her cousin a full week before calling her again.

But as before, the call went to voicemail. She left a message. Heather didn't call back.

Matty waited another week to try again. And this time she didn't call. Instead, early in the afternoon on the first Monday in June, she went to Heather's house. When she drove up, her cousin's Suburban was parked in the driveway. The odds were high that Heather was at home.

But when she knocked on her cousin's door, nobody answered. Matty waited, thinking that if Heather was in there, she might eventually stop being stubborn and let Matty in.

The minutes ticked by. Matty was just about to give up and leave when her cousin pulled open the door.

"The twins are napping," Heather whispered angrily. "And school's out, in case you hadn't heard. Will and Troy are with their grandpa at the moment, but they could show up any minute now. So say what you have to say and make it quick."

"This is ridiculous," Matty whispered back. "We need to work this out." She kind of expected Heather to shut the door in her face.

But instead, with an angry toss of her dark head, she stepped back and ushered Matty in.

They sat on the sofa. Meredith put her golden head on Matty's thigh. Matty scratched her behind the ears.

"I mean it. You need to keep it down," Heather warned with a stern look and a hushing finger to her lips, as though Matty had just jumped up and started shouting.

"I will," Matty whispered back. "I promise." Meredith whined softly and then, with a heavy sigh, flopped down on the floor at her feet.

For a long string of seconds, Matty and her cousin just stared at each other. Finally, Heather said, "You're really showing, you know that?"

"Tell me about it."

"Can I...?" Heather asked. At Matty's nod, she put her hand on Matty's belly. "Has she kicked yet?"

"Oh, yeah. Future soccer star here, no doubt about it."

Heather gazed off toward the stairwell and smiled. "There. I felt it. Just a nudge..."

"Heather."

"What?"

"You have to stop being mad at me."

"I know." Her eyes widened as the baby shifted beneath her palm. "Oh, I love that feeling. Nothing like it. She's going to call me Aunt Heather. You know how I feel about that."

"I do, yes."

"I don't give a damn that I'm really her first cousin once removed. Aunt Heather. Got it?"

"Yes, ma'am."

Heather flopped back against the sofa cushion and closed her eyes with a soft little sigh. "I loved every minute with my babies."

Matty leaned back with her. "I know, sweetie."

"I just... I'm having a really hard time thinking about never having a tiny one of my own again. When I look back at the happiest times, I always think of moments with a baby in my arms."

"Then remember those moments. Treasure them." Matty went too far then. "And let yourself move on."

Heather no longer slumped against the sofa cushion. Now her back was ramrod straight. "Easy for you to say," she hissed through clenched teeth. "With that little angel kicking inside you."

Matty closed her eyes and mentally counted to five. "Fair point." She met her cousin's gaze again. "I'm sorry."

Heather's shoulders drooped. "Me, too. Mat, I don't want to fight with you."

"So then, what do you say we don't do that anymore?"

"Deal."

They reached for a hug at that same time.

"So Heather's officially speaking to you again," said Ethan that night.

"Yes, she is."

"But not to Billy."

"Sadly, no. Not to Billy."

Matty and Ethan sat out on the front steps of her bungalow enjoying the mild weather. The June night was cloudless, the indigo sky awash with stars.

Earlier that evening, he'd driven them up to Sheridan for the first of three prenatal classes. She'd come home with a lot of information and tips, including detailed practical advice on how to get through labor and delivery.

Ethan was going to be a great birth coach. He listened so closely, jotting down important points using the notes app on his phone. He'd coached her through breathing techniques and helped her in the birthing ball exercises.

She smiled at him. "I think we're okay now, me and Heather."

"I'm glad," he said, his somber expression belying the words. "I feel pretty sorry for Billy, though."

"I feel sorry for *both* of them. From what Heather said, he's not budging on the baby issue. And neither is she. What she wants most is the thing he just won't give her." Matty stared up into the giant bowl of the dark sky seeking the brightest star. Somewhere nearby, a nighthawk let out its sharp, electric cry. "Watching them fall apart, it's so sad, you know?"

He wrapped an arm across her shoulders and touched his warm lips to her cheek. She shivered a little—not with cold but with the pleasure his kisses always brought.

Friends with benefits? Best. Plan. Ever.

Ethan's phone rang. "It's Gavin." He answered, "Hey, partner. What's up?" Gavin said something on his end. And Ethan replied, "How terrific is that? Congratulations... Yeah. Okay. Give her my best?... All right, then. No problem. It's handled." A minute later, he said goodbye and set the phone on the step beside him.

"Let me guess—Nicole had the baby."

He nodded. "An hour ago. A healthy little boy."

"Oh, Ethan. That's great news." She rested her hand on her belly. In about three months, she'd have her own little girl in her arms at last.

"Gavin's one happy man—and he wanted to let me know he probably won't be in the office at all for the next couple of days."

"Will you manage okay without him?"

"Oh, yeah. We have it worked out. There are some things he has to handle personally and he'll deal with that, but I can pick up the slack for most of it."

"What's the baby's name?"

"Charles. He's nine pounds, two ounces."

"A big boy."

"Oh, yeah. Gavin is so happy."

"I'm glad for them."

He nuzzled her ear. "You know, I was thinking…"

"Hmm?"

He kissed her cheek. "What about if Billy and Heather went off somewhere together, just the two of them?"

She pulled away enough to look directly at him. "A romantic getaway, you mean?"

"Yeah. We can watch the kids while they're gone."

She slanted him a disbelieving look. "Ethan. Didn't I mention that nowadays Billy's sleeping on the downstairs futon?"

"You did mention that, yeah." He said the words with resignation.

"They're hardly speaking to each other. I doubt they're ready for a romantic weekend together. At this point, if they could just talk to each other without the whole thing escalating into a pitched verbal battle, I would call that progress."

"Me, too." He leaned back on his hands and gazed up at the stars. "Think about it, Matilda. There's no rule that says a getaway has to be romantic. The two of them could use the time to talk things out."

"I don't know. The two of them trying to talk things out could so easily end up in a blood bath—metaphorically speaking. I'm starting to wonder if a breakthrough is even possible for them at this point. They've been on the outs for months."

"Oh, come on now," he said. "Think positive. If they each made a good-faith effort to actually communicate during the time they're off alone together, that would be a step toward them working things out."

He was right. Time away just might be helpful. And Matty wanted to do something for her cousin and Billy because giving up on them was not a solution. "I hear you," she said. "And your idea just might work."

He leaned in close again and pressed his warm lips to the side of her neck. "You're a good cousin."

"Yeah, well. I try." She tipped her head to the side, offering him easier access with a happy sigh. He kissed his way upward to nip at her ear.

And she thought of another problem. "Do you honestly think you're up for watching four kids under ten from Friday till Sunday?"

"You bet I am." His white teeth flashed with his bold grin. "We could take them out to the Rising Sun."

"Hmm. A weekend at the Bravo family ranch…"

"Yeah. It'll be fun. The boys can spend some time with the horses. The twins are a little young for that, but they can meet a few barn cats and get up close and personal with some baby chicks, maybe dig around in my mom's garden and hang out with my sister Jobeth's kids. And if babysitting Heather's children turns out to be too much for you and me, I'm guessing your folks and the Dolan grandparents will be happy to pitch in."

Ethan was quite proud of his getaway idea. And once he got Matty agreeing that a little time away together could be good for Heather and her husband, things kind of naturally fell into place.

Heather and Billy surprised them. They both said yes. Billy went online and booked a room at a gorgeous bed-and-breakfast in Denver.

And on an overcast Friday morning, two and a half weeks after Ethan came up with his plan, Matty's alarm went off at seven.

Matty grabbed the phone off the nightstand and silenced it. "Operation Save Heather's Marriage is officially underway," she announced with a big yawn.

Ethan, still half asleep, made a low sound of agreement.

Matty poked at his shoulder. "Wake up. We need coffee and then we need to pack." The plan was to be at Heather's by nine. Once Heather and Billy had left for the airport in Sheridan, Ethan and Matty would load up the kids and head for the ranch.

Ethan rolled over and pulled Matty close. He nuzzled the side of her throat. "Mornin'."

She laughed and wriggled away. "None of that. We've got to get a move on…"

They arrived at Heather's five minutes early.

Inside, it was chaos. The twins were clutching their baby dolls, crying. Ethan wasn't clear whether the tears were about their parents leaving or the argument they seemed to be having over whether or not they had traded dolls. Will sat on the sofa in his pajamas playing a video game on his tablet.

Six-year-old Troy was complaining. He didn't want his parents to go away for "…three *whole* days" because "Brandon and me, we've got stuff to do, you know?"

Brandon, Matty explained to Ethan, was Troy's best friend who lived next door.

As for Billy and Heather, they seemed awfully quiet—and also kind of grim. Had they changed their minds about the getaway?

If they had, they weren't saying so.

Ethan took charge. "Let's get going, everyone." He helped Billy load the luggage into the back of Billy's crew cab.

Then Heather handed Ethan her keys. "Three car seats," she said. "You'll need the Suburban."

There was more crying and complaining as the parents kissed the kids goodbye. Elissa whined, "I'm hungry, Mommy!"

Heather kissed her cheek. "You had breakfast half an hour ago."

"But I'm hungry *now*..."

Matty grabbed a banana from the fruit bowl on the counter, peeled it and gave Elissa a piece. She stuck it in her mouth and reached for more. By then, Claire wanted some, too. Matty divided the banana between them. Tears streamed down their cheeks as they munched away. The dog, Meredith, looked on anxiously.

Finally Billy and Heather went out the front door, three kids and Matty and Ethan trailing behind them. Only Will and Meredith remained in the house.

As Ethan followed the others out, he glanced back at the boy. Will hadn't budged an inch from his spot on the sofa. His eyes were glued to his tablet screen.

Five minutes later, following a flurry of intensified complaints and cries, along with a few hugs and another kiss or two, Heather and Billy drove away.

As Ethan and Matty herded the three children back into

the house, the twins were still crying. Inside, Ethan saw
that Will hadn't budged from his spot on the sofa. His focus
on his tablet remained absolute.

Troy loudly complained, "It's just not fair that I can't
stay at Brandon's..."

Matty sidled up close to Ethan and whispered, "You think
we should invite Brandon?"

He whispered back, "Do you know Brandon?"

"Never met him."

"Let's not go there, then. We've already got four to deal
with. Brandon might break us."

At least she was still in good enough spirits to laugh
at that one. "Okay, then. Let's get this show on the road."

The good news? The car seats were already in place in
the Suburban and Heather had packed for the kids—lots of
jeans, T-shirts, light jackets and sturdy shoes. Swimsuits
and towels, too. All they had to do was load up the car. The
golden retriever remained anxious as they buckled everyone into the car. When Ethan opened the back lift gate for
her, she jumped in eagerly.

The twins were still crying as they drove away.

But then Matty turned around and asked, "Who knows
'The Wheels on the Bus'?"

Troy groaned. "Oh, no. Not that one!"

Even Will glanced up from his tablet long enough to
gripe, "You know they will never stop, right?"

The twins were already singing, their cheeks and eyes
still red but their tears forgotten. When Ethan turned off
the state highway onto the ranch road that would take them
to the Rising Sun, Claire and Elissa were still singing and
Ethan was thinking he would need to disconnect Will from
his tablet at some point in the near future.

"Wow," said Troy, staring out at the grazing cow/calf pairs beyond the fences on either side of the gravel access road. "Look at all the baby cows!"

"It's a ranch, bruh," Will grunted as he fiddled with his tablet. "What'd you expect?"

By then, most of the cloud cover had burned off. The day would be a nice one. Up ahead, the hulking gray spines of the Bighorn Mountains marched across the horizon under a sky of unblemished blue.

Ethan smiled. Four kids was a lot. But it was a gorgeous day, and though he liked his life in town, he always loved coming home to the Rising Sun.

A few minutes later, they left the ranch road behind and turned onto the circular driveway that led them past the foreman's cottage to the main house. The house looked good, he thought. Built by his great-grandfather, Ross Bravo, back in the 1940s in a classic farmhouse style, it had dove-gray shiplap siding and a full-width front porch with a row of tall double-hung windows to either side of the door. His mom's roses, in full bloom, framed the front steps.

Matty waved out her window at Ethan's mom, Tess, as Tess came out the front door carrying Dustin, Jobeth and Hunter's two-year-old, on her hip. Seven-year-old Paisley followed close behind.

"We're here!" Claire announced and added, "Oooh. Pretty flowers!"

Elissa chirped, "Let's get out!" It wasn't a question. Latches clicked as the kids released themselves from their car seats. Surprisingly, Will, in the back row, set his tablet aside to lean over the seat and help his sisters with their safety harnesses. Three backseat doors yawned wide simultaneously and the kids clambered out.

Ethan and Matty shared a look, but neither of them objected to the mass exodus from the vehicle. At least no one had tried to escape while the car was in motion.

Matty said, "These kids are fast when they want to be."

Ethan's mom laughed as she hustled down the front steps to greet the thundering horde.

"Paisley!" Troy knew Paisley. She was a year ahead of him at Medicine Creek Elementary. The six-year-old gave Ethan's niece a shy smile. "I didn't know you had a ranch."

"I lived here *all* my life," Paisley informed him. "And this year I get to learn to ride a horse."

Troy seemed suitably impressed. "Cool."

Ethan's mom said, "Let's go in and have a snack."

Elissa concurred, "Yes! I am so hungry!"

Ethan let Meredith out, and she followed them all up the steps and inside, where they congregated around the big table in the kitchen. There were muffins and juice boxes.

Once the snack was decimated and everybody had a chance to use the bathroom, Ethan, Matty, Heather's kids and the dog climbed back into the Suburban. When Paisley asked if she could come, too, Ethan's mom gave permission. They transferred a booster seat from Tess's SUV, and the seven-year-old buckled herself in next to Will.

They set off, following a two-track road that branched off of the circular driveway. The two-track took them to the barn and sheds and a large pasture where horses grazed. Jobeth appeared from the barn with some apples to lure the horses to the fence.

For a while, they all hung out at the fence with the horses. Then Ethan and Matty took the twins off to meet the barn cats and check out the baby chicks. Paisley, the boys and Meredith stayed behind with Jobeth.

When Claire and Elissa got fussy, the four of them went back to the main house, where the other kids joined them an hour or so later. After lunch, Ethan took them all to his favorite swimming hole on Crystal Creek, which flowed east to west across the Rising Sun on its way to join the Powder River. The twins were exhausted by then. They put on their floaties and paddled around in the shallows for a bit.

Then Matty spread a big blanket under a pair of giant cottonwoods. The two little girls joined her there, one on either side of her, as Meredith flopped down at their feet. Matty began telling them a story, something about a big horse and a brave princess. Ethan got his phone from the pile of dry gear on the other blanket and snapped a few pictures of the twins cuddled close, Matty on her back, her pregnant belly round and proud.

When he stashed his phone back in his jeans and went to join the boys and Paisley, he couldn't help thinking that Matty was going to be a great mom. As for Will, there had been no need to ask him to cut back on his screen time. He'd left his tablet in the Suburban when they got out to visit the horses and hadn't picked it up since.

That evening, they had Rising Sun Cattle Company burgers and steaks grilled on the big cast-iron cooker in the backyard of the main house. For dessert, they roasted marshmallows on dogwood sticks over an open fire and made s'mores.

By full dark, Dustin was already sound asleep in his dad's lap. The rest of the kids were still trying their best to keep their eyes open. They knew they'd be hustled off to bed as soon as they dropped off to sleep. Ethan watched them droop in their chairs—and then snap up straight and blink their eyes wide, determined to stay awake.

The twins lost the battle first. Matty, in the Adirondack chair next to his, brushed his arm with her fingers, sending warmth scattering over his skin. She tipped her chin toward the chair a few feet away where the two girls sat together, their heads touching, both of them conked out with their mouths half-open.

Ethan grinned at the sight and then shifted his gaze back to Matty again. She leaned close and whispered, "Who knew four kids under ten could be so much fun?"

"Make that six, counting Paisley and Dustin." In the corner of his eye, he saw that his mom was watching them. Tess sat by his dad across the campfire. When he looked at her directly, she gave him a slow grin, like she'd figured out his big secret and just might be planning to do something about it.

But this thing with him and Matty—it wasn't a secret, not really. He wanted Matty and she wanted him and they were enjoying being together for as long as it lasted.

As long as it lasted...

He tipped his head up to the star-thick sky. It was a gorgeous night. And today had been pretty much perfect. No reason to darken his own good mood with thoughts of when he and Matty would end their pre-baby fling, how they would somehow transition back to friends-only after being so much more.

Uh-uh. Better just to let himself enjoy every perfect moment. The future could take care of its own damn self.

In the chair next to the one where the twins snoozed together, Troy yawned hugely.

Definitely time to think about calling it a night.

A few minutes later, everybody said good-night. Ethan's dad and mom returned to the house, their blue heeler, Winston, trotting along behind them. Jobeth and her husband, Hunter, took Paisley and Dustin back to their place across the yard. As for Ethan and Matty, they herded the Dolan kids and Meredith to the bunkhouse, which mostly served as a guesthouse nowadays. Ranch hands, as a rule, preferred to live in their own trailers.

Six years ago, Hunter, the family celebrity, had renovated the bunkhouse for his popular home-improvement show, *Rebuilt by Bartley*. Now it had several bedrooms, each with its own bath. There was also a large great room with a fully equipped kitchen.

Droopy-eyed and yawning, the children brushed their teeth. They were tired enough to fall into bed without bothering to bargain for a story or another half hour of screen time. When all four of them were tucked in with the lights off, Ethan met up with Matty in the central hallway.

"Where's Meredith?" he asked.

"She settled in Will's room."

He offered his hand. She took it. He laced his fingers with hers.

There were more than enough rooms for her to have her own. But Ethan didn't want that. He figured she didn't either or she would have said something earlier. He led her down the hallway to the room at the end, which had a comfortable queen-size bed covered in a blue quilt his mother had made. Pushing the door wide, he gestured her in ahead of him.

She hesitated on the threshold. "When I put my stuff in here this afternoon, I didn't really think about what we'd tell the kids in the morning when they wake up and find us in the same bed."

He pulled her over the threshold and shut and locked

the door. "Nothing." He clasped her shoulders. "We will
tell them nothing. When one of them knocks on the door,
I'll say, 'Be out in a minute!'" He let his hands wander up
the smooth sides of her neck to cradle her sweet face. "And
then we'll put on some clothes and take them over to the
main house for a big ranch breakfast."

She gazed up at him for a long count of ten. And then she
turned and went to the window that framed a moonlit view
of overlapping pastures rolling toward the breaklands and
onward to the foot of the mountains way out there at the horizon. They were silent as they stared out at the night together.

"Ethan," she whispered, turning to face him again.
"Thank you for today. I loved it. The kids did, too."

He bent his head and kissed her. She tasted so good, so
sweet and willing. She tasted like happiness.

Like home.

Sadness welled in him, the good kind of sadness that
comes from knowing life is too damn short and no fine,
perfect thing lasts forever—but that's all right. Because at
least this moment, right now, is about as fine and perfect
as any moment ever gets.

"It was fun," he said.

"Oh, yeah." She slid her hands up over his chest and
clasped them around his neck. "So. Much. Fun." She lifted
on tiptoe, offering that mouth again.

He took it, sliding his tongue beyond her softly parted
lips, tasting her more deeply. Slowly she began to walk
backward, pulling him with her as she went.

This, he thought, in wonder. *This is what happiness is.*
She took him down with her onto the pretty blue quilt. He
gave himself up to it—to *her*, to this perfect moment that
would never come again.

* * *

His mother cornered him after breakfast. Tess Bravo was highly skilled at getting her grown children alone no matter how many people were hanging around the ranch house.

This morning, she essentially cut him from the herd as soon as his dad and his brother, Brody, headed for the barns and sheds.

"Jobeth," Tess said with a gentle smile, "why don't you and Hunter and Matty take the kids outside? Ethan can stick around and help me straighten up the kitchen."

Jobeth shot him a look. She understood as well as he did that their mom would be probing for insights into his private life. She asked, "You good with that, little brother?"

Ethan hesitated. He did love his mother, and of course he would help her with anything she asked for. Not to mention, the one-on-one talk she wanted was bound to happen eventually. Tess Bravo wouldn't give up until she got him alone and he answered her questions.

Matty had noted his hesitation and tried to come to his rescue. "I'll stay to help clear off."

Still smiling way too innocently, Tess shook her head. "Thanks, Matty. But you go on out with the kids. Ethan and I won't be long."

In no time, it was just him and his mom. He cleared the table and put things away as she loaded the dishwasher and cleaned the pots and pans.

For a few minutes, neither of them spoke. Then Tess said in a wistful tone, "I do miss Edna…" Ethan, who was scraping and stacking plates at the table, glanced up to see her staring out the window over the sink. She went on, "I drove up to see her just the other day. Edna's sharp as ever, but she does have trouble getting around."

Edna Heller had been the housekeeper on the Rising Sun
for years. She was family—both figuratively and literally.
Her only daughter, Abby, had married Cash Bravo, who
not only had his own investment business in town but also
owned a third of the Rising Sun. Ethan's dad, Zach, ran
the ranch, but it was jointly owned by three Bravo cousins:
Zach, Cash and Nate Bravo. Nate lived and worked on his
wife's ranch, the Double-K.

Over the years, Edna and Tess had grown very close.
Last year, though, Edna had moved up to the Sylvan Acres
Retirement Community in Sheridan.

Ethan carried the stacked plates to the counter. "I hear
you, Mom. The place isn't quite the same without her."

Tess made a soft sound of agreement. She was looking
out the window over the sink, which faced the backyard.

Matty, Jobeth, Hunter and all the kids were playing capture the flag out there. Even two-year-old Dustin had joined
in. He toddled around, falling on his butt and then getting
right back up again, completely out of the loop on the rules
of the game but happy to follow anyone who happened to
wander past him.

Ethan smiled as he watched the twins. They adored
Dustin and spent more time hovering around the toddler
than playing the game. Once again, Dustin plopped to his
butt in the grass, spotted Elissa and gave her his goofy grin.
She darted right to him and tried to help him up. Dustin
wouldn't have it. He shook his head, levered up on his
hands and pushed himself upright butt-first all on his own.

Tess grabbed the hand towel. She dried her hands as
she turned to him. "So. You and Matty, huh?" He almost
laughed at her abrupt change of subject. As he considered

how much he was willing to say, his mom clucked her tongue at him. "Don't even try it."

"'It'? What?"

She patted his shoulder. "Matty's a fine person. I've always liked her. And her mom and dad, too. And *you've* always had a soft spot for her—no, not everyone knows that. But I am your mother, after all. I understand that Gabe was a brother to you, that you would never have made a move on his girl."

"Where are you going with this, Mom?"

She pressed her hand lightly to his cheek and then gave it a gentle pat. "Just be patient."

"Believe me, I'm trying."

"I was just wondering…"

"Say it."

"Well, what about Sylvia?"

"That's over."

"Whew." Tess nodded. "Good. And, though it's common knowledge around town that Matty is having a baby on her own. I know that she's a very direct sort of person. But still, I didn't know whether to ask her about it or…"

"Ask away. She won't mind."

"Excellent. When's the baby due?"

"September." He added, feeling inordinately proud, "I'm Matty's birth coach."

She gave him her softest smile. "That's lovely."

He almost groaned. "Seriously, Mom? 'Lovely'?"

Her nod was firm this time. "That is what I said—and don't give me that look, Ethan John. I'm happy for you. I truly am." Happy for him because he was Matty's birth coach? Clearly his mother had made a few assumptions—and now she was blinking and sniffling.

"Mom. Come on. There's nothing to cry about."

"Oh, Ethan…" She leaned in.

What could he do but give her a hug? "It's okay, Mom." He cradled her close and patted her back.

She sniffled again and then looked up at him, her smile kind of wobbly now. "So." Stepping back, she snatched a tissue from the box on the counter and dabbed at her eyes. "What about the baby's father?"

"Mom…"

"Please. Just tell me. Matty Hunt strikes me as a woman who has no problem with the truth. And you just said I could ask her anything I want about the baby. So why don't we simplify the process and you just tell me yourself?"

He gave in and explained, "Matty was living with someone in LA. It didn't work out, but before they broke up, she got pregnant."

"This someone…he still lives in Los Angeles?" Tess asked. At his grim nod, she frowned. "That will be difficult, sharing custody long-distance."

"He doesn't want the baby."

"Hmm. Well, all right, then."

"Mom. Just cut to the chase, okay? Tell me what you're getting at."

"It's just that it seems pretty clear to me. You should marry Matty and adopt the child."

He stifled a laugh of surprise that she would go so far. "Mom. Please."

"Don't try to tell me that's not what you're thinking."

"The baby isn't even born yet."

"Not my point. I'm simply suggesting that you go after what you really want. I'm saying, don't hang back. Make a real move."

"But Mom, it's really not any of your—"

"Business? Maybe not. But I'll never forgive myself if I don't speak up and tell you that were you and Matty to decide to be together, I would be so happy for both of you and I would welcome her and her baby to the family with open arms. As for you becoming that baby's father, I just want to remind you that in this family, adoption is a proud tradition."

Oddly enough, she was right. Jobeth had adopted Paisley when a relative in South Dakota gave her up at birth. Jobeth herself was the biological child of Tess's first husband. Ethan's dad had adopted Jo when he married Tess—and in some ways, Jobeth was more Zach Bravo's child than Ethan, Brody or Starr. Everyone in the Bravo family knew that Jobeth would someday be taking the reins at the Rising Sun.

And this conversation was getting way out of hand. "Mom, I really think—"

"It's okay," she interrupted. "I know I've said too much and you really need to get back to your guests. Just think about it—that's all I'm asking."

The truth was Ethan had already thought about it. A lot.

But bringing the idea up to Matty felt way more than dangerous.

She'd already made it painfully clear that she wasn't seeking a dad for her baby—and also that she was never getting married again.

No. His mom's *suggestions* aside, he and Matty had an agreement. Asking her for more than she was willing to give would almost certainly blow up in his face.

However, his mom's bold suggestions brought it sharply home to him that he had a serious problem. He was getting far too attached to this whole thing with Matty. He loved it.

And his mother was right, damn it. He loved *Matty*. And he did want to marry her. He wanted to adopt her little girl and spend the rest of his life being Matty's husband and that little girl's dad.

It was all so painfully clear to him now.

He'd spent years trying to tell himself he was over her— and during that time he'd almost come to believe his own lie. But then she'd come home and they'd started hanging out together, become friends with benefits just till the baby came…

Lying to himself wasn't working anymore. His eyes were wide open and he saw the truth crystal clear.

It was love that he felt for Matty. It always had been.

And these last months with her had only served to show him that he wanted Matty for the rest of their lives. He loved her. He truly did. It was real and it was deep and it was lasting.

And if she would only say yes, they could raise the baby together, build a fine, full life. Together.

Gabe had been dead for three long, sad years. That was the truth. Gabe was never coming back. It had taken Ethan a long while to learn to live with that truth. But he'd done it finally. He'd fully accepted that Gabe really was gone. That it would not be a betrayal of his best friend if he made a life with Matty.

Far from it. For him to make a life with Matty was how it *should* be. They were so good together. They could have so much together.

Damn. He wanted that, wanted a chance for that.

But he didn't know if he could make himself ask her for that. He couldn't even imagine himself going there with her.

Telling Matty he loved her—and as much more than a friend? That could so easily lead to disaster.

He could lose everything trying to win it all.

Chapter Eleven

Matty looked up when he came out onto the back porch. She patted the chair next to her. His heart pounding way too fast, he circled the lawn where the game was still in progress and sat down beside her.

Immediately, she leaned his way, her eyes alight, her scent of oranges and jasmine drifting to him on the wind.

Longing hit him like a punch to the gut. He couldn't wait to be alone with her, the two of them in that bunkhouse bedroom with the window looking out on the mountains. They had another night here at the ranch, and he couldn't wait to have her to himself.

"Just to bring you up to speed," she whispered. "Though your dad carefully explained all the rules to the kids, the twins and Dustin have no clue how the game of capture the flag is played."

He heard every word. But he wasn't really listening. He was too busy thinking how gorgeous she was—with her haphazardly pinned-up golden hair, her grin that spoke of equal parts mischief and intelligence, her blue eyes that sucked him in every single time.

Damn. He was a goner.

A goner and scared to death to tell her so because the

chance was too great that telling her would bring their *just till the baby comes* love affair to a screeching halt.

Several feet away, Dustin chortled as he struggled to his feet. Claire and Elissa, giggling, ran in a circle around him.

"Well," Ethan whispered back to the woman he loved, "at least they're having a really good time."

Will called out to his sisters, "Come on, you guys! The game! Play the game!"

Dustin announced, "I play!" as he staggered and dropped to his butt again.

Laughing, Paisley ran to him and tagged him. He looked up at her with a giant smile of greeting. "Pais!"

Will grunted and held the flag high. "Yeah, right. Like he's gonna freeze. I'm telling you—this game is not happening."

Laughing wildly, Elissa ran up and tagged him. Resigned, Will froze, and his little sister got the flag.

Matty asked, "So…what did your mother have to say?"

"Nothing exciting," he lied outright. "Just that she likes you and the kids and you're welcome back anytime."

"That's all?"

"Pretty much, yeah."

"Whew. I was afraid she was going to tell you that the kids are too much and we'd better head on back into town tonight."

"No way."

Right then, as if on cue, his mother came out the back door.

Matty whispered, "Uh-oh. Here she comes."

Tess Bravo circled the lawn and dropped into the empty Adirondack folding chair on Matty's other side. She leaned

Matty's way. "I'm so glad you decided to come on out to the ranch this weekend," she said.

"Whew," said Matty. "I'm relieved to hear that. It's a lot, four extra kids."

"I am loving every minute of it," Tess declared.

Matty's too-bright smile relaxed then. "Thank you. We're all having the best time."

"Oh, my!" Matty, on top, with her legs folded to either side of the gorgeous man beneath her, lifted a hand and raked her tangled hair back from her sweaty face. She looked down into Ethan's eyes. "I sincerely hope we didn't wake up one of the kids."

He gave her a wink. "Relax. Capture the flag kind of finished them off."

"I hope you're right."

"I know I am—listen." He held up a finger for silence.

She frowned, waiting. "What am I listening for?" she whispered after several seconds.

"Nothing. Because there is nothing. Those kids are out for the night."

"All righty, then." Carefully, she slid to the side and stretched out on the bed with him. Plumping her own pillow, she tucked it under her cheek.

He traced a slow finger down the side of her throat and up over the slope of her shoulder. "You're so beautiful, Matilda," he whispered almost reverently.

"Thank you," she whispered back. "You're not so bad yourself." And that was putting it mildly.

Because dang, he had it all going on, with that killer smile and those green eyes with glints of amber, that thick brown hair she constantly wanted to run her fingers through—good looking and smart, understanding and kind. No wonder all the women fell for him.

She lifted up enough to kiss the cute dent in his currently scruffy chin. "I'm a very lucky woman."

"Okay, I'll bite. What are you getting at?"

"It's just…you're so hot, Ethan."

He gave her the goofiest *aw, shucks* sort of grin. "You said that once before…"

"Probably. Why wouldn't I? I mean, it's true. And I am having the best time with you. I love this, being your friend *and* getting to spend the night with you. Plus, here you are taking all of my cousin's kids for a weekend at the family's ranch. That's above and beyond to say the least. The truth is I was more than a little worried that this weekend would go spinning off the rails. I pictured Will sulking and Troy complaining and the twins crying a lot, wanting their mom."

"Nah. Piece of cake."

"Please. I love my cousin's children, but have you noticed there are *four* of them? And I don't really have a lot of experience taking care of kids. Heather was always the one people asked to babysit, not me. Growing up, I secretly thought most kids should be sent to a desert island at least until they got old enough to carry on an interesting conversation."

"I remember you back then. Always with a book in your hands…"

"Yeah. While Heather was cuddling other people's babies and cheerfully offering to change their diapers, I was very happy working in the bookstore to earn my extra spending money."

He was looking at her kind of thoughtfully. "Are you saying you had doubts about ever having kids?"

"Absolutely not. I always knew I would have children. But not for a long, long time. I saw no reason to practice for motherhood by looking after other people's kids. That's why secretly, I've been picturing this weekend as something of a trial by fire. Instead it's been nothing short of terrific."

She leaned in and dropped a kiss onto his warm lips. "That's all because of you, Ethan. Because of you and Jobeth and your mom and Paisley, too, pitching right in to make this a getaway not only for Heather and Billy but for their kids as well. And on top of all that, I get to spend the nights in this bed with you."

He sifted his fingers through her hair, lifting it, then sliding his palm around to cradle the back of her head. For a moment, he just looked at her. She knew he had something important to say. But the seconds ticked by and the silence stretched out.

"What?" she prompted. "Tell me."

"Just…"

"Yeah?"

His gaze shifted away for a fraction of a second. She wondered what he might be thinking, what he hadn't said. But then he tugged her even closer, so they were face-to-face. His breath warmed her cheek. "You're beautiful and I love being with you."

And then he kissed her.

Oh, the way he kissed her…

He kissed her, and she forgot everything but the feel of his lips on hers, the hot glide of his hands on her body, the low, hungry sounds he made—all of it, everything. Perfect.

She was thirty weeks pregnant, and he still hadn't started

making noises about putting the brakes on these amazing benefits they were sharing.

And that was absolutely fine with her. She hoped they could go on like this straight on through until she went into labor. As long as he was willing, she was completely on board.

Monday on her lunch break, Matty went to Heather's. "So, how was your getaway?" she asked her cousin. "We didn't really get a chance to talk Sunday..."

The day before, as soon as Heather and Billy arrived at home, Heather had called Matty at the ranch. Then Matty and Ethan had piled everyone into the Suburban and headed for the Dolan place, where there was way too much going on for Matty to take her cousin aside and find out how things had gone in Denver. They had the car to unload and four kids talking over each other, eager to tell their parents everything about their weekend at the ranch.

Today, though, Heather's house was quiet. The twins were downstairs playing dress-up with Meredith. Billy had taken the afternoon off. He and the boys were out hiking.

For the moment, at least, it was just Matty and Heather. Both of them had shucked off their shoes. They sat close together on the sofa and spoke in hushed voices so that the twins wouldn't suddenly decide to come see who was upstairs with Mom.

"Well..." Heather began.

Matty waited for a good count of ten, but her cousin did not continue. "You're killin' me here. What happened? Was it okay?"

Heather frowned. And then she drew a slow breath. Finally, she declared, "Yeah. It was. It was okay."

Silence.

Matty resisted the urge to grab her cousin and give her a good, hard shake in the hopes that something more encouraging might find its way out of her mouth. "Just okay?"

Heather executed a thoroughly dramatic eye roll. "I have to tell you, Mat, relationships can't be fixed overnight. Problems in a marriage are rarely worked out in a weekend away."

Matty reminded herself not to yell at her cousin. She said in an excruciatingly civil tone, "All right, then. I understand. Your marriage has not been *fixed* by your Denver getaway."

"No, it has not." Heather granted her a gracious smile. "But..."

"What, Heather? Talk to me."

Heather's face flushed and her rosebud mouth trembled just a little. "Well, Billy did say he still loves me and there is no other woman for him."

That did it. Matty felt the tears welling. "Oh, honey..." She reached out.

Heather reached back. They were both crying now—crying and hugging each other good and tight.

"It's not a solution," Heather whispered between quiet sobs. "And we didn't, you know, have sex... But we're going to get counseling."

"That's good. Really good."

"You think so?" Heather wiped at her eyes again.

"I do. And if you want some recommendations, I can ask around about that, help you find someone you can talk to."

"I've already got someone."

"Wow. Just like that?"

"Pretty much, yeah."

Matty grabbed her in another hug. "Look at you. Not just *talking* about getting help. You are actively making it happen."

"Well, I'm working on it." Heather explained, "She's someone I met a while back at the Perfect Bean, a family therapist with an office on State Street. Last week, I was thinking about her, about how, if Billy and I did decide to get counseling, she might be a good choice. So I looked her up online and got references, made a few calls to check her out. This morning, I called her. Billy and I have a first appointment with her on Thursday. Billy's mom will watch the kids for us."

"Oh, Heather. Good for you."

"Well, the weekend did kind of motivate me, you know. It got me really thinking how much I love Billy—oh, Mat. I really don't want to lose him…"

"I know you don't. And you won't."

Heather teared up again. Matty grabbed the tissue box on the coffee table and held it out. They both blew their noses.

Then Heather lobbed her tissue at the wastebasket in the corner, looked Matty up and down, and said with a heavy sigh, "I have to tell you…"

Matty sat back. "What? Say it. Are you all right?"

"More or less—but this is not about me."

"No? Then…?"

"It's you. Just look at you." With a soft smile, Heather spread her hand on Matty's baby bump. "How many weeks now?"

Matty's suddenly racing heart settled to a more even rhythm. She glanced down at her cousin's hand on her belly, then up into Heather's eyes again. The tender look on her cousin's face had her choking up just a little. "Thirty weeks."

"I am so jealous—but in a good way, I promise."

Matty eyed her sideways. "You sure?"

"Yeah. I'm jealous and I'm so happy at the same time— that you're going to be a mom and I'm going to be your baby's auntie. It will be epic. Is Ethan still on board to be your birth coach?"

"He is. He went to the birthing classes, and he's been reading some books on labor and delivery. It's so sweet of him, really. He swears he's up for it."

"I believe it—and you have to know that after the weekend, my kids now adore him. Will declared him to be cool. And Claire showed me a boo-boo on her knee."

"Yeah. Ethan put a Band-Aid on it for her."

"She said Ethan took good care of her and she wants to go back to the ranch soon." Heather accused, "I also heard that you took my daughters to visit a litter of kittens in the barn..."

"Yes, we did. Really, there is nothing in this world like watching little girls and kittens..."

"Tell me about it." Heather was grim. "You'd better believe Claire and Elissa are tag-teaming me now, coming up with a thousand reasons why they should get to bring one of those kittens home."

"Uh-oh." Matty tried really hard not to grin.

Heather poked her with an elbow. "You love it."

"Well, yeah. I kind of do."

"At least so far, I'm holding the line."

Matty offered hopefully, "Well, if you change your mind—"

"Don't say it. Don't even think about it."

Right then, they heard footsteps on the stairs.

Elissa poked her head up first. "Aunt Matty's here!" She came running with her arms out, Claire right behind her.

Meredith appeared last. The twins had rigged her up in a doggy princess costume, complete with a plush golden crown held on her head by a wide pink ribbon tied in a crooked bow. The dog didn't look all that happy about the situation. Still, she followed the twins faithfully, wagging her tail and whimpering in greeting when Matty called her name.

The next weeks were busy ones for Matty. With Ethan's help, she bought and assembled a crib. They put up shelves in the baby's room and stacked them with baby things.

At the bookstore, Matty had been busy organizing events. She was now hosting two monthly book clubs, a quilting club and a group of chatty knitters. Also, Matty had reached out to Piper Bravo, who was not only the wife of Ethan's second cousin, Jason, but also the director of the Medicine Creek Library.

Piper was only too happy to work together with Matty. The librarian agreed that for author events, rather than ordering books directly from the publisher or distributor, Cloud Peak Books would bring the author's books and offer them for sale.

In return, the bookstore would give a discount to anyone who bought a book to donate to the library. People could buy and donate books they loved so that library patrons would be sure to have a chance to read them.

Matty set up a colorful display to honor everyone who donated and the books they chose. In the first few weeks of the program, customers had bought more than two hundred books for donation. People who shopped in the store loved it. So did Piper and her staff at the library.

Early in the second week of July, when Matty and her mom were closing up for the night, Simone said, "I always meant to get going on the library connection. Now you're on it. I'm so proud of you, Matty. I hope you know that."

Despite the sudden tightness in her throat and the emotions swirling in her chest, Matty teased, "It's kind of intimidating, walking in your footsteps, Mom. But I'm doing my best."

And right then, her powerful, unflappable mother started to cry. "Oh, Matilda…"

"Whoa, wait. Mom, what'd I say?"

"It's not what you said, sweetheart. It's…everything. All of it. It's you."

"Me?" Matty asked in a tight little squeak.

"Yes. It's that you're so…resilient. That you came home, that you're creating a whole new life here for yourself and the baby. That you seem to be loving every minute of your new life."

"Well, Mom, I do. I love it that I'm home, that I have my people around me, that my baby will grow up knowing what I always knew—that she has family and a community she can count on, that whatever big chances she needs to take, she's got backup and a safe place to land."

"Exactly." Her mom was nodding. "And I have a confession to make."

"Uh-oh…"

Her mom chuckled. "Don't be scared. It's nothing *that* bad…"

"Okay, then. Hit me with it."

"Well, it's like this…" The unflappable Simone took

a shaky breath. "The truth is it's always been my secret dream that you would come home someday, that you'd just get up and walk away from that amazing career you worked so hard to build because you'd suddenly decided you couldn't wait to run the store..."

Now Matty's throat was tight. "You're serious..."

"Oh, yeah. Not that I ever really believed it would happen. Surely you're well aware that I'm a woman with a firm grasp of reality and both feet firmly planted on solid ground."

"Mom. You are that. You truly are..."

Her mom sniffled, shook her head and drew her shoulders back. "So anyway, there was my dream and there was reality. And reality required that my dream would never be realized, that in time, when I was ready to retire, I would be putting the store up for sale."

Now Matty was starting to feel pretty emotional. "Oh, Mom..."

"There's more. As a matter of fact, when you called us at the beginning of February to say you were moving home, your father and I were already talking about when to put the store on the market. I was about to try to sell my life's work—and instead here you are back home, making my dream come true."

"I can't even..." Matty grabbed her in a hug.

When they pulled apart, Simone took her by the shoulders. "I have to say it..."

Matty didn't quite trust the look in her mom's eye. "What now?"

Simone caught her hand. "Come on. Sit."

Matty followed her mom to the corner reading nook in the front of the store. They sat in wing chairs facing each other. Her mom, who always knew exactly what she wanted to say, seemed suddenly at a loss for words.

"Just go ahead, Mom. I'm listening."

"Well, I have been wondering…" Simone let that sentence die unfinished.

"Mom. What?"

Her mom drew a big breath and let it out forcefully. "About you and Ethan…"

Matty felt a sudden tightness in her throat. She put her hand on her belly, where her baby slept. "What about me and Ethan?"

"Well, it's been pretty obvious to all of us that since you've come home, you and Ethan have grown close."

Where was this going? "We *are* close, Mom. Close friends."

Her mother gave her a sheepish smile. "Oh, sweetheart, I guess I just want to you to know that I think you two are perfect together. And, well, if you decided to make it official, your father and I would be so happy for you."

"Wait… *Official*. You mean like, get married?"

"Yes." Now her mother was beaming. "That is exactly what I mean."

Never going to happen, Matty thought. She'd kind of assumed that the people she loved understood that. But apparently she'd had it wrong. She answered gently, "That's sweet. But Mom, I've been married. I lost my husband. I just…no."

Her mom seemed puzzled. "No?"

"What I'm saying is Ethan and I, we are friends forever. We are in each other's corner. We have each other's backs…" And then there was the scorching-hot magic they shared in bed together—but no way was she getting into *that* with her mom.

Simone seemed to slump in her chair. "I don't like where this is going."

"I can see that. But Mom, Ethan and I aren't ever getting married."

"Oh. Well." There was a sad little sigh. "I see." Her mom folded her hands in her lap and stared down at them unhappily as Matty tried to decide what to say next to put this painful exchange behind them.

But then her mom glanced up with a frown. "Wait a minute. Who am I kidding? The truth is no, I *don't* see. Because I think you and Ethan have a lot more than friendship between you. I think you're in love with him and that he is in love with you. I think the two of you would be very happy together. And by that I mean married—married with a lifetime commitment to each other."

Would this excruciating conversation ever be over? "Well, yes." Matty took great care to speak calmly. "We are happy, Ethan and me. As friends. But marriage? Mom. No. That is not going to happen."

"Ah," said her mother.

"*Ah*?" Matty echoed. "What does that even mean?"

"Well, sweetheart, that means I really don't know what to say right now. Except that I, er, understand. And that I'm so glad you have each other, even if you're not willing to—"

"Willing? Mom. It's not about being willing. Not at all."

"Oh, please. What else can it be about? You're unwilling to take another chance."

"No. I mean, not exactly..."

"Honey, it's so obvious how you and Ethan feel about

each other, so clear to all of us that the two of you are deeply in love."

"In love? No, Mom. Honestly, we do love each other, but—"

"No *but*s about it. I think you need to—"

"Stop. Please."

Her mom pressed her lips together. They stared at each other. Matty cast about for a graceful way to finally lay this painful conversation to rest. Forever.

But Simone spoke first. "Well, I have to say I just don't get it. I honestly don't. But I support your choices and I… respect your wishes."

"Thank you." Was this the end of it, then? Matty desperately hoped so.

But Simone simply could not leave it at that. "Even though I do think you feel more for him than you're willing to admit right now."

Matty just sat there waiting for her mother to stop trying to tell her what her own feelings were.

Her silence must have gotten through somehow because her mom said, "Okay, okay. It's your life. I'll shut up." Simone rose and held her arms. Matty went into them for another hug.

And then, together, they finished closing up the store.

Chapter Twelve

From the bookstore, Matty went straight to Ethan's. After what had happened with her mom, she considered making up a story, texting Ethan that she was tired and going straight home alone to get some rest.

But she wasn't tired in the least. And they'd agreed to meet at his house tonight. Really, it wasn't his fault that her mom had jumped to conclusions. Ethan was her best friend. Matty didn't want to lie to him, didn't want to make up some fake excuse for not coming over tonight.

She didn't want to lie. And beyond that, she wanted every night she could get with him for as long as their hot affair lasted. Every woman should be lucky enough to have Ethan Bravo for a lover.

He pulled open the front door as she ran up the steps—and straight into his waiting arms. After that first endless kiss, they headed upstairs to his bedroom, where he reminded her of all the reasons she would keep spending her nights with him until...

Who knew?

Probably until the baby came, which would be about two months from now.

They were shameless, the two of them. He liked her on top and she liked it, too. Or on her hands and knees...

She loved that he so easily adapted to the changes in her body. Whatever was most comfortable for her suited him just fine.

Afterward, they took a quick shower together. The warm water felt so good. He got out first. She lingered under the spray as he dried himself off and pulled on jeans and a T-shirt. When she stepped from the open shower nook, he bent, kissed her giant belly and then rose to kiss her forehead, too. "Relax," he instructed. "I'll go pull dinner together..."

She watched him go, feeling sex-drunk in the most delightful way. Lazily, she grabbed a towel and dried off. Her phone, on the nightstand, started playing Brad Paisley's "First Cousins" as she wandered back into the bedroom.

Grinning, she grabbed it. "Hello, cousin."

"You sound sleepy," Heather said.

"Just...relaxed." Still naked, she stretched out on the bed. "What's going on?"

"I called about Sunday," Heather said. Her parents were flying in Friday from Florida for a two-week visit. On Sunday, Heather was throwing a family barbecue in her backyard.

"Let me guess. You have instructions for me."

"Yep. You're bringing that hot German potato salad that everybody loves. And something nice for dessert."

"I'm on it," Matty promised.

"Oh, and bring Ethan, too."

Matty frowned as she thought of that awful conversation with her mom. Yes, Simone had promised to back off on the subject of Ethan and marriage and love. But maybe it would be better not to bring Ethan around the family for a while. The last thing she needed was her mom observing her and Ethan together and making up more stuff in her head about what a great thing they had going on.

Not that they *didn't* have a great thing going on—they did. Just not a marriage-and-true-love-forever sort of thing.

"Mat? You still there?"

"Uh, yeah. Right here."

"Whew. I thought we got cut off. Anyway, about Ethan. He's such a rock. I need to pay him back for taking all my kids to the ranch last month. Plus, he's pretty much part of the family anyway."

Part of the family? Matty winced at the sound of that. Was Heather matchmaking now, too?

Her cousin went on, "Do you want to ask him, or do you want me to do it?"

Matty reminded herself not to be paranoid. Heather was grateful to Ethan, and she wanted to show her appreciation. "It's okay. I'll invite him." Maybe he would be legit busy with something he couldn't get out of.

Hey. It could happen...

"Be here at noon," Heather commanded.

"Will do."

And then Heather giggled like a kid. "I'm so excited. Seems like I haven't seen my folks in forever."

Matty's heart melted. "You do sound good."

"Yeah. I can't wait to see them."

Matty turned on her side. Nowadays, she grew uncomfortable lying on her back. "Can you talk?"

"Yeah. For a minute or two. I'm alone in the bedroom. Billy's keeping an eye on the kids."

"And how are things between you and Billy...?"

"It's better."

"Really?"

"Yeah. It really is."

Matty removed the big clip she'd used to corral her hair in the shower and set it on the nightstand. "Oooh. Good news. I'm so happy to hear that."

Her cousin backpedaled. "Well, I'm not saying it's great between us."

"Hey. I get it—I honestly I do."

"Me and Billy, we're real careful with each other now, kind of walking on eggshells, both of us trying to get along."

"That sounds...difficult."

"Yeah. It is. And it's sad. But it's better. A lot better. I just don't feel as angry with him lately. I have hope now that we can somehow work it out—especially after our first meeting with the marriage-and-family therapist last week."

"How was it, with the therapist?"

"It was a step. I feel good about it. I got some stuff off my chest, and so did he. But it's just the beginning, you know. Next week we go to separate sessions—one for me, one for him. Then probably after that, we'll be going to see her together to work stuff out."

"But you said that you feel good about the therapy?"

"I feel better now we have someone to talk to, yeah. Someone to guide us..."

"I'm so proud of you, Heather. You're taking steps to fix what's broken between you and Billy. You really are."

"We'll see. And Matty..."

"Yeah?"

"I do love him."

"Oh, honey. I know you do. And he loves you." Ethan appeared in the doorway to the hall. They shared a smile.

His gaze strayed slowly down over her naked body. She mouthed, *One minute.* He nodded and headed back down the hallway. "And guess what?" she said to her cousin. "Gotta go…"

"German potato salad, dessert and bring Ethan," Heather recapped.

"You got it." They said goodbye.

"Oh, Lordy," said Heather, leaning close to Matty so no one else would hear. "My poor ovaries. I swear, he's almost as good with them as Billy and my dad."

It was Sunday afternoon, and Heather's backyard family barbecue was in full swing. Ethan sat in a folding chair next to Heather's dad, Darryl, Sr. Heather's dad talked nonstop about the joys of retirement on the Gulf Coast. As Darryl gushed over the fishing boat he'd just bought, Claire and Elissa climbed back and forth from their grandpa's chair to Ethan's. Not only were they constantly on the move, the two little girls chattered away like a pair of surprisingly good-natured spider monkeys.

Matty sipped her ginger ale. "Ethan's always been good with kids. He's easygoing and he doesn't talk down to them."

"He really is a great guy," Heather gushed.

Matty nodded. That afternoon, she'd heard a lot about how wonderful Ethan was.

Not that she disagreed. It was just that after her mom had rhapsodized about his wonderfulness last week and suggested that Matty ought to put a ring on it, well, everybody seemed to be telling her how fabulous Ethan was.

She couldn't help wondering if they were ganging up on her, piling on the admiration for Ethan in an effort to convince Matty she ought to grab him and marry him. Because apparently they just couldn't bear the idea that she intended to be a single mom.

Was she overreacting?

She kept telling herself that she was.

Did they not approve of her because she was having a baby without the benefit of a husband?

No. She really didn't think that was the problem. They just wanted her to be happy, and they thought marrying Ethan would make her so.

Was she going to have to tell each and every one of them in no uncertain terms that she was not in love with Ethan and she had zero intention of marrying him—or anyone?

She hoped not. But if they kept it up, she just might.

On the last Saturday in July, Heather hosted Matty's baby shower.

It was a totally traditional affair. No men were invited. The shower started at noon and ended at 2:00 p.m. They played a few games, drank sparkling punch in champagne flutes—pink punch, because the baby was a girl—and ate yummy quiches and a pink-and-white baby buggy made out of cupcakes.

Heather had invited a couple of women Matty used to hang out with back in high school. It was fun to catch up with them a little. Both women had married the guy they'd been dating when they graduated from Medicine Creek High. They both had kids and they both seemed happy.

Matty got a stroller, a baby harness carrier, a high chair and a lot of adorable baby clothes. There was a changing table and a diaper bag. And a boatload of baby supplies. It was fun, and she was grateful to Heather, her mom and her aunt Leonie for planning it and making it happen.

But the best thing about the baby shower was Heather. She actually looked happy for the first time since Matty had moved home. The strained look in Heather's eyes had eased. She smiled more easily.

Matty caught her alone in the kitchen filling flutes with more pink punch and asked, "So. How's it going?"

Heather gave her a radiant smile. "Good, Mat. Real good."

Matty couldn't stop herself from getting specific. "With Billy, you mean?"

"Yes. With Billy—and guess what?"

"Tell me."

"Did I ever mention the Labor Day camping trip?"

"Yeah. It's Billy and the boys camping in the Bighorns, right?"

"For the past couple of years, yes. The last time I went was the year before Troy was born. I always stay home with the little ones. And since the twins came along, it's been Billy, Will and Troy—a guy thing. They're usually gone for the last week of August through Labor Day."

"I remember. And..."

"Well, Billy and I have been talking..."

Matty nudged her with an elbow. "Spill. What?"

"This year, we're *all* going on the Labor Day camping trip—Billy, the boys, the twins. And me, too."

Matty grabbed two full flutes of pink sparkling water and handed one to her cousin. "Here's to you and Billy and breaking the old patterns."

"To breaking old patterns," Heather repeated softly as she tapped her flute to Matty's.

A while later, as the guests were leaving, Matty hugged her aunt Leonie goodbye. She and Uncle Darryl were heading back to Florida in the morning.

That evening at Matty's house, Ethan helped her put away the shower gifts. She cooked them dinner. Later, they made love slowly. She was thirty-four and a half weeks along. And Ethan was so careful of her now, so tender and patient.

She loved him for that—as a dear friend, of course.

It seemed so hard to believe sometimes that she was due to deliver in a little over a month. The days were going by so fast. She would hold her baby in her arms in no time now.

Matty kept waiting for Ethan to say that it was time to end their pre-baby fling. Because nowadays, she waddled wherever she went. And her ankles were noticeably thicker. One of her high school friends had joked at the shower that there was a name for those—cankles, she called them. For when you can't tell where your calves end and your ankles begin.

Matty had to agree. Dr. Hayes reassured her that she was perfectly healthy and so was her baby. Her cankles would go away after the birth. Still, she was puffy right now. And so big. When she stood at the mirror she'd hung on the back of her bedroom door, she couldn't help thinking she resembled a walking beach ball.

As for her fling with Ethan, as August rolled around, the two of them were still spending every night in each other's arms. Ethan showed no inclination to call an end to the benefits they'd been sharing since March. Matty might look like a beached whale, but Ethan treated her like she was the sexiest woman alive.

And he loved to cuddle. She loved it, too. How many cuddles was she going to get once her little girl was born?

Better not to think about that right now. It was lovely being half of a temporary couple with Ethan. She never wanted to give it up—and she didn't have to. Not yet.

It was still summer, after all. And she wasn't due until September. Right now, the hillsides wore gorgeous cloaks of Indian paintbrush and columbine. The August days were warm, and the nights, while not always clear, were mild and beautiful.

Most evenings, after dinner as dark came on, she and Ethan would sit out on his porch or hers. They didn't need to talk, really. He would put his arm around her, and she would lean her head on his strong shoulder and think that after the living hell of losing Gabe, after all her fury at Ted and her disappointment in herself that she'd actually trusted that guy, things were looking good for her now. She was home and she was loving it. And soon now, she'd have her little girl to hold in her arms.

Heather and her family left on their camping trip. They returned on the day after Labor Day. And when Matty took her lunch hour on Wednesday, she headed straight for her cousin's house to find out how the trip had gone.

"It's open!" Heather called when Matty rang the doorbell.

Matty pushed the door wide, and there was Heather on the sofa, two enormous mounds of laundry piled on either side of her.

The sight brought tears to Matty's eyes as she remembered all those years ago when Will was born and Matty had walked in the door to see her cousin nursing her new baby surrounded by piles of wrinkled clothes, perfectly content.

"Mat!" Heather jumped up and grabbed her in a hug. "Hey!" But when she pulled back, she was frowning. "You okay?"

"Uh, good. Real good. Why?"

"Mat, your eyes are wet."

Matty laughed and swiped the tears away. "These are the good tears, I promise you."

"Good tears for…"

"You, Heather. You just looked so happy, sitting there on the sofa between two enormous mounds of laundry."

Heather laughed at that. "Well, if I'm happy, I swear it's not about the laundry."

"Whatever it's about, I'm glad."

They grinned at each other, and then Heather looked down at Matty's giant belly between them. "I can see your outie through that tent of a tunic you're wearing."

Matty grumbled, "Tell me about it—and you, on the other hand, look great. How is that fair?"

Heather, who was literally glowing, gave Matty a smug little smile. "Must be all the sex Billy and I have been having."

Matty gasped. "It happened?"

"Oh, yeah. Frequently. In our tent, no less. And it was so good—to be close that way again, just me and Billy. We couldn't keep our hands off each other, even if we did have to keep reminding each other to be quiet."

"You're kidding. With the kids right there?"

"Of course not. We brought two tents. Adults in one, kids in the other. We figured Will was old enough to help look after his little sisters at night. And he stepped up— he really did."

Matty tipped her head toward the stairs. "Speaking of the kids…"

Heather waved a hand. "No worries. The boys are outside and the twins are on a playdate. Iced decaf?"

"I thought you'd never ask."

They sat at the kitchen table with their heads together as Heather told all. "Oh, Mat. I'm getting it now, I honestly am. Having a new baby to dote on is one of the great experiences of life. But it's not everything. I see now that I have lots of good things to look forward to, so many life adventures that don't require me to have a baby on my hip.

"I've been blinded. I get that now—blinded by the fear of the unknown. I mean, I've been either pregnant, working on getting pregnant or caring for very young children for most of my life with Billy. And I have loved that, all of it. It was beautiful and meaningful. I was happy just being a young mom. It's been so hard for me to imagine moving on."

Matty took her hand across the table. "But you're doing it…"

Heather held on tight. "I am, yeah. I'm getting used to the idea, day by day." She looked down at their joined hands and then up again into Matty's waiting eyes. "I apologized to Billy for trying to trick him into having another baby."

"Good for you. How'd that go?"

Now Heather's eyes gleamed with the sheen of tears. She blinked them away. "Oh, Mat. He accepted my apology, just like that. Because he's a good man. He's *my* man. And Mat, I do love him. With all my heart."

"Oh, honey." Matty started to rise so she could circle the table and pull her cousin up into a hug.

"Wait." Heather squeezed her hand. "There's more."

"Okay..." She sank back to the chair. "I'm listening."

"Mat, I just want to thank you."

"Thank me? What for?"

"Because if you hadn't been here for me, if you hadn't kept after me to get honest and take the next step, I don't think I'd have come around in time to save my marriage."

That did it. Matty pushed herself upright, lumbered around the table and pulled her cousin into her arms.

As they stood there, together, holding on tight, Heather sniffled and whispered, "So thank you. I mean that. From the bottom of my heart."

Ethan found Matty waiting in the open front doorway when he got to her house that evening. Even from outside on the porch, he could smell dinner. "What's that? Bolognese sauce?"

"Yes—but forget the sauce for now," she said. "I have so much to tell you."

"Okay, then. But first things first." There in the open doorway, he pulled her close and kissed her. She kissed him back, a kiss both passionate and tender.

When she stepped back an inch, he put his hand on the hard swell of belly. "How are you feeling?"

"Good. Fine." For a moment, she brushed her hand over his. But then she caught his fingers, pulled him inside and shut the door. Her eyes were shining.

"Okay, Matilda." He shucked off his shoes. "What's going on?"

"Come with me." She led him into the living room,

pushed him down on the sofa and sat beside him. "It's about Heather and Billy…"

"Good news, I hope?"

She nodded. "They're reconciled. They're going to be all right. I saw her today and… Oh, Ethan. They really are working it out. I'm so happy for them."

"That's great…"

"I know, right? I was worried for a while there—I really was. But not anymore."

Her beautiful face was alight with happiness as she told him the details of her visit with Heather that day. He listened, feeling glad for her cousin.

And for Billy, too. Billy was a great guy who loved his wife. And now it looked very likely he wouldn't lose her— that they wouldn't lose each other.

In his years as a small-town lawyer, Ethan had represented a large number of clients in way too many divorces. Divorce was always sad and difficult and inevitably destructive to the whole family. Even an amicable divorce left damage in its wake.

That Heather and Billy seemed set now on staying together was a beautiful thing. He hoped it really did work out for them.

He hoped…

Damn. Here was Matty, beaming up at him with stars in her eyes, over the moon that her cousin and Billy weren't breaking up after all.

And what was he thinking about?

That it *seemed* they would work it out. That he *hoped* they would stay together.

Clearly he'd handled one too many divorce cases. He'd become a real cynic.

He didn't want to be like that. He wanted to believe that love really could overcome any obstacle. That people could change and grow and move on from tragedy. That couples like Billy and Heather could let go of the past and find ways to make their relationship work today and into the future...

He wanted to let himself trust that love was stronger than all the thousand and one things that tore people apart. He wanted...

Matty.

It was that simple. He wanted Matty and he *had* wanted Matty for a very long time.

True, in the past, he'd accepted the reality that he would never have her—not as his wife, not as his partner in life. That she was Gabe's and they were happy together and that was just plain reality.

But all that wasn't true anymore. It hadn't been true for years now. Gabe was gone forever. Nothing stood in Ethan's way now—nothing except his bone-deep fear that she would say no to him. That would hurt. That might just break him.

And what would she say when she learned that he'd been hiding his love for almost a decade? He'd had a damn good reason to keep his mouth shut. But still, Matty didn't care much for liars.

Even if she ended up forgiving him for hiding his true feelings all this time, there was no guarantee she would suddenly want to spend her life with him.

She'd told him in no uncertain terms that she was never getting married again. What made him think she'd somehow change her mind because he'd finally decided tell her the truth?

She said, "Ethan, what's wrong? Are you okay?" She searched his face.

"Fine," he said. "I'm fine."

"But you just checked out on me. All of a sudden, you just...went away."

He took her hand. "Sorry. I..."

That was when it happened—right then, as he hesitated over what to say next. That was when he understood what he had to do. That was when he saw that this woman was the center of his life. And he would never have even a chance to be with her, not really. Not without laying his heart on the line and telling her what he'd been keeping from her.

"Please Ethan," she whispered. "Talk to me."

He lifted her hand, turned it over and gently pressed his lips to the heart of her palm. "I love you, Matty." He made himself sit back just a little so he could look into her eyes. "I am *in* love with you. And I have been for a very long time."

Stillness.

For an endless count of five, neither of them moved, and the silence between them was absolute.

Then, too carefully, she eased her hand from his. "Ethan, I..." She seemed unable to go on.

He laid it right out there. "I've been in love with you since that year in LA."

Her sweet face showed pure bewilderment. "What year?"

"The year we all three lived in the same building in Los Feliz."

"No..." In her eyes, he saw all the memories—memories of the two of them, of the way they used to cook together, laugh together, even share each other's secrets. The way they'd become true friends that year, as close as he and Gabe had always been. "Oh, Ethan. *No...*"

"Yes. That's why I left, Matilda. I came back home be-cause Gabe was my best friend and I'd fallen in love with my best friend's girl."

"No!" She jumped to her feet, the move surprisingly agile given how hugely pregnant she was. "Ethan, really. Come on, now. That's just wrong..." She backed away from him, tears welling in her deep blue eyes.

"I realize that. I didn't like it, believe me. I didn't want to lie to you—to either of you. But no way was I about to tell you the truth. At that point, leaving LA felt like the only right choice. I said I missed home, and I did. But that wasn't all of it. I knew if I stayed, I would do something desperate—that I would tell you how I felt or maybe even tell Gabe. I didn't see how any good could come from that. So I lied about why I was going home. And I left."

She drew a shaky breath. "I... I knew there was some-thing else. Something more. I always wondered why you wouldn't tell us the real reason you couldn't stay..." She seemed to have no idea how to go on from there.

"What was there to say? Gabe loved you. You loved him. I left. It was the right thing for all of us. And over time, after I came back home, I even talked myself into believing that I was over you, that I'd moved on. I had a girlfriend I really liked. I'd convinced myself that eventually I would ask Sylvia to marry me, that we would do what couples do, buy a house together, plan a family...

"But then you came back. You came back to stay. It didn't take more than a few nights of us cooking together like we used to do in the old days, dancing to the oldies after dinner, staying up too late because we had so damn much to say to each other. In no time I realized what a liar I was. That I'd lied to everyone. Even myself. I realized that I love you. That I never stopped loving you—I just pretended that I had. I pretended so hard that for a while, I even had myself convinced that I was over you."

She was shaking her head at him. "But I didn't even... I mean, all those years ago after you moved back, when Gabe and I were still together in LA, we used to come home to visit. Everything was good between us. You two still hung out together. You were still best friends. I had no idea."

"And that was how I wanted it. You didn't need to know how I felt. It was better for everyone that you didn't."

Her sweet face was a portrait of pain and confusion. "I can't believe this is happening. I can't believe I never knew."

He rose, slowly, afraid that any sudden movement would send her reeling from the room. "Matty. How many ways can I tell you this? Nobody knew. I never told anyone. I was the only one who could have told you, and I was never going to do that."

"But you're doing it now." It was an accusation. "If you were never going to do it, then why are you doing it now?"

"Matty..."

She put out a hand, palm out. "Just stay there. I mean it. Stay there."

Slowly, he sat down again. She backed away and demanded, "Ethan. Just explain to me why you're suddenly telling me now."

"Because Gabe's been dead for three years. We buried him, and we know that he's never coming back. Because I love you. I have loved you since LA, and it's time that I told the truth about what's in my heart. It's time that you know how I feel. Matty, I want a life with you beyond this... thing we're doing now that's supposed to be just until the baby comes. I want a life with you, and with the baby, too. I love you, and I want you to give me a chance."

For a moment, Matty was absolutely certain she was going to throw up. She swallowed hard and breathed carefully through her nose and had no idea what to say to him.

Should she have known?

Yeah. Probably. She'd been a bad friend and a reprehensible wife for not figuring it out when he left Los Angeles all those years ago.

It wasn't Ethan's fault, what he felt. And as for his not telling her or Gabe his real reason for leaving back then, well, she understood that, too. His leaving LA was the right thing, the noble thing.

It was just...

If she'd only known sooner what was in his heart, she would never have taken such complete advantage of him over the past several months. She wouldn't have used him for a fling thinking they both felt the same, that they were simply two friends enjoying each other, with a mutual understanding that it was just for now, just until the baby came...

Ethan asked, "Matty, are you all right?"

No. She was not all right. But at least her stomach seemed to be settling a little. "I'm okay. And I'm so sorry."

"Sorry? There is nothing for you to be sorry about."

"Oh, yes, there is. Because, Ethan, I can never give you what you want."

He flinched. But then he dragged in a breath and said gently, "You know the truth now. It's a lot to take in. Just give yourself some time, okay? Just think about what I've said."

"There really isn't anything to think about. I can't go there with you, Ethan. I just can't. Knowing the truth doesn't change anything."

"Maybe not. But Matty, I think we've talked about this enough for tonight."

"No. No, really. I need to be honest here, too. We need to settle this. You said just now that you want a life with me and the baby."

"Yes. I do. But did you hear what *I* said? We can talk about all this later, when you've had time to—"

"No, Ethan. We can't. Because I want to be your friend, Ethan. Your *friend* and that's all."

He blinked. "You say that now, but—"

"I say it because it's true. If I'd known how you really felt, I would have done everything differently."

"What does that mean? You're blaming me for taking too long to tell you how I feel?"

"No! Of course not. I was angry at first, just for a minute or two. It's a lot to take in. But I get it. I do. You were in a bad position. How were you supposed to decide what to say and when? I see that you only wanted to be true to Gabe. And you have been true. To Gabe. And to me, too."

"Matty, I—"

"Stop. Please listen. I love you, I do. I love you as a dear friend. And that's all. So when you say you want more than a fling, more than our friendship... Ethan, that's just not possible."

"Of course it's possible." His voice was so tender, his eyes so very sad.

"No. It's not. Ethan, I am never getting married again. I'm never living with a man again. I'm simply not going

there. After losing Gabe and that awful thing with Ted—
no. Just no. Never again."

"Matilda. You say that now. But—"

"No *but*s. No hashing this all out again later when I've
had time to change my mind. I'm not going to change my
mind. That's not going to happen. I can't do it. I'm not ready
for love again, and I don't believe I ever will be. I only want
to raise my baby and run the bookstore and never again
take the chance of having my heart torn in pieces by a loss
I'll never get over or a cheating, worthless jerk willing to
turn his back on his own child."

"Matty, I would never—"

"Stop. Please. Can't you hear what I'm saying? We agreed
on a fling. That's all this is for me." She made herself say
it again. "A fling, Ethan. That's all."

"You're serious." His voice was hollow now.

"Yes. I am."

"You want me gone."

It was the last thing she wanted. "What I want is our
friendship back. But as for more than that… Ethan, no."

"You won't even give yourself a little time—give *us* a
little time? You won't even think it over?"

"No. I'm sorry. I won't change my mind."

He was silent. She watched his eyes change, saw the
light of hope go out of them. He looked at her distantly now.
"Friendship isn't going to be enough for me."

She kept her mouth shut. What more was there to say?

"Bye, Matty." He said it quietly.

And it hurt. It hurt so bad. "Goodbye, Ethan."

He turned for the door. She stared straight ahead until
he was gone.

Chapter Thirteen

The bed was too damn big without Ethan in it.

Matty hardly slept at all that night. She kept throwing off the covers, picking them up off the bedroom rug and settling them back over herself again. Really, she'd gone and done it now, let herself get in too deep with the man who was supposed to be her dear forever friend in the strictly hands-off kind of way.

She missed him. Already. And he'd only been gone for a matter of hours. Over and over that night, she reached for the phone to call him—to ask him to come back, to beg him to work with her, so that they could find a way to be friends again the way they'd been for so many years now.

Around 2:00 a.m. she weakened. She called him.

He picked up on the first ring. "Matty. What's up?" He sounded tired and bleak.

Because of her. Because she just couldn't do the love thing again.

She wanted to beg him, *Please come back. Please don't leave me...*.

But she knew that would be wrong. "I'm sorry I called. Never mind."

"Matty, wait..." he said as she disconnected the call.

The phone rang in her hand. It was him. She couldn't contain herself. She swiped up. "Ethan."

"Is it the baby, Matty? Are you in labor?"

"What? No. I just…"

"Okay, then. Good night." And the line went dead.

She waited, the phone in her hand. But he was stronger than she was. He didn't call back.

She was miserable. It took every ounce of willpower and self-respect she possessed not to call him again.

Plus, she was having contractions. She timed them for a while. They were pretty far apart. Eventually she faded away into an uneasy sleep—and then woke at six with a mild contraction.

After that one, it was more than fifteen minutes before she had another. Over the next hour, as she showered, got dressed and ate a light breakfast, she had three more weak contractions. Really, they weren't strong enough or close enough together to mean that she was in labor.

And those weak contractions weren't going to keep her from going to work—no way. She needed to go to work, needed to keep busy, to keep her mind off the man she would have to learn to forget.

When she let herself in the back door at the bookstore, her mom was crouched on the storeroom floor scratching Xo Cat's belly.

Simone scooped up the purring cat and stood. She looked Matty up and down. "Tell me now. Who died?"

"Har-har, Mom. It was just a bad night."

"Are you having contractions?"

"A few. But they're not close together and they're not all that strong."

"You know what today is…"

It was her due date. She was officially forty weeks pregnant. "So what? First babies are rarely born on time."

"Go home, Matilda. Take it easy. Check in with Dr. Hayes and call me at once if you need anything. I'll come right over."

Matty waited patiently for her mother to stop talking. When Simone finally fell silent, Matty said, "I'm a grown-ass woman, Mom. *I* get to decide whether or not to call my doctor *and* when I'm well enough to work."

Her mom had that look—like she was barely restraining herself from taking extreme measures. Whatever those might be. "Did you eat?"

"I did. I'm fine."

"Sure. If you say so…"

"I just want to get through the day, Mom—if that's all right with you."

"Fine. Have it your way."

"Thank you. I will."

The store did a brisk business that morning. Matty was grateful to keep busy. The contractions didn't stop, but she did her best to ignore them. *Really*, she kept telling herself, *they aren't that bad.*

She was proud of herself for keeping it together. Losing her best friend was killing her. But still, she kept moving. She needed to work in order to keep her mind off her own misery.

She'd just rung up a big purchase and thanked the customer with a forced smile when the bell over the door chimed for the umpteenth time that morning. Heather walked in.

Matty met her cousin's eyes. Scowling, Heather made a beeline for her at the register counter.

"Oh, dear Lord," Heather whisper-shouted. "Are you all right?"

Before Matty could answer, her mother appeared at her side. "I'll take over here," Simone said flatly. "Heather, talk to your cousin."

"Did you call her?" Matty glared at her mom.

"So what if I did? You refuse to listen to me. Maybe your cousin can talk some sense into you."

Matty opened her mouth to tell them both to butt the hell out.

But by then Heather had stepped around to Matty's other side and clasped her arm. "We'll be in back, Aunt Simone." She tugged on Matty's arm. "Come on."

Matty gave in and went where Heather took her.

In back, Heather led her toward the two straight chairs and the small table in the far corner. "I wish there was somewhere more comfortable," she muttered.

Matty pointed at the door to what used to be extra storage space. "Mom and I set up a little nursing area through there, for when the baby comes."

"Let's try that." Heather pulled her into the small room and shut the door. "Sit." She eased Matty down into the big, comfortable chair with the porta-crib on one side and a small table on the other. Heather took the folding chair on the far side of the table. "All right, now," she said, "What happened?"

Where to even start? Matty sighed and shrugged.

"You look like somebody just died," Heather cried. "What happened? Please. Talk to me, Mat."

Matty opened her mouth to say *Mind your own business*, but something else entirely came out. "Ethan said he loves me, that he's loved me for years—and not just as a friend. He says he loves me like a man loves a woman."

"Oh, Mat..." Heather got up again, took Matty's hand and knelt by her chair. "Sweetie, I know you want me to act surprised right now. But honestly, it's about time you faced the truth."

"What is that supposed to mean?"

"You know exactly what that means. Don't try to tell me you haven't noticed the way that man looks at you. He's a goner, plain and simple."

"Wait. You *knew*?" Matty tried her best to drum up a little outrage. "You knew how he really felt, and you didn't say a word to me about it?"

Heather reached up, ran a soothing hand down Matty's arm and then pressed her palm to Matty's cheek. "You two have been together nonstop for months. It doesn't take a genius to figure out there's been more than—what'd you call it—a *pre-baby fling* going on."

"It's just that I..." Matty lost her train of thought. She moaned and clutched her belly as another contraction came on, crested and faded away.

When it was over, Heather demanded, "Are you timing those?"

"Don't get on me, Heather. I know what I'm doing here, okay?"

"Oh, sweetheart. I love you with the power of a thousand suns. But you need to face it. You haven't got a clue."

Matty tipped her head back and let out a groan of pure frustration. "I don't know whether you're talking about Ethan right now or this baby I'm having."

"Let me put it this way. You have yet to get real about

your true feelings for Ethan. And that contraction you just had is more serious than you're letting yourself realize."

"I know exactly how I feel about Ethan."

"Yeah, right."

"And as for the contractions, they've been weak ones..." Or they had been until a little while ago. "Probably just Braxton Hicks," she said—and tried really hard to believe that. "The baby's not coming yet."

"You're sure?"

"I am positive."

Heather stared up at her as though assessing her sincerity—or possibly her sanity. Finally, she shrugged. "So then tell me more about what happened with Ethan."

"Oh, Heather..."

Her cousin rubbed her arm again. "Stop stalling. We both know you desperately need feedback right now, and I'm here to give it to you." Though Heather spoke impatiently, her dark eyes were full of love and understanding. "Talk to me..."

"I just... I can't..." Matty's vision blurred with tears, tears that kept coming. They slid down her cheeks and over her chin. She swiped them away with the back of her hand.

"Oh, honey, don't cry." Heather stood long enough to whip a tissue from the box on the table between the chairs. "Here you go." Kneeling again, she pressed the tissue into Matty's hand. "Keep talking..."

"I just... We agreed, Ethan and me. We both knew where we stood, that what we've had together these last wonderful months, it was all just for now, you know? Just between friends."

"Okay, and..."

"It turned out he was lying to me, that it was more than

that for him. And now it's all a mess, and I miss him so much, like he's been gone forever when, really, it's only been since last night that he told me how he felt and I turned him down..." More tears spilled over. "Oh, Heather. I don't know what to do..." Matty sniffled and blew her nose. "What if I've lost my best friend?"

Heather groaned. "Oh, please."

Matty glared at her. "I don't think I like your attitude."

"Well, too bad. You need to get real, Mat."

"Will you please stop telling me what I *need* to do?"

"No way. You need to hear what I have to say."

"That's what you think," Matty grumbled out of the side of her mouth.

"Mat. You need to face the truth."

"Great. More things I *need*."

"Drop the attitude. Face the truth. This is me you're talking to. I've seen you two together. You need to stop lying to yourself. You're in love with him, and you need to take your own advice."

"What advice?" Matty demanded—and then instantly wished she'd kept her mouth shut.

Because her cousin had the nerve to give her own advice right back to her. "Sometimes you have to grow and change. Sometimes you have to see a new way to be in your life. Sometimes you have to take responsibility for your actions—and not only that. You need to listen to your heart. Matilda Gage Hunt, it's time for you to admit that you love Ethan Bravo and you're not going to stop loving him no matter how scared you are to love again..."

Matty opened her mouth to tell her cousin that she was full of crap.

Unfortunately, all that came out was a long, loud groan

as she doubled over with a real, full-out contraction—
one that seemed to take forever to crest and fade away.
"Breathe, honey," Heather coached. "Just breathe…"

Matty breathed. What else could she do?

When it was finally over, Heather said, "Grab your
phone. We're going to the hospital. You can call Dr. Hayes
on the way."

Matty clutched her giant belly. "Omigod. It's happening. It's really happening. I'm having my baby today…"

"Yes, you are, and we need to go."

"Heather. This is terrible."

"No. It's wonderful. It's the miracle of birth."

That did it. Matty burst into tears—a flood of them this
time. "I need Ethan! He's my birth coach…"

"Fine." She helped Matty to her feet. "You can call him
after you call Dr. Hayes."

"But I *can't* call him." She grabbed another tissue and
mopped up the streaming tears. "We aren't even speaking."

"But you will be as soon as you call him. Where's your
purse?"

"I just told you—I can't call him!"

Heather blew hair out of her eyes with a hard breath.
"Answer the question. Your purse…?"

"Under the counter out in front," Matty sobbed.

Heather patted her back. "It's okay. I promise you. Everything's going to be okay…"

"Easy for you to say!"

"Listen, now. I'm going to go get your purse and tell
Aunt Simone what's happening."

"Heather, I'm not ready."

"And your baby isn't waiting for you to be ready."

"I'm not prepared!"

"Didn't we just cover that?"

"I packed a suitcase, but it's at home."

"Somone will bring it to you. Right now, though, I need to go get your purse."

"Maybe we can just wait a while. Maybe this really isn't what you think it is…"

"Maybe it's not. But we're still heading for the hospital. Now, you stay here, and I'll be right back with your purse. Do. Not. Move."

"Fine. Go. My life's a disaster, but what do you care?"

"All righty, then."

Another contraction came on as Heather darted off. Matty focused on her breathing, on getting through it. When that contraction finally ended, Heather was standing in front of her, the purse slung over her shoulder. "Off we go. Your mom will be there as soon as she can."

"But the store…"

"Matty. Forget about the store. Aunt Simone will get your dad over here or put a sign on the door. Right now your job is to breathe and time your contractions."

"I can't believe this is happening. I can't believe what a mess I am."

"You're not."

"Don't lie to me, Heather Marie. I *am*, and we both know it."

"All right. Have it your way. You're a mess, and we both know it—now, come on. We're out of here. My Suburban's right outside the door…"

During the drive up to Sheridan, Matty called her doctor. When she said that her contractions were three to four minutes apart and lasting about a minute, he said to get checked in and he would be there shortly.

When Matty ended the call, Heather said, "Call Ethan."

Matty just shook her head.

Three hours later, she was installed in a birthing suite waiting for Dr. Hayes to examine her again—and maybe this time give the go-ahead for her to start pushing.

The nurse had just left the suite. Matty had her mom on one side and Heather on the other, and she tried to be grateful for the wonderful women in her life.

She *was* grateful for her mom and for Heather. But she wanted Ethan. She *needed* Ethan—needed him so bad. Bad enough that in the past hour or so, she kept forgetting all the reasons she couldn't let herself take a chance on him, couldn't let herself just be honest and admit that she...

With a groan, she cut herself off in mid-thought. There was no point in going there. She'd made her decision. It was better this way.

Heather said, "You're crying again."

Matty puffed out soothing breaths, hugged her knees to either side of her beach-ball belly and glared up at her cousin. "So?"

"It's just...you're so unhappy, and I don't understand why you won't do what you have to do to make things better."

"I have no idea what you're talking about."

"And lying doesn't help, either."

"I am not lying."

"Liar," Heather muttered.

"Girls," Simone cut in then. "Please..."

Matty ignored her mom and asked her cousin, "What do you want from me?"

"You're just so dang stubborn."

"Stubborn? I'm having a baby. It's a big job."

"You're not crying because of the baby."

"You don't know what you're talking about, and I…" Just then, another contraction hit. Matty threw her head back and groaned at the ceiling as it rolled from the top of her belly all the way down to the core of her.

When that one finally ended, Heather said, "I need a minute. I'll be right back."

"No problem," Matty's mom agreed cheerfully. "We'll be here."

"*You* need a minute!" Matty shrieked, grabbing hold of Heather's hand. "I need a lot of things, including that damned epidural." She had the nitrous oxide mask in her free hand. It just wasn't cutting it.

"It's okay, honey." Her mom rubbed her shoulder. "Use the laughing gas when it hits so you're medicated at the peak of the contraction, just like the nurse and Dr. Hayes explained. You can do it…"

"I'm *trying*. I really am. But the gas just isn't enough."

Right then, Heather managed to free her hand from Matty's vicelike grip. "Be right back…" Before Matty could call her a long string of mean names, she was gone.

"Here." Matty's mom offered a plastic spoonful of ice chips. Matty took it. It didn't help all that much, but the coldness was kind of refreshing.

The door to the hallway opened again. Matty turned toward it, ready to say something snippy if it was Heather and to cry out in relief if it happened to be Dr. Hayes.

It *was* Dr. Hayes, with Heather right behind him.

"At last." Matty smiled at the doctor, relieved enough to see him that she forgot to yell at her cousin some more.

Dr. Hayes examined her and gave her the unwelcome

news that she still wasn't ready to push. Instead of the baby, he delivered a little pep talk about her pain level and how she really could work through it with proper management of the nitrous oxide. He reminded her—again—to breathe the gas at the first twinge of a contraction.

All the reminders of how to manage the gas renewed her determination to hold off on the epidural for a while more at least.

When the doctor left, Heather kissed her on the forehead. "You are so brave."

"No, I'm not. I'm a mess."

"But such a brave, brave mess."

Before she could think of a suitably crabby reply, she felt another contraction coming on. She put the mask over her face and breathed....

"That one went pretty well," she said a minute later with a wobbly attempt at a smile. "Maybe I don't need that epidural after all."

The door opened again, and the nurse poked her head in. "Matilda, your birth coach is here."

Matty gaped in sheer disbelief. Because it really was Ethan, so tall and broad and handsome in faded jeans and a T-shirt. He nodded at the nurse as he entered the birthing suite.

Relief swept through her, as sweet and cool as those ice chips her mom kept feeding her. "Ethan! You came..."

He looked at her so steadily. "Of course I came. I'm your birth coach."

She turned to her cousin and accused, "You called him."

"Yes, I did," Heather said proudly. She grinned at Matty's mom. "Aunt Simone, we need a break."

"Great idea," Matty's mom agreed.

"Work it out, you two," instructed Heather as she followed Simone through the door to the hallway.

With a small cry, Matty reached out. He came right to her and took her hand. She had no idea what to say, so she didn't say anything. He didn't speak, either. They looked into each other's eyes. A lovely sort of peace settled over her.

She thought, *This...*

This is what it's all about. The two of us, together, solid. And strong.

She wished that this perfect moment might go on forever.

But then she winced as another contraction began.

"Use the gas," he said in a low, soothing tone, just as they'd taught him in their labor-and-delivery class.

She put the mask over her face, and then, her gaze locked with Ethan's, she breathed in slow and steadily.

A couple of hours later, her little girl was born. They laid her on Matty's belly to take the Apgar score that determined how well the baby had survived her birth. Everything was looking good.

After the second Apgar test—again, perfectly normal—they weighed the newborn. She was seven pounds, six ounces.

A little later, Matty's mom, her cousin and then her dad all came in briefly to meet the newest member of the family. Ethan stayed with Matty and the baby the whole time.

Eventually, they moved Matty and the little one to a regular room. Not long after that, Matty's parents and her cousin said goodbye. Then it was just the three of them—Matty, Ethan and the baby, who was making little cooing sounds from the hospital bassinet beside Matty's bed.

Ethan asked, "Is it okay if I...?"

"Go for it."

He bent close and gathered the little girl into his arms.

"I want to name her Gabrielle," she whispered as he gently rocked the newborn back and forth.

"Gabby," he said. "For Gabe…"

"Yeah."

He was nodding as he adjusted the receiving blanket under Gabby's tiny chin. "It's the perfect name for her, a beautiful name for a beautiful little girl. Good choice."

Her eyes had misted over. *Happiness*, she thought. *This is happiness…* And suddenly, the tears were streaming down her face. "I love you, Ethan. I do. I've been terrified to admit it, but I love you so much. And not only as my dearest friend. I love you as a man, as the man I so want to be with, the man I trust with my heart, the man I hope is still willing to trust me, too."

Holding Gabby close to his heart, he bent to Matty and brushed his lips against her cheek. "Finally," he whispered on soft exhalation of breath.

She confessed, "I know. I made it harder than it had to be. I was just so set on never, ever loving any man again— not even you. So I freaked and tried to ruin everything."

"But you didn't ruin anything. You just needed a little time to figure things out."

"I'm so glad to hear you say that."

"I've loved you forever, Matty. That's not going to change. Not ever. You should take all the time you need to decide how you want it to be…"

She stared up at him, her heart so full it made her chest ache in the best kind of way. "I swore I would never take a chance on love again. But when you walked in the birthing room door two hours ago, I knew. One look in your eyes and I got it at last. I saw that it was too late to be afraid, too late for denials, too late to send you away."

"You really mean that?" he asked.

"Yes, I do. Ethan Bravo, I am deeply, completely, over-the-moon in love with you. I have been for months now, all my denials to the contrary. And I sincerely hope I'm not too late, that you haven't given up on me."

"Never," he said on a low husk of sound. "And I have to tell you, over the years, I have tried to get over you. I've lied to myself and promised myself that I *was* over you. I even believed it, I honestly did. I told myself that I'd moved on. And maybe, in some alternate world where Gabe is still with us, where you're still Gabe's girl—maybe in that world, eventually, somehow, I really would have gotten over you." His voice had gone ragged. "But Matty..."

She lifted her hand and pressed it to the side of his face. Her eyes steady, holding his, she nodded and waited for him to go on.

"Right now," he said, "I'm just glad. That you want to be with me. That I can finally be with you in the real way, the truest way. Because for me, it's you, Matilda. It's always been you. No one else will do." He took her hand, pressed his lips to the back of it.

They were silent together for a little while.

Then she whispered, "It's all so unreal. The baby. And you..."

"You think?" He gave her a slow grin.

She grinned right back. "I'm so glad you're here. After all the awful things I said, well..."

"You needed time. It was a lot to deal with."

"I think I knew what a fool I was being when you walked out my door last night. Because I do love you, Ethan. So much. I am *in* love with you. I tried to move on with Ted, and we both know how that went. I told myself then that I'd had my one true love, that I would never again find that someone who could fill up my heart and make every day better. But here I am, looking at you, knowing it's really happened for me. Lightning has struck twice, and I just might be the luckiest woman alive."

"Damn, Matilda. You really mean that?"

"Oh, yes, I do."

With Gabby cradled close against his chest, he bent and kissed her again, a deep kiss, one that spoke of promises, of the future they would share.

And then Gabby started fussing again.

He gave her back to Matty, who put her to her breast. The baby fussed and squirmed. But eventually she latched on for the first time.

Ethan settled into the chair by the bed. They were quiet, the three of them, together.

A little while later, Matty straightened her gown and whispered, "She's sleeping, I think…"

Ethan got up to check, bending near again. "Looks like it to me." Their eyes met and held. Matty lifted her face to him. They shared another slow, sweet kiss.

And then he said, "It's probably the wrong to time to ask you, but—"

"Just do it," she said. "Just say what you need to say."

"Will you marry me, Matty?"

"Yes," she replied. "I will, Ethan. I will marry you…"

He kissed her yet again, slowly, sweetly—and very gently in order not to wake the tiny baby in her arms. And then he said, "I want to adopt her. I want to be her dad for real."

Matty breathed a happy sigh. "Yes."

"Remember what I told you?"

She nodded. "If we're married and Ted signs away his paternal rights, you can legally adopt her."

"Exactly. That's what I want."

"It's what I want, too, Ethan. With all my heart."

"Okay, then. We have a plan."

"Oh, yes, we do." And then she yawned.

He chuckled. "Rough day, huh?"

"Brutal." She covered a second yawn. "But you know what? Overall, I think it just might be the best day of my life—so far."

Epilogue

On the last Saturday in September, Matty married Ethan in the backyard of her parents' house. It was a nice day, with just a few fluffy clouds drifting around up there in the pale blue Wyoming sky.

Matty wore a blush-pink tea-length dress and a short veil. Her mom and Heather and Aunt Leonie had gone all out with floral pillars and other lavish arrangements from the great little flower shop, Betty's Blooms, right there in town. They'd set up a white silk canopy over the refreshment table and hired a string quartet to play the wedding march and to provide music for the small reception after the ceremony.

Matty had three attendants—Heather and the twins. Elissa and Claire were the cutest flower girls ever, strewing petals from rose-bedecked baskets, preparing the way for Matty, who walked down the aisle created between the rows of folding chairs to meet her groom and the sleeping baby he held in his arms.

The ceremony was brief. Matty looked up into her husband's handsome face, and he gazed down at her, his green eyes steady on hers. She marveled that she'd found a second forever with her dear friend after honestly believing that deep love and a future with just the right man would never be hers again.

Ethan smiled against her lips as he kissed her. The baby he cradled between them stirred and yawned. "I love you, Matilda," he whispered.

"Oh, Ethan. I love you. So much. With all my heart."

And he kissed her again.

That night, they went home together, the three of them, to begin their new life as a family. By then, Matty and Gabby had already moved into Ethan's house. Matty planned to sublet the bungalow until her lease ran out.

In March of the following year, Ethan arrived home from the office with a giant bouquet of white roses.

"They're so beautiful," she said. "Thank you." Something in his expression had her asking, "And what's the occasion?"

"Does there have to be one?"

"Absolutely not. But why do I get the feeling you have good news…?"

That was when he told her that Ted Lansing had formally relinquished all parental rights to Gabby. Now Ethan could adopt the baby he already considered his child.

"Oh, Ethan. That's amazing!" She went straight into his arms, the enormous bouquet still clutched in one hand.

He danced her around the living area as she sang "Yes Sir, That's My Baby" loud enough to wake the baby who'd been sleeping upstairs. Ethan took the flowers and put them in water as Matty ran up and got Gabby from her crib.

Back in the great room, he took them both in his arms to continue the dance. Matty burst into song again—but softly this time for the baby's sake.

* * * * *

*Watch for Joe Bravo's story
coming in October 2025
only from Harlequin Special Edition.*

Harlequin® Reader Service

Enjoyed your book?

Try the perfect subscription for Romance readers and get more great books like this delivered right to your door.

See why over 10+ million readers have tried Harlequin Reader Service.

Start with a Free Welcome Collection with free books and a gift—valued over $20.

Choose any series in print or ebook. See website for details and order today:

TryReaderService.com/subscriptions